THE QUEST FOR FREEDOM

*After forty years, could there be
hope for six forgotten POWs?*

THE QUEST FOR FREEDOM

J. L. Rothdiener

NAVIGATOR BOOKS

SAN DIEGO, CALIFORNIA

THE QUEST FOR FREEDOM

Copyright © 2013 by J. L. Rothdiener

Biblical references taken from the HOLY BIBLE, New International Version (NIV), New Living Translation (NLT), and King James Version (KJV).

Navigator Books

www.navigator-books.com

ISBN-13: 978-1-940397-91-7

Printed in the United States of America

ACKNOWLEDGEMENTS

Thanks to my wife, Joy, and Burton & Sylvia Murdock, whose combined effort made '*The Quest for Freedom*' all that it could be.

DEDICATION

For those who have loved ones who did not return home from the Vietnam War, God bless you.

May the memories of your loved ones give you comfort. Our prayers are with you.

"You are not forgotten."

To Tom

Not only were you my brother, you were my friend.

You will be missed.

Freedom is never more than one generation away from extinction. We didn't pass it to our children in the bloodstream. It must be fought for, protected, and handed on for them to do the same, or one day we will spend our sunset years telling our children and our children's children what it was once like in the United States where men were free.

— President Ronald Reagan

He will make your righteousness shine like the dawn,
the justice of your cause like the noonday sun.

Psalm 37:6

PROLOGUE

Arlington, Virginia

Arlington National Cemetery—this beautiful, hallowed ground is a military cemetery and the final resting place of many of the nation's brave heroes. Scores of men and women whose lives were cut short defending America's freedom rest here. Others died after years of torment, still haunted by the horror of war. At this sacred memorial, the famous are buried among the unknown.

It was a crisp autumn day, and a touch of chill lingered on the air. The fall leaves stirred in the breeze, rustling pennants of red, orange, yellow, and brown.

A man of Vietnamese descent sat on a blanket spread across an ornamental concrete bench. He was a frequent visitor to this place, and he always sat on the same bench, directly across from the gravesites of five courageous American servicemen. Although the names of the five men were not well known, they had all been extraordinary heroes, who had fought for freedom and their country in a way that most people could never imagine.

At a casual glance, the visitor might have seemed out of place. His yellow ivory skin, high cheekbones, and large, dark almond eyes were common Vietnamese characteristics, but his face revealed something atypical. Perhaps it was the seriousness in his eyes, or the way he stared at the graves, as if he were lost in time—somewhere in the past.

Since the death of his wife a few years earlier, his visits to the Arlington National Cemetery had become practically a daily routine. He arrived early in the morning and often stayed until sunset. It was a quiet vigil, dedicated to the bravest souls he had ever known.

The world would probably never give these men the respect they had earned. The public might never understand what they had done. But *he* knew. And so, he spread his blanket on the bench, day after day, and honored these fallen warriors in the only way he could.

The groundskeepers knew him by sight. So did the handful of other regulars who came to the cemetery on a frequent basis.

If he happened to glance up and notice someone, he would nod or wave. But his attention was usually on the five gravesites, or on the laptop computer resting across his legs.

He typed haltingly, but with steadfast determination. Bit by bit, the story of these incredible men was gaining shape and detail on the screen of his laptop. It was a good story—an important story. And he was determined to share it with the world.

When it was done, the truth of their courage and fortitude would be revealed for everyone to see. Their lives would touch the hearts of many.

Curious people sometimes stopped to question the man on the bench. He usually managed to impart at least *some* of the story to these people in passing. Occasionally, school-aged children would place a wreath on a nearby grave, paying their respect to a fallen soldier. Other times, youngsters gathered around the man, listening with interest as he spoke passionately about the unbelievable lives of the men who rested beneath the five headstones.

He was the only one who could tell the account properly and accurately. He knew the whole truth. He had lived some of the story, and had heard the rest from the lips of the men themselves.

It had begun in 1970, halfway around the planet, in a place called Vietnam. The tiny Southeast Asian country had been desolated by war, and nearly torn apart by the clash of political ideologies in direct and bloody conflict.

It was a dark chapter in the history of the United States. The nation was polarized by frequent protests, many of which crossed the line into mob violence. Newspapers and television programs covered the daily events in Vietnam, along with body counts, and gruesome photographs.

A swirling maelstrom of disagreement surrounded the Vietnam conflict. The protesters, news reporters, and politicians screamed the loudest, while the patriots who fought the war went virtually unheard.

Whether or not they believed in the war was irrelevant. Thousands of brave young American soldiers put their lives on the line for their country.

Many young people today know little about America's involvement in Vietnam. They have only the haziest idea of the purpose, or who was involved. They are either baffled by unanswered questions, or (worse) completely indifferent to the entire affair.

It would be difficult to explain how the man on the bench felt about the war in Vietnam, because that complicated period of American history had occurred before he had been born.

Yet sometimes he wondered...

Did the South Vietnamese people deserve their freedom from the oppressive force of the North? Yes, he believed that they did. Were they free? No, they were not.

Despite America's military might, and the many lives sacrificed in the attempt, the freedom of South Vietnam had been lost. And the oppressions there continue to this day, out of the public eye, but never out of the mind of the man on the bench.

So he continued to tap out the story of the five soldiers, laboring slowly to bring truth to a world that had somehow managed to ignore it. The words emerging on the screen of his laptop would be difficult for most people to believe, but they were true. The events chronicled in his narrative had actually happened. The proof lay before him, under five plots of grass on the lawn of Arlington National Cemetery.

ONE

The Forgotten Battle
Vietnam; August 1970

Colonel Lawrence Moore entered the crowded mess hall where over one hundred men stood anxiously awaiting his orders.

"Atten-hut," the sergeant major yelled.

Every man immediately snapped to attention, eyes fixed on the colonel.

"At ease men," the colonel commanded; his face, his dark eyes signaled the urgency of the moment.

"I'm going to make this short," the colonel said. "Intel reports that the enemy has dug in at a province about ten miles from here. Our job is to seek out and destroy all the Cong in this region. The choppers will drop you near the villages, and you will sweep the area carefully. We do not want the enemy getting any closer to this base. If they do, we will be within mortar distance. I don't have to tell you twice—shoot first… ask questions later. Do you understand?"

The men chorused a hearty, "Yes, sir!"

"Let's get a move on. The choppers are spinning up now. You have ten minutes to be in the air. You've got your orders. Now, carry them out."

The colonel did a quick about face, and left the room. The men sprang into action.

Captain James McCarter joined a fellow pilot as they hurried to their barracks.

"It doesn't sound like it's going to be a good day," he murmured.

"I'm with you, Deacon. This is not the way I had planned to spend my weekend."

Some of the men referred to McCarter as 'Deacon' because of his strong religious beliefs. Highly respected by his fellow soldiers, many of them tried to curb their foul language when he was within earshot.

Captain Richard "Goldie" Jenson murmured, "I hate it when the colonel says that."

"Says what?"

"'Shoot first, ask questions later.' You and I both know when the press gets hold of something like that, there's going to be big trouble for us. The reporters don't have a clue what it's like to be in battle, facing an enemy you can't see. They ought to be here a while! The VC's idea of a good day is to burn our eyes out, or cut off a limb. They're heartless and we all know it."

With resolve in his tone, James grumbled, "I know what you mean, Goldie. We do what we have to do to survive. We'll face the consequences later."

"Did you hear the scuttlebutt about Captain Santiago?"

"Do you mean the children who got burned up?"

"Yeah. Don't get me wrong, that whole thing was tragic, but how was he supposed to know there were kids in those huts? All he saw was the Cong firing from inside, so he ordered his men to torch the huts. And naturally it all got captured on film. Next thing you know, the top brass were throwing the captain to the wolves."

Jenson swore under his breath. "Pitiful! Those guys should have defended him to the last man."

Nearing their quarters, McCarter quickly questioned the other pilot, "What was the latest you heard?"

"All I know is his life is ruined. Too bad. He was a good man. Even if he gets off, the press has made it impossible for him to go home. They call him 'baby killer.' I heard his wife and family are getting hate mail and threats almost every day."

The men reached the barracks, each deep in thought.

"We'll just have to do everything by the book," McCarter replied.

Goldie flashed a look of skepticism. "I don't think it's possible. You can't always fight a war by the book. Not *this* war especially."

The pilots wished each other luck.

"I'll see you when it's over," McCarter declared, punching his friend lightly on the shoulder.

The men rushed to their bunks and hurriedly grabbed their gear—anything they might need in battle—mostly guns, and ammo.

They also snatched keepsakes from home—photos of a loved one—a wife, girlfriend, or child. Some held pictures of their mothers. One of them clutched a cross necklace, kissed it, and gently placed it around his neck.

A couple of GIs looked in the mirror, combing their hair precisely, as if they were getting ready for prom.

And then they were rushing to the choppers, which sat on the landing pads with their rotors turning. The air was sharp with the kerosene odor of aviation fuel and exhaust of turbine engines.

"Move it, move it," the sergeant blared through the thundering roar of the rotors.

The sergeant in command flashed Captain McCarter the thumbs-up, indicating all men were present and accounted for.

The captain signaled back as the last soldier jumped aboard.

McCarter pulled back on the collective, and his helicopter mounted the air quickly, trailed by eleven additional choppers.

Gunners positioned themselves on both sides of the aircraft as they soared toward their assigned destination. They were ready for action.

The men were quiet. Experience told them that mental preparation was vital in winning a battle. They all knew what was at stake. Some took the few tense moments to pray, asking God for guidance and safety. Others reflected on their loved ones at home. A few men sat nervously puffing on cigarettes, dealing with the stress of war by flirting with a different kind of death.

Three choppers, led by Deacon McCarter, approached the first village. The other nine helicopters split off into flights-of-three, vectoring toward other engagement zones in nearby villages.

Hovering over his own target village, Deacon could almost smell the tension of the impending battle. A split second later, the enemy opened fire.

The Viet Cong's bullets and tracers whistled through the air, seeking— and sometimes finding the American helicopters.

The door gunners on the Hueys returned fire, and the hammer of machine guns nearly drowned out the heavy thump of the rotors. Anything below was fair game. The gunners reasoned that the women and children had taken shelter inside the huts around the perimeter. At least, they hoped so.

The center of the village became the focus of their fire, where the Cong stood sniping at the choppers. The firefight raged on, rifle bullets and machine gun rounds flying in both directions.

One-by-one, the aircraft darted to the ground, disgorged their cargos of soldiers, and leapt back into the air. When the strike force was on the ground, the three choppers circled the village—door gunners still firing at the VC.

In the first village, the firing at the helicopters tapered off when the Cong centered their attention on the bigger problem—the GIs approaching on the ground.

The three choppers circled overhead, waiting for the smoke bomb that would signal the "all clear." The white smoke signal appeared in less than ten minutes, indicating that the soldiers were ready for pick up.

"Sir, look north!" hollered one of the gunners.

Deacon's gaze followed the gunner's pointing finger. Smoke was rising from one of the other villages. Not the color coded white, orange, or green mist of a chemical smoke bomb. This was black oily smoke—the mark of burning oil or fuel.

Deacon shook his head. That was not a good sign.

McCarter and the two other choppers prepared to land and pick up the ground troops. Suddenly, an urgent voice blared through the radio, "Red Dog! Red Dog! We need back up now. Red Dog, come in."

McCarter replied quickly. "Goldie, this is Red Dog."

Goldie's voice was frantic. "Deacon, we need help, fast! We've been downed! The VC overran the village. We're surrounded!"

"Hang on, Goldie. We're on our way."

McCarter relayed the message to the other pilots. "Choppers are down in the next village. We can make the pick up here later."

The choppers immediately spiraled skyward.

"Gunners, be ready," McCarter shouted. "There's trouble ahead!"

As they approached the village, the atmosphere in the choppers remained tense. Through patches of smoke, McCarter could see dozens of Cong swarming from the jungle. From the air, it resembled a horde of army ants attacking their prey. There seemed to be no end to their number.

On the ground, there was chaos everywhere. Three helicopters crippled in the center of the village caught McCarter's attention. One lay on its side, trailing smoke. Smoldering wreckage littered the landscape.

Some of the GIs had taken shelter in the huts. However, they realized that at any moment the American choppers would attack the village and fire at the Vietnamese dwellings, not knowing their comrades had taken refuge inside. Meanwhile, other injured men stranded in the downed aircraft hoped for rescue.

The billows of dark smoke obscured McCarter's vision, hiding some things completely, and rendering others hazy and difficult to distinguish.

He knew that time was running out for the soldiers. The enemy persisted aggressively, as the GIs on the ground fought for survival.

The three choppers fired at the VC below for support.

The remaining choppers from the other villages swiftly arrived for reinforcement.

Another pilot's voice boomed through the radio, "Who has room to pick up?"

McCarter's voice echoed, "Our three choppers are empty. Cover us. We're going down for pickup."

"That's a go, Deacon. We've got your back."

The hovering aircraft fired in the area of the downed units, while the other choppers landed to pick up survivors. The barrage of firepower from the gunners ravaged the jungle and obliterated some of the enemy soldiers.

The scene was frenzied; the situation confused and bleak.

McCarter radioed one of the downed pilots. "Goldie, do you have any casualties?"

"Deacon, it's a blood bath. There are no civilians here, just VC. We walked right into a trap. Smith's helicopter is in flames. Davidson's and mine are disabled. Only my two gunners are here. Somehow they keep shooting, even though they're wounded. The rest of the men have taken refuge in the huts; I don't know their conditions."

"Goldie, we can't be on the ground long."

"Got it."

Immediately, McCarter shouted into the radio, "We need fire, we need fire."

"Read you loud and clear," another pilot's voice sounded as his gunners opened fire on the enemy below.

McCarter's unit and two others landed close to the downed aircraft while the rest circled the village, shooting in all directions. The survivors from the crippled choppers, and those in the huts, ran to their rescuers while firing at the enemy.

McCarter caught a glimpse of Goldie struggling out of his downed helicopter.

The two men had a long, intriguing history. James McCarter chuckled the day he saw photos of Richard Jenson as a child with his golden, curly locks. He understood why he received the nickname, "Goldie," that he carried most of his life. Now a captain in the Army, Goldie's hair is short, but still honey-colored.

The friends served together at basic training, then flight school. They always helped each other through trials and lonely times away from their families. The comrades learned to depend on one another when times were rough. They laughed together when the opportunity arose.

Goldie confided in James when he received word that his wife gave birth to a stillborn son. He would never hold the infant he dreamed of having. His baby, his own flesh and blood, would never have a chance at life. He would never be able to watch his son take his first steps, or toss a football to him. Goldie felt completely helpless during those days. It devastated him to be thousands of miles away in Vietnam, while his lovely, young wife grieved alone in Dallas, Texas. Both were lonely and heartbroken, longing to hold each other, and dry each other's tears. James was available to listen to him during that dark time, even though he had no answers. He knew more than anything, Goldie just needed his friendship.

McCarter prayed many times for his friend, Goldie—for healing of his heart and for his salvation. Goldie did not believe in God, at least not a personal one. He felt if there were a God, he certainly would be too busy for a person like him.

"Maybe later in life my faith will be stronger," he told James on more than one occasion.

Goldie assisted his wounded gunner as the men piled into McCarter's chopper.

When a bullet ripped into his leg, he instantly knew what hit him. The searing pain took his breath away, stinging in unrelenting agony. Horror overwhelmed him. A warm wetness streamed down his leg. He grasped his wound, falling toward the aircraft.

"There's just room for one more. We're already over our weight limit," a soldier in the chopper warned. "One of you will have to catch another ride," he shouted to Goldie and the injured gunner. Goldie knew too much weight in the chopper could make it crash, killing everyone onboard. He realized the GI was just doing his job.

Goldie's leg wound made it difficult for him to make it to another aircraft. Still, he ordered the wounded gunner he was assisting onboard. Stumbling to his feet, he hobbled toward another aircraft.

"Goldie!" McCarter hollered, opening the door and jumping out of the pilot's seat.

McCarter put his arm around his friend's waist for support, and helped him to the door of the chopper. He carefully lifted Goldie into his pilot seat. "Get out of here. Fast! The Spookys are on their way!"

Goldie realized his pal was willing to make the ultimate sacrifice for him, he was deeply moved. No words could express his gratitude.

"Go on. I'll hitch a ride on one of the others," McCarter shouted.

They looked at each other for a few seconds, both unable to speak.

A barrage of VC bullets striking the helicopter startled them back to reality.

"Go! Go! Go! Get out of here now!" McCarter boomed. He drew his pistol, downing three enemy soldiers.

The injured Goldie piloted James' helicopter into the dark, smoky sky.

The battle scene on the ground below was surreal; the VC continued their invasion of the village. Flames shot from the downed choppers. Chaos reigned everywhere. Thick, black smoke and fire made it difficult for anyone to see or breathe. VC bodies were strewn throughout the village.

The GIs on the ground realized that the American AC-47 gunships, known as the Spookys, would be on site within minutes. At a firing rate of six thousand rounds per minute, their guns would obliterate this village and everything in it.

Anyone who wanted to survive would need to evacuate quickly.

The last time anyone saw Captain James McCarter, a number of VC were chasing him toward the opposite side of the village.

The gunners opened fire at the remaining Cong, and McCarter disappeared into a cloud of choking smoke. He fired the final rounds in his pistol, and a couple more attackers fell to the ground.

The sound was deafening as the ceaseless rapid gunfire, and the screaming bullets, joined the roar of the helicopters.

In the chaos, McCarter lost sight of the other helicopter.

The last chopper lifted off for its return to base.

On the return flight, Goldie saw the Spookys in the distance, heading toward the village. Comforted by their sight, he knew they would finish the fight swiftly. In a matter of seconds, there would be nothing left in the village—the enemy and everything in its path would be eliminated.

It was not until all aircraft returned to base that they discovered Captain James McCarter had never made it to any of the other choppers.

On the ground, McCarter watched the two remaining choppers lift into the ominous sky. The gloom of the sky matched his emotions at that moment.

Frantically, he ran for his life, discarding his empty pistol on the way. Racing by a downed chopper, he heard what he thought was moaning. A shudder ran through him. Peering in the chopper, he noticed movement.

An apparent head wound had knocked a soldier out, and he was regaining consciousness, noticeably wracked with pain.

"Can you move?" McCarter hollered over the bedlam, as he picked up a nearby M-16.

The dazed, wounded soldier looked behind McCarter and saw the VC approaching in the distance. "If I can't, we're both dead." He stumbled out of the chopper, holding onto McCarter for support. Together they scurried in pursuit of safety.

"The Spookys will be arriving any second. We need to get out of here. Everything in its path will be shredded," the captain yelled, firing his M-16 at the nearing enemy.

The two soldiers used the smoke to their advantage—it provided cover for escape. They quickly disappeared into the dense jungle, fleeing for their lives.

Seconds later, the AC-47 military aircraft dropped a number of bombs, and riddled the village and nearby jungle with lead. The village lay in smoldering ruins.

The men sprinted through the bush until they collapsed from exhaustion. They had no choice but to take a much needed breather.

"What's your name, soldier?" McCarter tried to catch his breath.

"Specialist Anthony Williams, sir."

"Looks like you have a nasty wound there." McCarter reached into the young man's backpack, pulling out a handful of bandages.

"We've got to keep running!"

"We need to dress that wound, or you won't be running anywhere." As McCarter bandaged Williams' head wounds, McCarter discovered the man was a medic in the United States Army.

"Where is home for you?" McCarter asked.

"Wells Bridge. Little town in upstate New York. Where are you from, sir?"

"Colorado Springs, Colorado."

A sudden rustling in the leaves arrested their attention.

"We better get moving." McCarter whispered.

The men immediately hit it off. They realized right away they had one major thing in common—their Christian faith. While on the run from the VC, they prayed for safety and rescue.

The men traveled alertly through the hostile country, always looking out for the enemy. Wearily they trekked through rice paddies, and leech infested swamps, as well as forested areas, but fear and anxiety kept them pressing on. At times, the humidity was overbearing, their clothes dripping with perspiration.

They assumed that if they kept heading south they would eventually run into some "friendlies."

Late afternoon on the third day, a few Vietnamese children spotted the soldiers. When the terrified children ran off, the two friends realized they would likely meet their fate soon.

Within hours, enemy soldiers surrounded them. The GIs knew fighting was out of the question, only certain death would occur. They surrendered reluctantly, knowing they would face hardship and torture, perhaps even death. At that moment, it was impossible to imagine the extent of the brutality ahead.

Words cannot describe the cruel treatment they endured. It began immediately following their capture, and never ended for the captives. How any human being could force such inhumanities on another person is incomprehensible.

TWO

The Prison Guard
Vietnam; 2010

For four years, Le worked as a guard at a prisoner of war camp, deep in the Vietnam jungle, just east of Laos. The disgusting, heartless acts he witnessed during that time were more than most people could bear, but all part of his daily routine.

Le Huu Trang entered the world, February 13, 1985, in a small village in Vietnam. He was the only boy out of four children. His parents worked in the rice paddies, a common routine in Vietnam.

The dog tags around Le's neck identified him as "Daniel Sparks," a corporal in the United States Army. For forty years, Sparks existed in the prisoners' minds as an American POW. In reality, he was a young Vietnamese guard named Le. After dark, in the cells, he was also known as "Saturday."

How could a twenty-five year old Vietnamese be an American POW for forty years? The answer goes back to that horrific war in Southeast Asia four decades earlier.

The real Corporal Sparks died in General Yo's prison camp. The exact date was unknown. There was no body, just scorched bones, along with those of twenty-six other brave, young men. General Yo burned the bodies, hoping to destroy the evidence. He had a personal vendetta with each of these men because they were from America. His hatred ran deep against all Americans.

As a North Vietnamese soldier, General Yo was known for his destructive, cold-hearted techniques of warfare. He made his presence known by capturing, torturing, and killing South Vietnamese soldiers in the most inhumane ways imaginable.

When bombs from an American plane leveled his village, killing his entire family, his focus became clear. All American soldiers he captured would be victims of his gruesome revenge and hatred.

13

To keep the prisoners hidden, they were relocated a number of times over the course of forty years. They ended up on Yo's personal property. Most Vietnamese officials were unaware that these men were in captivity in their country. They were Yo's "secret project."

Thirty-three prisoners began the imprisonment—only six remain. All the others died in captivity from wounds, torture, or suicide. Sadly, not one died of natural causes. Every death devastated the comrades who survived. With each death, the prisoners would sink further into their pit of despair.

The last attempted escape was a trap. Evidently, the guards listened to the men's conversations and were prepared for the breakout. The failure resulted in seven fellow prisoners being tortured to death.

General Yo recruited Le because of his knowledge of the English language. The Vietnamese guard took pride in learning what many believe to be the international language. He studied each word, understanding its meaning, and enunciating it with clarity. His job was to listen to the prisoners' conversations and report the findings to General Yo.

Le wondered what information Yo expected to get from them. Why the endless beatings and interrogations? They knew absolutely nothing of value to him.

Undoubtedly, it all went back to the bloody attack on the village when the evil tyrant's family was killed.

All who remain are six men who refer to each other by the days of the week. For personal safety, the prisoners' cell names are Sunday, Monday, Tuesday, Wednesday, Thursday, and Friday. Le was Saturday.

However, Le knew the real name of each of them.

Years of maltreatment emaciated the prisoners' bodies. What was left of their teeth had yellowed and decayed. Their bodies were afflicted with open sores, unable to heal. Their feet callused, due to not wearing shoes for as long as they can remember. Their eyes were sunken. Their hair was almost gone from lice and mange. All that remained were dirty shells of what used to be strong human beings. They literally resembled walking zombies with sunburned, scarred, dry skin covering their weakened bones.

Their two meals a day were always the same—a handful of rice, usually mixed with dirt and insects. Sometimes they received rotten fruit or potatoes as a special treat.

Bathing was not a part of their life, but a monthly lime wash while they were fully clothed was routine. Designed to keep them tolerable for the entire month, it did not work. Their stench became unbearable, especially toward the end of the month. The last time they had clean clothing was almost a year ago.

There is an old saying, "Home is where you lay your head." Their home was a cell, which was nothing but a wooden cage with a dirt floor, just big enough to sit up or lie down, uncomfortably.

The treatment of the prisoners by General Yo and his guards was merciless. They starved the men for days, sometimes weeks. Beatings were frequent. At times, they were whipped until they could no longer walk; some were beaten to death.

One of the worst punishments was what the prisoners called, "The Hole." It was a small, dark, hot building, which served as a cell. There was just enough room for a man to stoop. He was unable to sit or stand for hours, sometimes for days, often crying out in agony.

Not only did the prisoners take new names, but they also created a voiceless way to communicate with each other in order to keep anonymity. They developed a unique system of communication similar to Morse code by tapping their feet or hands on the wall of the adjoining cells. It was vital their captors did not know who was tapping.

The men soon learned what various "taps" meant. Their contact among themselves could not be stopped, and their favorite topic of conversation was always the same—home!

The prisoners had one day a week to talk about whatever they chose. It wasn't actually "talking" because no one heard any of these men speak aloud for years. They might scream, or cry out in pain from torture, but never talk to each other, not even a whisper. Their captors never permitted speaking aloud except during interrogations.

When they returned, exhausted from slaving in the rice field, digging holes, or some other meaningless, drudgery for twelve hours or more, they sat in their damp, dingy cells and watched the same rat night after night, begging for food. Many times, the men were tempted to grab the rodent and eat it. However, they never did, maybe because they considered the rat their friend; some of the men even named the nightly visitor. The cockroaches and other bugs were a different story—they were fair game.

When night descended, the men sat in their cages and listened to the tapping. Tap, tap, tap. They seldom asked a question. While one man tapped, the rest of the men listened without a sound. In the dark hours, their tapping gave them a sense of closeness with each other. A reminder they were not alone; they realized an identity…in misery.

At the end of each brutal day, they eagerly looked forward to that special time of voiceless communication. Maybe because when nightfall arrived, they knew they survived one more day. Perhaps, because much needed rest would soon overtake them. Sleep was the one time when all seemed okay, unless the nightmares took over as they often did.

The tapping was important because they talked about what used to be. It was their time to reflect about happy times in their lives, when all was good. It was the only time that each man lost himself in the past, forgetting the present indescribable despair. He could forget the loneliness, the pain, and even the torture, briefly.

It did not matter if the memories were his, or a fellow prisoner's, because they all became part of each other's lives. The fragmented assortment of one another's memories became interwoven. As time passed, their own recollections faded, but others in the group helped them remember their special times.

Five words came to the forefront as Le listened to the prisoner's conversations. They were significant words: Life…Hope…Faith…Love…Responsibility.

Life meant just being able to survive one more day. It could have a positive or negative connotation, depending on their outlook.

Hope evaporated over time. They believed that the American people and their military comrades no longer remembered them. All hope was gone.

Faith in God had faded. Some of the men once had a strong faith, but over time, their faith in a higher power had diminished. They felt their unanswered prayers meant that God had given up on them. Some of them wondered if God really ever existed. Did even He abandon them?

Love was the most difficult word to understand. After forty years of separation from their parents, wives, children, brothers, and sisters, there was no evidence of love anymore. Was it still an emotion any of them were even capable of feeling?

Responsibility was another complicated concept. What responsibilities could there be? All they had was each other, in a sense "they" were their only responsibility.

Hope, faith, love, and responsibility were in their past. For the prisoners, the words held no meaning in the present, or for the future. Life merely existed.

THREE

The Days of the "Weak"

The imprisoned men rarely talked about the last forty, miserable years. It may have been self preservation, a way to keep their sanity, or possibly simply a survival instinct. Each day was the same as the previous one. No one remembered a good day.

Although, they couldn't forget the countless beatings and abuse they suffered at the hands of their captors. The excruciating pain—both physical and emotional, was a daily reminder.

Each week on their day to tap, they looked forward to sharing their recollections of home. It was all they had left—faded memories of past lives, when life was joyful, simple, and contented. Maybe that is all that kept them alive.

The men never talked about their capture.

However, Le knew about them. He was aware of exactly what happened that hot summer in the humid jungle in Vietnam. In fact, he knew all about the men's lives—past and present.

Sunday

Sunday lay on the dirt floor and watched a cockroach scuttle down the rough wooden wall of his cell. The roach was a big one, nearly the size of his thumb, and Sunday thought about trying to catch it. After a few seconds of consideration, he decided that he was too exhausted to try. Like all of the prisoners in this camp, he hovered constantly on the edge of starvation, but tonight, his fatigue was stronger than his hunger.

They'd had him in the rice paddy today, wading calf-deep in tepid brown water for at least fourteen hours, tending the endless rows of rice stalks. His lower back was a solid knot of pain from bending over for hours at a time. He'd learned long ago that the guards wouldn't allow him to straighten up, even for the few seconds needed to relieve cramped muscles. Any attempt to stand upright would earn him a rifle butt in the face, or a boot to the ribs.

He was a tall black man, and once he had been handsome and physically fit. But, four decades of unceasing brutality had leached away his strength and the chiseled features of his face. He looked more like a scarecrow than a man now—a bag of dried sticks held together by sunburned flesh and scar tissue.

His real name was Specialist Anthony Williams, but it had been years since anyone called him that. At some point, he even stopped thinking of himself by that name. He was *Sunday* now, his nickname chosen because Sunday was his day to tap, and also because he had a tendency to preach to his fellow captives. His desire to share the Word with the other prisoners faded over the years, along with Sunday's belief in the possibility of rescue.

During their first few years of captivity, he and Monday tapped out messages of faith and encouragement to each other, sharing bits of remembered scripture and thoughts about God. As their months in this pit of misery stretched into years, and the years dragged into decades, their discussions about the Lord had fallen silent.

There had been a time when all of the prisoners prayed daily. Not that they were all religious men, but even the least devout among them wanted to play the odds, just in case there really was a God out there somewhere. But, if their prayers for rescue had been answered, the answer had apparently been *no*.

Sunday still held to his faith the best he could manage, but it wasn't easy to keep believing in this hideous place. God seemed distant. Far off. Maybe even nonexistent.

Anthony Williams entered the United States Army as a conscientious objector. His father, a protestant minister, raised him to believe in the sanctity of human life. Anthony's father held a deep conviction that all life was sacred—young or old. He used to say, "I believe God created human life to be treasured, not destroyed... even in a bloody battle like this."

As a youngster, Anthony dreamed of becoming a doctor, bringing the God-given gift of healing to some third world country. He also had a heart for missions. Many governments would not allow missionaries to enter their countries, but borders were rarely closed to doctors. To Anthony, it seemed like a perfect way to get into a country that needed him, and fulfill both of his dreams at the same time.

He married Abigail, his high school sweetheart, only a month after graduation. Abby shared his faith. She shared his dreams. And, she was ready to share his future.

The draft notice showed up in the mailbox a week before Christmas, and Anthony's plans changed instantly and dramatically. He had no desire to fight, but he loved his country and he would not refuse its call.

He left his home in upstate New York to serve in the Army. Despite his love for peace, he was a proud soldier, putting his dreams on hold while serving his country.

Almost immediately, the young soldier experienced the horror of war. At only nineteen, the Army shipped him to Vietnam. Abigail was pregnant by then. When Anthony climbed aboard the Army transport plane, he left behind his young wife, his unborn child, and his lifelong desire to become a doctor.

On Sunday's turn to talk, he often tapped out memories of his beloved Abigail. Like his relationship with God—his memories of her became more distant over time. Through the years, he often thought about his bride. Sometimes, his thoughts of her seemed like his only link to the past, to a world beyond the pain and degradation of his life in the prison camp.

Once, when the guards had looped parachute cord around his thumbs and hoisted him to the ceiling, he tried to summon Abby's beautiful face to take his mind away from the searing pain. The weight of his hanging body pulled the thin nylon cords tight around his thumbs, cutting deep into his flesh until the blood coursed down his arms. He searched his mind for one memory of her face. Anything to pull his thoughts away from the ripping agony in his brutalized hands, but nothing came to him. He could no longer remember what she looked like.

Certainly, he could call up a hazy impression of her, but the image was no longer clear in his mind.

Often, he tapped about Abigail. "I wonder what she's like today. I loved her beautiful dark eyes and the funny snort when she laughed. I wonder if her smile still lights up the room."

Other times he tapped, "We used to laugh together at the simplest things, sometimes to the point of embarrassing ourselves. We enjoyed life to the fullest!"

Then he would tap the question that no one could possibly answer. "Did she remarry and find love in the arms of another?"

That comment stirred up thoughts in the minds of all the prisoners.

He recalled how Abby couldn't control her laughter when she saw somebody fall down. To her, every stumble was like a miniature comedy routine.

One incident was imprinted indelibly in his mind. "We had just arrived at church on a snowy, January morning. I was dressed in my powder blue leisure suit. I stepped out of the car and headed over to my wife's side to open her door. Suddenly, I slipped off the icy curb, disappearing out of sight. She was laughing hysterically, and barely noticed my head appearing next to her window when I used the door handle to pull myself up. My nice suit was torn, wet, and dirty. Abigail laughed uncontrollably, falling to the floorboard, tears streaming down her cheeks."

He continued tapping, faster than normal. "When I finally made it into the car, I glanced at her and tears had smeared makeup all over her face. That set us both into another wild bout of laughter. We were a sight to see, and never did make it to church that day. We went home and cleaned ourselves up. That was the day we conceived our baby."

Every day Sunday wondered about his baby. *Did I have a son or daughter? He or she would be forty-years-old. Has life treated him or her well? Did my child learn about God and His sovereign power?* He prayed for his family daily.

Sunday and Abigail had a short relationship, but it was happy and fulfilling. She taught him to be a better person—how to live, love, and laugh.

Forty years later, still in the enemy's prison, his dreams were no more than fading memories. Occasionally, one popped up in the back of his mind, almost as if it belonged to someone else.

Death seemed to be all that awaited him. At times, he yearned for it, knowing it would be his only escape to freedom. Life's finality was something he did not fear.

Monday

Hordes of mosquitoes hovered around Monday as he attempted to sleep. He had no choice but to cover up with the ratty, filthy blanket they threw in there years ago. Even with the excruciating heat, wrapping up in the blanket was better than being attacked by the disease-laden flying insects.

He tossed and turned, trying to get comfortable—what a sick joke! *Comfort...what was that?* The most he could ever hope for was a couple of uninterrupted hours away from the horror of imprisonment through sleep, but it certainly wasn't comfort. Never would be!

Monday's real name was Captain James McCarter, but his comrades nicknamed him "Deacon." He was a United States Army helicopter pilot, and the high-ranking soldier of the group.

He came from the scenic city of Colorado Springs. Sometimes he wondered if his life could be any more of a contrast than it was. *I traded the cool mountain air for the hot humid jungle. The comforts of home...and there were plenty, for this hellhole.*

It was difficult to imagine what he looked like when he entered the military, young, and physically fit. Undoubtedly, he was a good looking guy with a headful of thick, dark hair, deep blue eyes, and stood over six foot tall.

Now, just an empty shell, his skin and bones hung loosely on his gaunt frame.

As he lay on the hard, dirt floor, he would do his best to envision his wife, Wendy, in her rose garden, pregnant with their first child, leaning slightly to trim one of her beautiful rose bushes. At first, he distinctly recalled the fragrance of the roses. In later years, the stench of the prison camp overpowered it—the vomit, diarrhea, filth, and the smell of death itself were the only familiar odors.

Sometimes in the stillness of the night, he would whisper "Wendy, my Wendy." Then he would drift off to sleep, dreaming about their years together.

He and Wendy were the envy of many of their friends, who used to kid them saying, "You guys are living in a fairy tale, certainly not the real world. Life just isn't that perfect."

He had everything he ever wanted—a gorgeous wife who stayed at home to care for their two healthy, energetic kids, a luxurious home, and a great church family. He even loved his career—as owner of a thriving insurance agency, which his father had started.

Life seemed perfect!

He recalled how he used to walk into his comfortable home after a busy day at the office, and break out singing the classic sixties hit, *Wendy*. His wife would run to him, and wrap her arms around him in a loving embrace, smiling.

Their Christian faith was a high priority for the couple. He served as a deacon in his local church. Often, he and some of his friends visited schools or nursing homes to give away small Bibles. Every Sunday they eagerly attended their local church to worship and often visited with friends after the service.

James earned his pilot's license his senior year in high school. Flying was the main reason he joined the Army Reserves following graduation. He took up gliding, which quickly became his favorite hobby. The freedom he felt soaring through the vivid, azure Colorado skies in total silence, exhilarated him, helping him feel closer to the Creator.

He also enjoyed flying his twin engine plane, using it for both business and pleasure flights. Occasionally, on weekends, he piloted his family across the majestic Rockies for an outing. They stared silently in awe at the magnificent, deep purple mountains, knowing they were seeing one of God's most beautiful creations. He called it a "God's eye view."

Special surprises delighted Wendy, so James looked for ways to please her. One day they flew to the other side of the mountain range, just the two of them, for a romantic picnic. The moment was perfect as they toasted each other with sparkling apple juice. He had slipped champagne glasses in the picnic basket when she wasn't looking. That day they both wondered if life could be any better, or their love any stronger.

They were soul mates, their lives mapped out, far into the future.

Life as the loving couple knew it, ended abruptly when James received the dreaded letter from the government—his draft notice. The time had come to pay his country back for his extensive training in the reserves.

Words can't begin to describe how difficult it was for James to leave his family and travel across the ocean to a bloody war, to a conflict no one really understood.

At the airport, when his son, Braden, clutched his leg crying, "Daddy, don't go," his heart shattered into a million pieces.

"I love you Daddy," were the last words spoken to him by his daughter, Kaylie, with tears streaming down her cheeks.

When it was time to part, he bent down and held his children tight as they cried in his arms.

Then he rose to face Wendy. Through muffled sobs she cried, "You come back to me, my love. Promise me, you'll take care of yourself. I'll be praying for you every day."

James' voice cracked. "God will protect me." He assured his family of his love.

"I'll return in a year," he pledged. Turning to walk away, his blue eyes were moist as he waved a final goodbye.

He walked with his unit to the waiting airplane and the tears started flowing freely. As they boarded the flight that would take them to active duty, he was not the only soldier with wet eyes. Each one had his own reasons for deep contemplation when the plane winged upward into the unknown.

The haunting memory of that final goodbye to his family still lingered in his mind. Many times McCarter wished he had spent more time with his family—people usually do when they lose someone they love.

Not a day went by that the men didn't wonder about the loved ones they left behind, four long, hard, decades ago.

The day of his capture, McCarter received a letter from his wife, which reported his father was critically ill. It was priceless to him, a rare, tangible possession from Wendy. That day he read it repeatedly, until he memorized it. He thought he could even smell the faint scent of his wife's favorite perfume on the stationery.

On that horrifying day, the captors ripped the letter from James' hands and maliciously burned it in front of him. That was typical of the enemy's heartless tactics.

McCarter watched through misty eyes. His body shook with rage at the cruel, insensitivity of his captors. Torment, dread, grief, and fear were etched in his countenance.

After the capture, there was no more communication from home. He never knew what happened to his father, but prayed for him every day.

The leader of the captors was a North Vietnamese army officer, named General Yo. He used any kind of mental or physical torture he could devise—the more vicious the act, the more pleasure it gave him. The more gruesome the scene, the more satisfaction he gained.

During McCarter's first interrogation, Yo ripped the soldier's wedding ring off his finger and put it on his own finger, kissing it—the ultimate act of mental brutality.

McCarter was not beaten as much as the others. He never understood why. Perhaps it was because he was an officer, or perhaps Yo thought mental anguish could be just as debilitating as his physical pain.

One of the things Yo often did in his sadistic way was concoct stories about the men's families—news that something terrible had happened to a child or wife—horrible things to cause mental torment. His vile deeds were detestable. He was evil incarnate.

Lies or truth, McCarter never knew which. In order to preserve his sanity, he gave up trying to sort it all out, trying not to dwell on Yo's claims. He would focus on the first twenty-three years of his life, which he knew were real.

Personal faith in God was a priority to both McCarter and Williams, and the main reason the two men formed a close bond from the beginning.

Monday was the high-ranking military leader, but Sunday was the spiritual leader. Together they helped each other make it through every agonizing day.

The other four GIs appeared to have lost all hope and faith. Yo's unimaginable cruelties savaged any semblance of hope they had at the beginning of their captivity. They were left with no faith in God, or hope in America.

Sunday and Monday seemed to have accepted their fate, perhaps because they didn't fear death. Yet, their faith had changed. Little by little, their spiritual talk faded, no longer part of their nightly tapping ritual.

They realized they were still there for each other—a small bit of encouragement was only a tap away. Together they would face the outcome…whatever it might be.

The other four men had only their fractured recollections to keep them alive. They merely existed, perhaps for only one more day.

Monday and his comrades were mere skeletons; they resembled the walking dead, each awaiting his demise. They no longer had the strength to attempt an escape, and guards watched for any possible suicide attempts. The men would never be permitted to award themselves the ultimate prize of death...they wanted it too badly. Yo would never allow it!

Tuesday

Tuesday's skin was literally crawling. The more he dug, the more it itched. Lice had so totally infested his scalp that every time he scratched his scarce, dingy gray strands of hair, his hands would be covered with blood. He had almost forgotten that he once had a full head of golden brown hair, let alone, what it looked like. That was a different world...a different life...a different person.

Tuesday's real name was Sergeant Brent Pfingston, and he was from Indianapolis, Indiana.

When deployed, he left behind five sisters, his mother, and father. He doesn't recall what they looked like. He often tried to capture their images in his mind, but after forty years of horrific beatings, those memories were gone.

As a kid, Brent was teased because he was short and round. He withdrew from social activities, becoming a loner. He was content in his bedroom by himself, and grew accustomed to the quiet and isolation.

Now, the silence makes him feel like he's going crazy. He would love anyone to talk to...anyone!

Even in the Army before his capture, his fellow soldiers would joke with him about being the shortest of the group, but he learned to take it in stride.

Sometimes he told his friends how much he weighed before the military. He would laugh. "I was a little overweight, but not too much— just some left over baby fat."

The military routine quickly turned his baby fat into muscle. He was never overly athletic, but certainly no longer "plump," as he called it.

That was then...this is now.

Captivity embedded its scars on him, as it had the rest of the prisoners. After four decades, he was frail and thin, looking much older than his years. His body evidenced harsh abuse. Any muscle he once had was long gone.

The year was 1970…the year that Tuesday's life changed forever.

It began when he received his draft notice. At first it stunned him, but the more he thought about it, the more honored he felt to be selected. He was proud to be in the United States Army, and even prouder to be an American. He would serve with his head held high.

Then came the day that the horror began.

The Viet Cong brutally attacked the supply depot where Pfingston worked. Sadly, it was just a couple of days before his scheduled return home to his family.

He was one of the fortunate ones—he survived. At least, that's what he thought at the time. He quickly realized that the lucky ones were those who died in battle.

Many times, he sarcastically asked the question, "Why do they torture a supply sergeant? What possible information can I give them—how many squares are in a roll of toilet paper?"

Between the lice and the oozing open sores—the pain at times was unbearable, and it seemed to be worsening with time. Sometimes the pain was so intense, he stuffed the filthy blanket in his mouth, so he could cry or scream without being heard. He didn't need another beating for making noise…that much he knew.

The only relief he could ever get was when he slept…which never was very sound…or very long. Oh, he wished he could! At least then, he could escape his pain and misery and relive what once was.

On Tuesday's day to tap, he usually talked about the Indianapolis 500, especially his favorite racecar driver, A.J. Foyt.

Before his deployment, he worked part-time at the famous Indianapolis Motor Speedway. He met many of the well known racers of the time: Foyt, Andretti, Unser, the great British driver—Graham Hill. He recalled those days fondly. *It was a tight squeeze, but I even got to sit in some of their racecars…it doesn't get much better than that!*

Since he was the oldest of the siblings, he felt protective of his sisters and took his "big brother" role seriously. Fortunately, for his older sisters, he left for Army basic training before he could scrutinize their dates.

During his conversations on his day, Tuesday often expressed concern about his sisters. He would tap, "I hope they married good men…they deserve the best."

When Tuesday was in high school, he would turn up the volume on his car radio to booming music, like a typical teenager. He would listen to his favorites: The Beach Boys, Jan & Dean and their "car" songs like, "*Hey, Little Cobra,*" and "*409.*"

He loved cars and continually talked about what car had the biggest and best engine, as if any of the men really cared. However, they all let him tap about his cars because it was his turn to talk and those cars were his love.

Pfingston seldom conversed about relationships. Occasionally, he would lose himself and talk about his dating days in his '67 Camaro. He said it was not a good car to take to a drive-in movie. It had bucket seats and a very small back seat, which meant he could not get close enough to his date.

Tuesday never talked about his faith—in God that is. He had faith in certain engines, and race drivers, and even cars, but he never mentioned trusting in a higher power.

Only Sunday and Monday ended their days with a prayer. Eventually, it became a silent prayer as the years dragged by. Usually their prayers were for others, mostly their families.

How religious the others were before captivity was not clear, judging by the wild lives they lived, and the stories they told. There is an expression, "There are no atheists in foxholes." There was even more truth to that in a POW camp, at least, in the beginning of confinement.

Wednesday

It just won't heal! Of course, it doesn't much matter, it will only be replaced by more wounds, the thin, pale prisoner whispered to himself.

Staring at the gash on the outside of his arm, he replayed in his mind what happened causing his latest injury.

The guard in charge, pushed him full force to the ground. He smashed against the sharp edge of a boulder. I couldn't go any faster. He was walking to the guard's disgusting latrine—not his favorite job, of course, not anyone's—cleaning the filthy toilets the guards use. How humiliating! The stench… the flies... the mosquitos, and the malaria they caused.

His mind drifted back to a time earlier in captivity when he suffered from that horrible disease. Alone, curled in a ball on the dirt floor in his cell, he drifted in and out of consciousness. He didn't know how long he was teetering between life and death. He hoped and prayed that the malaria would end his suffering once and for all…but somehow he stayed alive to face more torture. That's when he stopped praying to God. He stopped believing! Why would a loving God allow me to suffer this way? The only thing that died during that time of suffering was Wednesday's hope… his faith. He never talked to God again after that. What was the point?

His name was Thomas Traber. Better known as Wednesday.

Before enlisting in the Army, Traber worked as a mechanic in a small town in central Kansas. People came from miles away, so Traber could work on their vehicle. He had a reputation for being the best mechanic around.

He joined the military fresh out of high school. He could hardly wait to enlist because he desired further education, desperately wanting to be a helicopter mechanic.

After basic training, he arrived at helicopter mechanic school. He only enjoyed three short weeks of instruction before his company deployed to Vietnam.

Somehow, he became a gunner. "The man in the doorway," the other GIs called him. He was working with helicopters, but not repairing them as he hoped.

The gunners had a difficult job. They operated the guns on each side of the aircraft and were indispensable in fighting the war. Sometimes they would see where they were firing, other times they fired blindly into the jungle, hoping to hit an enemy target.

His job was essential. "The man in the doorway," was to get his fellow soldiers on and off the chopper as quickly as possible. The men were vulnerable when they were getting off the chopper, but even more at risk when they were getting on, because their backs were exposed to the enemy. Traber believed it gave new meaning to the term "Watch my back." There was no way of knowing how many people he killed in his military career—he tried not to think about it.

One day on a routine mission, Traber's helicopter crashed in the jungle. All ten soldiers aboard were captured by the Cong.

Years later, he was the only one of that group still alive.

On Wednesday's night to tap, he often tapped about his fishing trips to Wilson Lake. "Every weekend during the summer, I'd go to the lake for fun. One of my friends owned a speedboat. We'd ski, fish, and drink a lot of beer. I mean a lot! Oh, to smell those sizzling burgers again."

As a teen, Wednesday had several small jobs to earn spending money. One of his favorites was mowing the yard for a senator in Kansas, an influential politician.

He often talked about one summer in particular. "I was fifteen. The senator was relaxing on his back porch, watching me mow his huge yard. I still can feel that hot Kansas sun. The stifling wind made it hard to breathe."

He paused, letting his memory catch up to him. "Often the senator brought out a couple glasses of lemonade and called me over for a break. We both enjoyed the conversations about life in Kansas. I had utmost respect for that politician. Wounded in World War II, he still limped from his injury. He told me once how it happened, but I don't remember the details. All I recall was a kind, gentle man who cared about me, and took time out of his busy schedule to visit with me. I wonder whatever became of him."

One day, Le ran a computer search of the senator's name. Wednesday would be surprised to learn that the man ran for President of the United States. He would be proud of the fact that as a youth he was close to one of America's most influential politicians. Le could not share that news with him, although he wished he could.

The two favorite topics for Wednesday, as well as the other prisoners, were Thanksgiving and Christmas. Le could repeat hundreds of stories about those days. The memories of special holidays seemed embedded in the prisoners' minds, more than any other times.

Thursday

The rat inched closer. Thursday layed motionless, hoping his four-legged friend would appear for his nightly visit. If he didn't come, the prisoner would fear someone had hurt him, or possibly eaten him for a meal. That would be devestating!

Scrounging for food, the rodent stepped onto Thursday's boney hand, then crawled midway up his arm. Then, almost like it was on cue, the rat watched the prisoner, waiting.

It was the routine that had become all too familiar for both of them. And probably the only thing that kept the prisoner sane—companionship!

The prisoner was known as Thursday, his real name was Specialist Robert Freeman.

The rat…well, the rat was a dependable patient, who rarely ever missed his appointment. He fondly named his rodent friend "Professor Mortimer," but he called him "Mort" for short—the name of his favorite college professor.

Robert Freeman was an only child of divorced parents.

He was raised in Cooperstown, New York—home of "The Baseball Hall of Fame." No wonder he was a diehard baseball lover, a New York fan. Some would say he was obsessed with the sport as a young boy. He believed if the Yankees did not make it to the World Series, there was always the Mets. His philosophy about New York and baseball was interesting. If they play each other at the Series, it was no contest—it would be the Yankees all the way. If neither team made it, then it really was not a World Series after all—at least not one he'd be watching. He felt strongly that the Yankees were the team of the century.

He talked about two specific World Series. He remembered the Series in 1961 as the most exciting one ever. His only regret was how it turned out. Yankee pitcher—Ralph Terry, pitched to Pittsburgh's Bill Mazeroski, and the result was a game winning homerun. Freeman believed Pittsburgh played well and deserved their win that day.

However, his favorite of all times was the 1969 Miracle Mets. He talked endlessly about that Series. He boasted, "Tom Seaver was one of the greatest pitchers of all time. Players like him were one in a million."

Freeman's father, a prominent New York City lawyer, had many famous clients—none more important than the New York Yankees Organization. This gave him the privilege of having season box seats just a few rows behind the team's owners.

One of the biggest highlights in Freeman's life was the day he witnessed Roger Maris break Babe Ruth's homerun record. What an experience for a young boy—a memory of a lifetime that no one can take away—not even General Yo.

After that legendary game, his dad proudly took Robert to meet the man who broke the remarkable record. To his amazement, the giant of a man shook his hand and autographed a baseball for him.

When he left for war, the ball was still protected in a glass case at home.

The thing Freeman remembered most about Maris was his humility. He did not boast about his exploits. He just thanked the lad for watching the game, and told him that next time he would take him down to meet all the great ballplayers. Maris did not realize that to most people, at that moment in history, he was considered the greatest ballplayer in the world.

Freeman modeled his life after that baseball legend. He always tried to be kind, considerate, polite, and true to his word, just like his hero.

The past forty years in this hole they called "home," he has done that. Whenever he could help a fellow prisoner he would, no questions asked, no expectations in return.

Thursday's dream in life was to become a psychologist. He was fulfilling that goal in college, when drafted into the Army.

As a soldier, he worked with a medical unit as a psychologist, treating neurotic disorders caused by the stress of war. His job was to determine if certain men, after being in battle, were mentally fit to fight again. He had cases when the stress of war was too much, resulting in the men taking their own life or lives of others.

During the Vietnam War, it was referred to as "Post Vietnam Syndrome," more commonly known as Post Traumatic Stress Disorder (PTSD). Unfortunately, the illness has been around as long as there have been wars. In Civil War days, it was called "Soldier's Heart." During the First World War, it was known as "Shell Shock." During World War II, it was called "Battle Fatigue" or "Combat Fatigue." Whatever the name, it was the same thing—severe emotional problems caused by a traumatic event in one's life, such as the horror of war.

While on duty, Thursday was heading to a base with a man suffering from PTSD. The soldier's name was Specialist Ronald Lomack—a medic in the Army. Lomack had recently been active in a bloody battle, where he saw three of his comrades torn apart by a VC explosive.

The Cong designed a technique to stretch a line with mines or grenades attached to it across a path, or through the jungle. When GIs combed an area, if their feet touched the line, the explosive was detonated, and the results deadly.

Lomack was walking behind some comrades the day they tripped one of the lines. Three men were killed instantly, but the medic lived, the shocking images fixed in his mind. When he returned to camp, no one could quiet him—such a gruesome, horrific experience affected him immensely. He tried to get it out of his mind, but the scars stamped into his memory haunted him day and night.

One day, his memories erupted in uncontrolled rage. In a fit of anger, he exploded shouting expletives at those around him. Crazed, he took his M-16, walked to the front of the headquarters, and fired haphazardly, shots scattering everywhere. Fortunately, everyone was at the mess hall eating lunch, so nobody was hurt. This action caused him immediate admittance into the hospital psychiatric ward where Freeman was assigned to evaluate him.

While moving to a larger hospital facility, Lomack and Freeman were traveling in a caravan. The VC attacked and captured them, along with several other soldiers. Through the years, all the others in that attack died. Freeman and his patient were the only ones still alive.

That other prisoner is "Friday." Freeman felt compelled to help him, whenever and wherever he could, including in the miserable prison cell. Although, tapping was not as beneficial as face-to-face counseling would have been, Specialist Ronald Lomack still had forty years of evaluation.

So did the rat.

Friday

It was happening again. The smothering sensation. *I can't breath.* He tried to catch his breath, but couldn't get any oxygen. His heart beat faster, louder, and his chest started to burn. *Am I having a heart attack?* The shaking and profuse sweating would follow—he knew the routine. Next would come a terror that was paralyzing. *God, if you're there...please let me die!*

In fetal position, on the hard ground, he sobbed, quietly. *Calm down, deep breathing*, he thought repeatedly. *Calm down. Calm down....*

After a few minutes of self talk, his breathing started to return to normal. *Oh good, this isn't as bad as some of my episodes.*

Freeman once told him that he suffered from panic attacks.

Although he wasn't sure exatly what that meant, he knew he hated it. He knew it made him feel like he had lost his mind... totally out of control.

The panic attacks happened often...but only when he was awake.

Unfortunately, what happened when he slept...that was just as bad.

The recurring nightmares. They wouldn't stop. If only he could escape the horror! Screeching tires, shattering glass, fire, screaming...or else it would be a gruesome explosion.

Not surprising after all he had been through in his life.

To the other prisoners, he was known as Friday, but his birth name was Ronald Lomack.

Specialist Ronald Lomack tried to get a deferment from the military on the basis that his family farm in Missouri needed his help. The Army denied his request, and he received his draft notice shortly after.

The farm had been in the family for three generations. His three younger brothers took over the responsibilities on the farm when he left to serve his country.

Lomack attended a small school near his home. Ronald's graduation class consisted of nine students—six girls and three boys. He would say quite seriously, "The senior prom was fun for the boys, but not as much for the girls." He often talked about what good friends his schoolmates were. "Eleven of us started out in first grade. We remained close through the years."

Many times in Ronald's young life tragedy struck.

A dreadful farm accident killed his best friend, Ken, who was only twelve-years-old. While baling hay, he hit a stump, falling off the tractor. The baler crushed him.

The heartbreaking incident happened only a month after Ken's sister, two years older than he, drowned in a swimming accident. She hit her head on a rock while diving into a shallow lake.

Lomack tapped about Ken's attractive sister and told how much he missed her. "I had a secret crush on her. I think all my friends did, too. I wondered if she ever knew how much I cared about her."

In his senior year, another friend in his class died tragically in a car accident. Lomack tapped the story repeatedly. "The police report said the cause was reckless driving. I wasn't sure about that—it raised many questions in my mind. A couple of days later, I went to the scene to investigate and discovered what really happened. Tim had hit a deer. A piece of the car's headlight still clung to the animal's hide. It lay decomposing in the nearby ditch. I figured Tim managed to control the car until he hit the ditch, and then went airborne, eventually crashing through a large hay barn. The car and barn both caught fire. The officers believed Tim was conscious when he burned to death in the car—alone, and terrified. What a horrible way to die!"

His friend's death haunted him. In his nightmares, he heard screeching tires, glass shattering, and Tim screaming when his car burst into flames.

Lomack dwelt on that thought and it was overwhelming, deeply traumatizing him.

He visited the accident scene frequently and would sit silently reflecting on life and death. At his young age, death had stung him far too many times. He vowed to stop caring because it hurt too much when he lost someone he loved.

At times, he looked upward, crying out in pain, "Why God, why? Why did You take three people that I loved with my whole heart? How could a loving God allow this to happen?" He raised his clenched fist toward heaven in a fit of rage. Filled with torment, he yelled, "Where were You God? Why didn't You help?" Sometimes he even cursed God.

Friday often tapped about those he lost. If there were any tears left they would have flowed, but there weren't any—empty, dry, hollow eyes were all that remained—and a heart filled with lingering resentment.

Unlike the other prisoners, Lomack talked bitterly about his imprisonment. Clearly, the hatred he felt towards the enemy consumed him.

That was why Friday suffered more than the others did at the hands of his evil captors. The enemy sensed his hatred and bitterness, and he paid for it through extra beatings and unconscionable abuse.

The other prisoners mellowed somewhat. Not in a cowardly way, but almost as if they had no feelings left. No emotions. No expectations.

When ordered to do a lowly task, the other captives said nothing. There were no dirty looks or muttering under their breath. They just went ahead as ordered—like dead men going through the motions.

They would never acknowledge their captor's superiority by saying, "Okay," or "yes." Certainly, they would never answer, "Yes, sir." All the soldiers refused to do that—they would rather die first.

General Yo wanted them to feel subservient to him. After years of torture, he finally gave up. Just seeing them suffer was enough. He continually sought new and more bizarre methods of inflicting pain on his prisoners, especially on the one that he hated most, Friday.

Friday was different from the others. When he received an order, he would insult the guards using vulgar language.

One thing he would never do was bow down to his evil captors. Even though he knew it would result in an immediate beating, he would not yield to them. Friday despised Yo and his men, and wanted to be sure that they knew it.

Once he insulted General Yo by swearing at him in front of the guards. The maniacal leader had him tied to a nearby tree, with his arms stretched above his head. Yo brutally beat him nonstop with a bamboo stick for almost an hour. Then he stomped repeatedly on the prisoner's bare foot with his military boots, grinding his heal into it. The shattered bones caused intense pain making him convulse, resulting in both of his shoulders being dislocated. He screamed in agony.

Yet, the worst part was the gloat—the devilish grin on Yo's face, all the while, laughing in sordid glee.

Sunday doctored him the best he could, but Friday had a lasting limp from the many broken bones that never healed correctly. Medical care from the captors was nonexistent in the prison.

In recent years, General Yo eased up on the beatings. He knew the men would not survive in their weakened conditions, unless he did. He wanted them to continue to suffer. Death would be a means of escape and put an end to their misery, so he preferred them to feel miserable, to grovel in subjugation.

Saturday

"Saturday" was the remaining prisoner, also known as Corporal Daniel Sparks.

He had a different perspective in his cell. His cell was not quite as filthy, or as cramped as the others were.

And he was never brutally tortured like the other men.

Although, he did deal with the excess heat, the insects, and the rodents, it wasn't to the same degree.

Saturday's food was tolerable, even enjoyable.

On his day to tap, he manufactured stories…what he thought America would be like.

And the biggest difference…when the prisoners were finished tapping for the night, Saturday would quietly step out of his cell in the dark of night, and go home to his family.

In reality, Saturday was a Vietnamese soldier named Le Huu Trang. Most people called him Le.

The real Daniel Sparks died forty years ago.

Le was a spy within the group, a mole, planted by General Yo. In other words, he was a spy among the "weak."

FOUR

The Plan

Le Huu Trang's life began to change one rainy day when he met some Americans who had established an orphanage in a nearby village.

He had often heard about the children's home from his wife, Linh, who volunteered there regularly. When she saw a need, she eagerly jumped in to help whatever way she could. She lived up to her name, "Linh," which in Vietnamese means *Gentle Spirit*. She assisted the cooks in the kitchen. Other times, she changed beds, washed linens, or whatever else needed to be done. Mostly, she loved spending individual time with the orphans, patiently teaching or reading to them. Her heart broke for the children, knowing most of them came from deplorable backgrounds.

While working with the Americans, she sensed a void in her life. She realized they had something she was missing. Through talking with the staff, and reading the Bible they had given her, she discovered Jesus was the answer. Her quest led her to discover a personal relationship with Christ.

When she came home one evening, she told her husband about how different the people at the orphanage were. "Those Americans are amazing. They demonstrate such compassion and love to the orphans. They are very different than what we are used to in our country."

As the days went by, Le noticed a dramatic change in his wife after her conversion. It triggered his interest and he began to visit the orphanage more frequently, hoping to find an answer.

The orphanage housed twenty-five children ranging from ages three to fifteen. All were needy children—rejected by parents and society. Some were abandoned on the orphanage steps because they were an inconvenience, or as in the case of many of the girls, simply not wanted. The orphanage became the only home many of these youngsters ever knew.

The well-built, rough-looking, black man in charge of the orphanage was one of the kindest people Le had ever met. Samuel Jefferson came from New Orleans, Louisiana. Everyone just called him, "Sam."

The Vietnamese locals respected him as he worked among them, caring for the needs of the children. Le could see the loving interaction between the Americans and the little ones in their care.

Le was not a believer in Jesus, but enjoyed spending time with Sam whenever he had the opportunity. The Vietnamese guard spoke fluent English so the two men would talk for hours. They chatted about their families, each other's cultural traditions, and life in general.

Almost every time they conversed, Sam would tell him about a special friend he had met. He told him how Jesus Christ changed his life.

Occasionally, Sam talked about his life before he met Jesus. He told Le, "I was a man filled with hate, willing to fight anyone at any time. It would only take an action, a word, or even a look to infuriate me. Fighting was my way to settle differences with others. It was the only way I knew."

Sam served in the United States Army Special Forces. It seemed the right fit for him because of his background and fighting instinct. He was in many firefights and battled numerous enemies. Sam never talked about the men he killed, but the number was high. One of the young men at the orphanage told Le that he heard rumors about Sam killing over a hundred men in close combat fighting in Iraq and Afghanistan.

Le found it hard to believe that such a gentle person, who compassionately cared for orphans, could have previously been a man filled with such hatred. It piqued his curiosity about the One Sam called, "Jesus."

Often the two men would get into lengthy conversations about God. Sam talked about the role Jesus played in his life, but it always left Le with many questions. He was confused and hungry to know more. *How could Jesus change a person that much?* When they talked about spiritual matters, Sam would explain how Jesus loved the unlovely and defended the lowly. He stood up to the authorities when something was wrong, or when he saw someone treated unfairly.

Le realized that Christians, like Sam, had something he wanted for his own life. He soon came to know Jesus in a personal way. His life changed immediately.

Together, Le and Linh would study the Bible and pray. They had a purpose, a commitment to a higher calling.

The Vietnamese guard often asked Sam questions about America. "What is it really like… are all the people as friendly as you?"

Before Sam could answer, Le asked another question. "Can ordinary citizens own their own business?" He had only heard stories and they were never favorable. He began wondering if America was really their enemy as he had been taught.

Sam told him what freedom was like. Passionately he proclaimed, "In the United States you have the opportunity to become wealthy, no matter what class you come from. You can fulfill your dreams if you work hard. I came from the bottom, the slums of New Orleans, and now I have college degrees in economics and theology. I'm not rich, but I'm content."

Le sat spellbound as Sam continued. "America is the land of unlimited opportunity and prosperity. There is freedom of religion and speech. It is a democracy where you vote for the officials you want to serve you. Your opinions matter, regardless of your heritage. Even though America has problems, it's still the greatest country on earth."

Le imagined what Sam's homeland must be like. Sometimes in the stillness of the night, he would dream about America, picturing it vividly in his mind. He hoped his family could someday visit the land Sam loved.

The American planted a desire in the Vietnamese guard, which would only grow stronger with time.

The freedom Sam talked about seemed unbelievable, unattainable. Yet, Le could only take him at his word...and continue to dream. Freedom is a difficult concept to grasp for someone who has never experienced it.

His word—that was the trait Le respected most about Sam. He always spoke the truth. When he said he would do something, he did it. He followed words with actions.

Le observed the American stand nose-to-nose against Communist soldiers and officials, never backing down. Le wondered why the government tolerated his friend. Maybe they feared him. Perhaps it is the reason they turned their backs on many things he did—actions that others in the oppressed land could not get away with.

Sam walked the talk. He was available to assist the local people when they needed help. He often was the first on the scene after a storm—repairing roofs, rebuilding homes, and serving where needed. He tended to physical ailments of the people—brought medical supplies, bandaged wounds, and even helped bring a baby into the world.

Le and his wife respected Sam and the other Americans. They watched closely day after day, and Sam never wavered in his compassion, loyalty, or values.

One day Le asked him, "Why do you do what you do? After all, there is no money involved, no material gain, really there's only hardship—both physical and mental anguish. I can only imagine how difficult it is to keep an orphanage going with the Communist government always watching and threatening you. Why do you tolerate that? What's really in it for you?"

Sam's reply was simple, and it was always the same. "It just seems like the right thing to do."

Le's upbringing in Vietnam drilled Communist doctrine into him. It taught that only Mao Tse Tung, the former leader of China and the Communist movement, and Ho Chi Minh, who he referred to as "Uncle Ho" were right, and never to be questioned.

However, since Le became a Christian, he could see the control his leaders had over their subjects. He questioned the cruelty. He had a gnawing realization that it was wrong to treat others with such brutal, atrocious tactics.

Le heard about freedom, but never understood the concept. In the military, he saw what the Vietnamese government called freedom, but also witnessed hatred and controlling power. Many times, he observed his fellow soldiers beat innocent civilians simply because they disagreed, or hesitated before following an order.

During the last four years, Le listened to the prisoners talking about their past lives and the freedoms they once enjoyed. It triggered thoughts of what Sam had said about freedom.

As he mulled it over, he began to realize that he was not free, and this life was not for him anymore. He loathed the brutality and the harshness of the helpless, tortured prisoners. In his heart, he knew it was wrong, but what could he do? *I am only one man, just a lowly prison guard.*

Vietnamese citizens did not have the freedom of full access to the internet. Their government filtered it tightly. Propaganda was rampant; news was controlled.

Thanks to Sam, Le learned how he could get around many of the internet limitations.

A few months earlier, Le completed an internet search on each of the prisoners. He explored the "Vietnam Veterans Memorial Wall" website. Many names had personal messages posted by friends or family. Williams and McCarter had sites designated in their honor. One read, "Until they all come home." Another said, "Remember to pray for our POWs."

It captured his interest. Le expanded his search secretly, researching what happened to some of the prisoners' family members through the years. Of course, he never mentioned it to any of the captives.

If his superiors found out he knew the information, they would have him and his family imprisoned or killed. The control the Vietnamese government held over its citizens was terrifying, causing mindless obedience.

Through the years, Le frequently asked the other guards what the prisoners did to deserve such demeaning treatment. In return, the reply would always be the same. "They are Americans who fought in the Vietnam War. They killed our babies and women. They are the enemy." The authorities gave the rehearsed answer, never wavering.

As Le studied the conflict, he found out differently. There were accounts of soldiers who went into villages and dug wells, built orphanages, or flew sick or pregnant Vietnamese to hospitals for needed medical care. He was stunned. It certainly was not what he was reared to believe.

One night, Saturday (Le), tapped a question. "Were you ever in a position where you had to kill innocent people?"

The prisoners agreed that innocent people were not killed deliberately. One prisoner tapped, "Sometimes the Viet Cong hid in villages among civilians, and women and children might have been caught in the crossfire. At times, it was difficult to identify the enemy. We never intentionally killed the innocent."

Le finally realized that the only crime the men had committed was being American. General Yo found them guilty, gave them a life sentence, imprisoned, and tortured them, simply because they came from the United States of America.

The guard was keenly aware of the treaties Vietnam and the United States had signed freeing all POWs.

Le knew something had to be done.

On rare occasion, Le would catch a glimpse of the six prisoners working together, never uttering a word, staring at the ground as they dug or hoed. He noticed their sweaty faces wore only a blank, expressionless stare—all visible signs of emotion had been erased from their lives.

One night as they walked back to their cells, the captain quickly glanced at Le. Their eyes met briefly. Monday noticed something out of the ordinary on Le's face; it resembled pity. Le smiled at the prisoners on other occasions after making sure no one was watching, but this time was different. That strange look confused Monday. He wondered if he saw a glimpse of compassion on the guard's face. *What did it mean?*

Monday would never forget what happened next.

Le nodded to him, looked around to make sure no one was watching, and unmistakably smiled.

Monday walked by, his eyes locked on the guard.

Le never knew why he voiced three words to Monday, but they came out clearly, "I'm sorry, GI."

Monday's eyes widened, staring back at the man who kindly spoke to him.

Then Le repeated the strange words. "I'm sorry, GI."

Was it a joke, or another method of Yo's torture?

Fearfully, Monday lowered his gaze to the ground. As he turned away, he looked one last time at the guard. There was no mistake—his eyes showed compassion. *Why? What did that look mean? What did those words imply? Was it a trap?*

That night when Monday returned to his cell, Le listened for tapping about what had happened. *Would Monday refer to the unexpected exchange that took place that afternoon?*

It was never mentioned.

A confused Le went home after his shift and talked to his wife, Linh. They chatted about the situation—the men, their conditions, and Le's convictions. He related how his heart and mind were tormented by the continued persecution of the helpless men.

Laying his head on the pillow that night to get some much needed rest, he noticed the smell of fresh sheets. The laundry had been washed and hung outside to dry in the gentle breeze. Taking deep breaths, he tried to capture the fresh scent, and make it last forever. The fragrance triggered another thought of the soldiers in their repulsive cells, and the foul smells they dealt with every moment of their captivity. *When was the last time they smelled fresh sheets? They didn't even have sheets—only smelly, bare, dirt floors, and a torn, filthy, old blanket.*

As these thoughts raced through his mind, Le turned over in bed and faced Linh. "I must help them. I am their only hope."

"Yes, I agree. We are in this together, my dear," she whispered. "What can we do?"

They talked about the prisoners until dawn.

For days, these thoughts haunted them, monopolizing every conversation when they were together.

One sweltering day, the prisoners had been forced to go all day without food, and little water. Le observed the prisoners toiling under the blistering sun, and it became painfully evident how exhausted and demoralized they had become. Their emaciated bodies could hardly walk, and their faces grimaced in pain. *How much more can they endure?*

The guard could no longer sit idly by; he felt compelled to intervene. He made a momentous decision to help free the prisoners, no matter the cost. As for his family, only God knew what would become of them, but he must take the risk.

Le and his wife began developing a plan of intervention.

Linh angled her head. "Le, we both know you are the only person who is in the position to help. We are in this together. We will find a way to gain their freedom."

Le immediately began investigating possible strategies. Linh thought of ways she could assist their effort. They brainstormed each possibility, weighed the advantages and disadvantages, determined to find the correct solution.

It was not an option to report the tyrant, General Yo, to the Vietnamese authorities. The Vietnamese government had signed several peace treaties with the United States, and had agreed to help locate all the POWs and MIAs. If Le turned Yo in, the Vietnamese authorities probably would not believe him, or be forced to eliminate the POWS. Either way, he and the prisoners would surely lose their lives.

After much thought, discussion, and prayer with Linh, he reached a conclusion. *The only possible solution is to help the POWs disappear. But how? And when?*

Le was fully aware of the risks. The stakes were enormous. Everything in the plan must synchronize perfectly. One small mistake and all would fail. The consequences would be devastating, no escape. Death for the prisoners would be a better option.

Le and Linh considered their three children. He also was concerned for his parents. *Would their suffering be worth the freedom of these men?*

Linh flashed a painful look at her husband. "What will happen to our children, your parents? They are innocent bystanders."

"It's not time to walk away; we must commit our family into God's hands."

They sat in silence, asking for divine guidance.

Everywhere Le went, he kept his eyes and ears open for an escape route, or help of some kind. He knew he could not accomplish the mission alone. *Am I facing an impossible task? Is our goal attainable?*

One evening, Le realized he had exhausted all possibilities. He could not think of any way to achieve their objective.

Over a cup of tea, the couple sat down to pool their ideas.

Le looked distressed. "We still don't have a plan. I'm at a loss. I just know we can't pull this off without help. "

Linh asked, "What about Sam? Could he help?"

Le's eyes brightened, and his voice revealed his excitement. "Yes, Sam! He's ex-military, and I've heard stories about him being in covert operations years ago. Why haven't we thought of him? Maybe Sam is the answer we are looking for."

The more Le contemplated his wife's suggestion, the more apprehensive he became. *Can Sam be trusted? How much should I tell him?*

Le had other concerns. *Will anyone believe that just a few miles away, hidden deep in the jungle, there are six American POWs left from the Vietnam War? How could they have survived in those harsh conditions for forty years? Why would a Vietnamese prison guard want to help them?*

He knew Sam's knowledge and experience could prove beneficial. That is, if the American was willing to risk helping him with the dangerous mission. The more he considered it, the more he realized that Sam was their only option.

Unexpectedly, Le heard that Sam and his staff had been ordered to leave the country—he knew it was his last opportunity and he needed to move fast.

The first part of his plan would be to convince the prisoners to trust him—a huge challenge. Only then could he prepare for the escape.

Next, he would deal with Sam.

Le believed with his whole heart that within a few days the prisoners would walk to freedom, or die trying.

FIVE

The Plea

It was Monday. Actually, it was Thursday, but the prisoners lost track of time years ago. To them it was Monday, which meant it was Monday's turn to tap.

The men rarely talked about the day of their capture. All they discussed were past occurrences, reminiscing about happy times, events that took place before their capture forty years ago.

As usual, that night Monday talked about his wife and family. He tapped about the time his daughter Kaylie fell, badly gashing her head. "We could not stop the bleeding. Wendy and I rushed our disoriented, frightened daughter to the hospital, praying the entire way. If anything had happened to her, I would never forgive myself. I felt responsible. It was my job to protect my children." Something about the way he tapped allowed the prisoners to sense how much he cared, how much he loved his family. In a strange way, they felt his emotion.

"I wonder what kind of woman my Kaylie grew up to be," Monday tapped. "She was always smiling, and fun loving. Oh, she enjoyed making new friends."

Le envisioned a smile on Monday's face when he spoke about his little girl.

"One day when we were Christmas shopping at a mall in Denver, Kaylie spotted a helpless young man. He had a coarse beard and reeked of body odor. He was dressed in wrinkled Army fatigues and an old, worn U.S. Army hat. He sat slumped in a wheelchair. She asked if she could give the man some money because he looked lonely and poor.

"I remember thinking that the man was most likely taking advantage of people, just looking for a handout. Reluctantly, I gave my trusting daughter a dollar to give him. I was considering the best way to explain to my innocent child that sometimes people take advantage of others and are willing to do anything to make a buck.

"Then something happened that I will never forget. The man smiled at her when she handed him the bill, and then a tear trickled slowly down his cheek. It appeared the man was moved because one sweet, little girl showed him compassion."

Monday continued tapping his story. "As I stood watching the scene, a woman walked up beside me and told me the man's story. When drafted, he had a wife and young daughter. Six months into his tour of duty in Vietnam, he was severely wounded and came home paralyzed. Some doctors believed he might be able to walk again, but he had given up all hope. When he returned to the states, his wife left him, taking their little girl. She said she could not handle his problem—it was too big for her. They meant the world to him, especially his daughter. He never saw them again. How he missed them! Every day he went to that spot and sat helplessly in his wheelchair. He no longer cared if he would ever walk again."

Monday shared his heartfelt thoughts. "Words cannot explain what I felt at that moment. I stared at the veteran in the wheelchair. He did what his country asked of him. He paid a high price and returned home to face rejection, not only by the American people, but also by his own wife. That was too much for me," Monday said. "I opened my wallet and gave that man every bill I had."

The tapping stopped briefly as Monday reflected on the life changing event.

He continued. "As the disabled veteran took the money from my hand, he looked directly into my eyes for a long moment. I saw raw pain and loneliness."

I looked down at my daughter who was tenderly touching my arm, with a huge smile on her face." Monday began to tap slower. "Then, Kaylie turned to that dirty, rugged man, leaned over his wheelchair, and gave him a hug and soft kiss on his rough face. Then she did another amazing thing...she said, 'Jesus loves you.'"

Even though tapping relayed the story, the prisoners could feel the experience, picturing the episode vividly in their minds.

"I watched, absorbed by the scene before me. That simple act of love by my daughter brought me, as well as many onlookers, to tears. What a lesson I learned that day! Compassion for someone less fortunate should never be withheld because of preexisting ideas or stereotypes. Children look through eyes of love, uncolored by prejudice. I remembered how Jesus reached out to people in need, like the woman at the well, and I vowed to do the same from that moment on."

Silence reigned in the cells when everyone pondered what Monday shared.

Le listened to the heartbreaking story with the others. He decided to tap a question that weighed heavy on his heart. "Did you ever see that man again?"

There was complete stillness. No one, nothing, not even a rat made a sound.

Finally the tapping resumed, "It's funny you should ask that. A few days later, I contacted a client in Denver who owned a cabinet shop, and asked him if he could use a disabled veteran. I knew the owner of the business was a Korean War vet. I didn't have to ask twice. Not only did he hire him, but he gave him his upstairs loft at the factory to live in—complete with a convenient elevator."

Monday continued telling more captivating stories about his wife and children.

It was getting late and Le knew it was time to cut in. That was something they seldom did unless they had a question. He knew he had to make his move before the prisoners fell asleep.

To safeguard their identities, nobody ever knew who asked questions, but on this rare occasion, Le (Saturday) identified himself. He needed them to know they could trust him. Certainly, if the escape was ever going to work, he had to gain their confidence.

He tapped, "Saturday here…do you ever feel like leaving this place?"

There was absolute silence for a full thirty seconds. Then came, tap, tap, tap. Of course, Le did not know who it was.

"Leave? How?"

"Escape," Le replied.

"Are you crazy? We would be killed!"

"After they torture us," another added.

"I know how to do it," Le responded.

"This conversation is over," one of them insisted.

"No, hear me out. I know how to get away…all of us."

Dead quiet! Nobody answered—probably out of fear that the guards would overhear, and all would suffer the consequences. Why would anyone bring up the idea of an escape now? They had been there too long!

Le pressed on. He had gone this far. He knew this was his opportunity. "I have figured out a way to get out of here. I mean all of us. We can do it, but only if we all agree."

A hush came over the cells. For what seemed like an eternity, there were no sounds. Nothing!

He decided to continue down the path he established. "I want to see my family again. I want to experience freedom." As Le tapped on the wall, he realized that he was not only talking about the prisoners, but also himself. He desired to experience true freedom for the first time in his life.

He thought of Sam and the other Americans at the orphanage. He recalled a Bible verse Sam had once shared with him. Le tapped, "Jesus said, you can be free."

"The only way Jesus can free us is through death. If we try to escape, we will face certain death. You are right...we will be free with Jesus in heaven," someone tapped back.

"Why are we afraid? What do we have to lose?" Le asked boldly.

"I don't fear death. I fear another beating. I fear being whipped to the point that I won't be able to walk again. I fear that I will be left to die, suffering and alone—that's what I fear."

"Don't we have to at least try?" Le asked.

"We have tried many times. All we got in return is more beatings. Almost thirty men are dead because they tried to escape."

"I agree," another soldier replied. "We will not face death when we are caught, that's too easy. We will face more beatings... I can't take anymore of those."

That ended all communication for the night. Not another word was tapped.

Le was disappointed that the prisoners were not open to his plan, but he also understood. As he reflected on the details of the night, he realized he did not know who or how many men joined in the discussion. *Perhaps they were afraid to say anything. Could there be a couple silent men who agree with me? Or even just one?*

The next day, Le traded duty with another guard. He knew time was running out, and he had to make the prisoners understand before it was too late. He felt his best chance was to convince their leader, the captain, also known as Monday. Then, perhaps Monday could persuade the others to join him.

As Le helped deliver the prisoners to their jobs, he inconspicuously stayed close to Monday.

Occasionally, Monday would glance at Le, still surprised by the three words the guard had recently voiced to him—"I'm sorry, GI."

When Le flashed him a smile, Monday, confused by the guard's bizarre behavior, didn't know what to think.

As the blazing sun beat down on them, the other guard stationed with Le, motioned that he needed a break. This gave Le the opening he wanted.

Noticing the sweat pouring off Monday's brow, Le offered him a drink from his water bottle.

Monday looked at the Vietnamese guard with skepticism.

Le nodded his head. "Go ahead."

Monday's canteen was filled with dirty water from the river. Cautiously, he reached for the guard's canteen. At first he hesitated to drink, but then took a big swallow. He glanced at Le, watching for his reaction. Then he swigged the rest of the cool, clean water down, almost to the last drop. Suddenly, he realized what he did and abruptly stopped. Water ran down his chin. He eyed the nearly empty bottle. As he apprehensively handed it back to the guard, Monday flinched, knowing a beating would come next.

Without wavering, Le raised the bottle to his lips and finished the last few swallows.

The act of kindness baffled Monday. He wondered about the bizarre behavior of the guard.

The rustle of the nearby brush gave warning that the other guard was returning. Le hurriedly nodded to Monday, and whispered, "It's a beautiful day to be alive."

He stared directly into his eyes.

Shocked, Monday realized those were the kindest words he had heard in forty years, or maybe the cruelest, depending on how he looked at it.

Monday glanced at the guard a few more times that day, but quickly looked the other way when he noticed Le smiling at him.

That night, Tuesday tapped about a time when he took his girlfriend to the 1967 Indy 500. "What a heartbreaker! Parnelli Jones in his whistling, turbine racecar lost with a lap to go because of a faulty two-dollar part."

Le didn't know if Tuesday's story was accurate. In fact, he did not really understand it.

Nevertheless, Tuesday was noticeably excited as he was tapping his story. "Just before the car broke down, I was jumping up and down. I felt confident I was seeing a sure win, so I turned to the beautiful brunette on my side, and planted a long kiss on her lips. I almost married her. In fact, I would have, if I had not been drafted."

More silence.

"I wonder whatever happened to her," he added. There was stillness as he thought of what might have been.

After so many years, the prisoners knew when to be quiet, and when to help each other through a difficult time. Their survival depended on mutual support.

In the hush of the night, Saturday knew it was the ideal time to speak. "Saturday here…I have been thinking of a way to get out of this place. I have devised a plan to get all of us home in just days. What do you think about it?"

Again, nothing.

"What about it? Does anyone want to be free again?" Le persisted.

Finally, one prisoner tapped, "Free! Free! Who are you kidding?"

You could almost feel the anger as another soldier expressed his feelings, "Are you being cruel? Why are you saying this? You have to be kidding. Free! Only death will make us free."

Still another, or perhaps the same soldier, added, "America has forgotten us. To them we are dead. Probably, not even a memory. We will never be free. We are weak, and our enemy is strong. Home is too far away. Escape is impossible."

"No, it isn't. We can do it," Saturday protested.

Another soldier tapped fearfully. "I think this conversation needs to end. What if they are listening?"

Saturday tapped, "So…what if they are?"

Exhausted and discouraged, one prisoner offered, "I am sick of the beatings. I just want to die. I am tired. Please…just let me die."

Even through the tapping, the sadness could be sensed—pure hopelessness, only despondency.

What more can I say? How can I convince them? What more can I do? Le was at a loss.

Most of them had attempted to take their own lives, more than once, only to be brought back from death's escape.

Friday tried suicide several times. Once he jumped off a cliff, broke an arm, and the same foot General Yo injured years before. The others nursed him back to health, but he walked with a limp. The pain in his arm was a constant reminder—some days worse than others.

Wednesday once slit his wrist with a sharp rock. He lost a lot of blood, teetering on death's doorstep for days, but lived through it.

Both men were still angry at Sunday for saving their lives.

General Yo would not have let them die anyway. Their suffering meant too much to him; somehow, he would keep them alive and miserable as long as he could.

There was an eerie absence of sound the remainder of the night. Le wondered what was going through the minds of these men. *Were they fearful it was a trap? Were they so broken and adapted to this horrible life they simply accepted it? Didn't they have any hope left, only despair?*

Le recalled reading about how the Nazis captured the Jews in World War II. They forced a man to dig a hole, and then fill it again, repeating the process until his will was broken. At that point, the prisoners did anything the Nazis told them to do, including walking to their death.

Le believed this situation was similar. These also were broken men. He had to get their attention another way. If escape would ever be a reality, he needed to discover a method to obtain their trust and cooperation...fast.

The Vietnamese guard went home exhausted that night. He collapsed in bed, but could not get the vulnerable prisoners off his mind. As he tossed and turned, he wondered what else he could do to gain the prisoners trust. Time was getting short. The window to freedom would close for all of them soon.

Finally, he drifted into a restless sleep.

Morning came too quickly.

Fortunately, Le would be working with Monday again. *There must be a way to reach him. I have to get him to understand the urgency of my plan.*

Le recalled a recent conversation with the American at the orphanage. They were discussing people and their complacency. Le asked Sam, "How do you get through to someone who is contented with his life? How do you explain that he is missing something?"

Sam replied, "Share scripture with him. Tell him how much God loves him. I use John 3:16 often."

Le became familiar with the well known scripture and memorized it. It quickly became his favorite verse: *For God so loved the world that he gave his only begotten Son, that whosoever believeth in Him should not perish, but have everlasting life.*

Sam was a wealth of information for the guard. He was knowledgeable in many areas: the Bible, history, geography, military, and even relationships.

Another time Le asked his American friend, "What great speech would any American know?"

Sam thought for a moment and then blurted out, "I know! It's the Gettysburg Address!"

Le was obviously confused, but Sam explained, "It was a speech made by the sixteenth President of the United States after a great battle. The final words are powerful. '…and that Government of the people, by the people, for the people shall not perish from the earth.'"

Le replayed those words in his mind. It was a concept he could not fully understand, but the idea sounded remarkable.

When Le recalled the conversation with Sam, an idea came to him.

As Monday worked tediously, Le approached him and quietly asked, "Can you recite the last line of the Gettysburg Address?"

Monday stared back at the guard, not saying a word.

Le took pride of his mastery of the English language. Therefore, he was not sure if his good English or the question astounded the American more. Probably both did.

Le looked straight into his eyes and said, "…and that Government of the people.…"

Monday joined in slowly with his gravelly voice.

Together they finished, "…by the people, for the people, shall not perish from the earth."

It was a moment neither of them would ever forget. Two men who ought to be enemies, reciting an influential speech written one-hundred forty-five years earlier by one of America's greatest leaders. The scene was powerful.

With a small tear in his eye, Monday stared back at the guard. *What just happened?*

Le added, "Those were great words by a great leader. Were they not?"

Monday continued studying him, intently. Reluctantly, he nodded his head in agreement.

Le offered him another drink from his water bottle. Monday drank a few sips and handed the flask back.

Shielding his eyes from the sun with his hand, Le looked upward, just as a bird flew overhead. Both men watched it glide effortlessly through the air.

The guard took a drink from the bottle and stated, "Oh, to be free like that bird."

Monday stood spellbound, astonishment written all over his face. He fixed his eyes on the man who guarded him the past four years. "Who are you?" Monday quizzed the guard.

The young Vietnamese guard looked around to make sure nobody was watching. He replied softly, "I'm a friend." He paused, and then added, "A redeemer. John 3:16. Do you remember it?"

The aging POW, touched by the familiar verse, nodded his head. "I remember saying it to myself every night. During the first several years in this hellhole, I recited the verse as often as I could. Unfortunately, somewhere along the way, it stopped." *When did my faith begin to dwindle?*

Le continued to look at the peaceful, blue sky. He took a whiff of the humid air, and glanced at the dense jungle, colored with every shade of green. He hoped to ease Monday's fears, but also kept a lookout for the other guard to return.

He knew he must act quickly. "I believe what it says in Psalms 33. *Behold, the eye of the LORD is upon them that fear him….*" He looked directly into the eyes of the prisoner and finished the verse. "*…to deliver their soul from death.*"

A look of amazement crossed Monday's face, mixed with confusion, and a faint glimmer of hope.

Le whispered, "Do you remember Proverbs 3:5?"

Monday shook his head, lowering his eyes, ashamed. "It's been too long. My mind does not even remember yesterday."

Thankful for the opportunity, Le quickly recited it, *Trust in the LORD with all thine heart; and lean not onto thine own understanding.*

As Le shared the verse, a sparkle appeared in Monday's eyes. "Yes. Yes, I do remember it. But, what does that have to do with me?"

"Trust," Le said confidently. "You need to trust."

The older American looked at the young Vietnamese guard with a blank stare, not fully understanding what he meant.

The crackling twigs under foot indicated the other guard was returning to resume his duties. The conversation ended.

Nonchalantly, Le walked away uttering the words, "Just think of 'Saturday' when you remember those words tonight."

He could not see Monday's expression when the prisoner's jaw dropped, astonishment on his hardened face.

Another guard took Le's shift for the rest of the day freeing him to go to town to pick up supplies. Before he left, he looked back at the feeble POW toiling in the rice paddy. The pain in Monday's back was noticeable, agony written all over his face.

Monday managed to turn his head, glancing at the guard who had given him a spark of hope…*dare I believe?*

Meanwhile, Le prayed that Monday understood what he meant.

SIX

The Decisions

Le's trip to town took longer than he expected, so he could not hear the conversation that took place on the walls that night; he did not know if anything about the events of the day was shared.

However, it gave him the perfect opportunity to set the second part of his plan in motion.

He finally had an opportunity to visit Sam at the orphanage.

Earlier in the week, Le heard from one of the other guards that Sam and his team were being forced out of the country because of their Christian teaching. Word spread that the orphanage would close soon, and all the children would be moved to state facilities. Sam was responsible for giving the devastating news to the children. It was the only home most of them had ever known; they loved Sam and the rest of the staff.

After much thought, Le still was not certain how much information he should reveal. It was obvious the authorities were already suspicious of the American.

As Le and Linh sat eating a bowl of hot noodles, he looked around the humble orphanage. His heart broke for the children; he hoped they would be content in their new home.

Linh, raised in an orphanage herself, felt at home with Sam and his staff. She never knew her parents. Her only family was the other orphans until she married Le. Perhaps that explained her burning desire to volunteer with the children she had grown to love.

Sam joined the couple at the table.

Le looked at him and boldly stated, "Sam, I have a favor to ask."

"Shoot," Sam replied hastily.

"Sam, I have a confession." He paused, contemplating what to say. "I'm a guard at a prison, which is hidden deep in the jungle."

Sam's eyes widened. "Well, that I did not know."

Le spoke carefully, wanting to tell his friend as little as possible. "Sam, I don't know how to tell you this, but there are six innocent prisoners at that prison. They need to be free, and I want to help make it happen. I need to get them out of the country as quickly as possible."

He blew out a deep breath and continued. "At the same time, I need to be sure my family has escaped safely. Do you have any idea how this can be accomplished?"

Trying to gather his thoughts, Sam pondered for a moment, not wanting to appear as surprised as he felt. "I can see that you are serious, my friend. Let me start by saying that my first responsibility is with this orphanage. Does anyone know you visit, or that your wife volunteers here regularly?"

"I'm sure they do. We are here often enough."

"Then if the escape fails, or even if it succeeds, wouldn't the authorities know to find you here and punish all of us?" Sam challenged him. "What happens to the orphanage and the children?"

Le studied him thoughtfully. "Sam, I happen to know the Vietnamese authorities have already asked you to leave the country, or should I say, ordered you to leave within three days. I heard that the children will be put in state facilities tomorrow."

Each man was trying to learn what the other one knew without divulging more information than necessary.

Cautiously, Sam proceeded. "That's true. Your sources are right."

Taking it a step further, Sam issued a challenge. "Is it because of you, Le? Did you turn us in?" He glanced around at his fellow helpers, other young Christians who had given a couple years of their lives to work with helpless children in an underprivileged country.

"No, I'm only a guard. That's all I do." Le looked at Sam for a second, and then added, "Until now, that is. Now, I guess I'm sort of a freedom fighter."

Sam stopped eating, staring at Le. "You're serious, aren't you?"

"Yes, I am." His expression conveyed his sincerity.

"It's really important for you to do this, isn't it?

"Yes, it is. I've thought of nothing else the past few months. I have a plan that I think may work. You often told me that Jesus died doing what was right. You said that sometimes missionaries in other countries sacrificed their lives doing what is right, helping others. These prisoners have suffered many years for no reason. I have to help them. I believe it is my duty. It is what is right." Le's face showed pure determination.

Sam knew his Vietnamese friend well enough to know his mind was made up. No matter what, Le was resolved to follow through with his plan with or without his help.

Le interrupted his thoughts. "My concern is for my family and for these six men. I am not worried about myself."

Sam stared at Le, and then looked at Linh for a sign that she agreed with her husband.

With a hint of a smile, she gently nodded her head.

Sam remained thoughtful. He sipped a drink and sat up straighter in his chair. "I know some people in Thailand who may be able to help. I will contact them and see if we can set up a rendezvous. When do you want this to happen?"

"In two days."

"Two days? Again, are you certain you want to do this? It sounds awfully risky."

"Yes. I am positive." Le confidently nodded his head.

Sam continued, "That's pretty short notice. The authorities are watching us all the time. How will we deal with that?"

"We will have to move quickly. I do not want to put your lives in jeopardy. Therefore, you and your team need to leave Vietnam tomorrow. Since the children will be gone by then, they will be safe. The plan is quite simple. I suspect your people in Thailand are the same ones who bring your supplies every couple of months. That helicopter can pick up the prisoners and fly them to freedom."

"You know about that?" Sam said with a look of astonishment.

Le nodded.

"If you know about it, does the Vietnamese government know about my special shipment of supplies for the orphanage?"

"I don't think so. Your secret is safe with me. Be assured my friend, I am on your side. I would have done this last month, but I was not certain I could completely trust you. To be honest, I didn't know who could be trusted. Since I heard you were leaving and the orphanage would be closing its doors, I knew it was time to proceed with the plan. This way the children will be safe, and if the plan works, we all will be free."

Le sipped his hot tea. "I also believe when the international community finds out what has been going on, the Vietnamese government will do everything in its power to distance itself from the whole situation. Everything will be denied."

As they sat facing each other, their eyes locked.

Sam sought additional facts as he tried to comprehend what Le was revealing. "Why should we help six of your people escape? Are there not hundreds of innocent Vietnamese people stuck in Communist prisons?"

Le thought hard for a second. He knew Sam served in Desert Storm and believed he could trust him. Everything depended on what would happen next.

The young guard glanced over at Sam's laptop on the table and asked, "Is your computer on?"

"Yes."

"May I use it?"

Perplexed, Sam nodded his head, pushing the computer over to the guard.

Le typed, "Captain James McCarter."

Immediately, the prisoner's POW web site came up. Le looked at it, and then turned the laptop so Sam could see it clearly.

The former GI stared at it, his eyes grew large, and the expression on his face changed. It was obvious Sam was beginning to understand what Le was telling him.

Sam looked directly into Le's eyes. "You're not saying...." He couldn't finish his sentence.

Le nodded enthusiastically.

Sam looked around making sure they had privacy. The three missionaries cleaning the kitchen were busy with their duties, unaware of the conversation.

"I need proof that what you say is true. I can't risk my life, or put my friends in danger. This could be a trap."

Linh finally spoke. "Sam, this is real."

Le added, "Sam, you talked many times about Jesus dying on the cross between two thieves, right?"

Sam looked at him with an intense look. "Yes."

"One of the criminals asked Jesus to save him. The Savior responded, *Today you will be with me in paradise.*"

Sam wondered where Le was headed. Curiously, he answered, "Yes, I know the story. What does that have to do with me?"

"The thief never questioned that Jesus would do what he asked of him. Why was that?"

Sam considered the question. "I'm the one who is supposed to give you Bible lessons. Has the student surpassed the teacher?" He chuckled, and then moved his hand up to his chin as he thought long and hard about the question. "I would have to say, because he had faith. He trusted Him."

"You're right. He believed Jesus would do what He said. All I ask is that you believe and trust me. I have no pictures. I have no evidence except what I have witnessed the past four years. You have to take me at my word. I'm asking you to trust me, completely."

Sam stood, pushed his chair under the table, and looked closer at the website. He saw a forty-year-old photo of a young man in uniform, with his wife and two children— a man who may be just miles away, longing to be free after four decades of bondage.

"I was getting a shipment in three days, but since I was ordered to leave, I planned to cancel it. Could we do it then?"

The ideas of the two men were now converging.

"No. I will have an eight hour window two days from now. That is when I will be in control of the prisoners...we must act then!" Le insisted.

Sam considered his options. "Talking about the Word of God has become more restrictive. It's getting more difficult all the time." He shook his head sadly.

After a pause, he continued. "Okay...since we are leaving the country, and won't be permitted to return...I'm going to trust you."

Deep in thought, Sam stated, "You do realize the helicopter only has room for ten to twelve people, don't you? In my head, I count fifteen." He paused. "You are going to leave too, aren't you?"

Le's dark eyes showed concern. "My family will leave tonight, heading straight to Laos. I have contacted some friends who will help smuggle them into Thailand."

He paused briefly. "I will lead the men to the rendezvous point. From there, your helicopter will take them to the American Embassy in Bangkok. At that time, I will escape into Laos and catch up with my family. Everyone here must be out of the country within forty-eight hours. It will take the authorities a little time to figure out who was behind this— but they will. Timing is critical."

Sam scratched his head. "You're telling me...you're saying...that there are six American POWs alive this many years after the war...and they are close to where we're standing?"

Le nodded his head, grinning.

"Six?" Reaching across the table, Sam grabbed Le's shoulders with both of his large hands, and repeated emphatically, "Six Americans!"

Sam's eyes were wet, and for a split second, Le could tell his mind was in a distant place. "My own father was a POW for nine months. He was finally freed, but had been tortured brutally."

"I know about your father...that's why I thought I could trust you," Le confided.

Sam questioned Le further. "When were these six men captured?"

"1970."

"Forty years ago!" Sam asked excitedly, "Do you know if there are others?"

"I do not know. Maybe. This is an unusual circumstance, unknown even by the Vietnamese government."

"How can they not be aware of the atrocities?"

"That's a long story. Maybe I can fill you in some day."

"American POWs are alive! I can't believe it." Sam shook his head. "There's not a moment to waste. I'll contact my people and move the rendezvous time up."

"Do not tell anybody about this, Sam? Not one word to a soul."

"You don't have to worry about that," Sam stated. He noticed the three workers were puzzled by his excitement. A chill ran up his spine. "Forty years… just like Moses and the Israelites in the desert."

Le grinned. "I need to head back now. I will be at the pickup site at exactly 10:00 on Saturday."

"Wait a minute." Sam inquired, "Don't you need to know where the rendezvous point is?"

"No, I followed you a couple times. I know exactly where your pickup location is."

The American teased the young guard. "You've been doing your homework, haven't you?"

"Sam, my friend, please pray about this." Le hesitated, looking directly into his eyes. "If anything goes wrong, we are all dead—you, me, and your friends...." Le glanced at Sam's volunteers. "…and my family, as well as the prisoners."

Le walked over to his wife who stood, smiling at him in a show of support. Embracing her, he whispered, "We are doing what's right, aren't we, Linh?"

Unwavering, his wife reassured him. "You don't have to ask that question. We are!"

Speaking straight from his heart, Le spoke to his wife. "What if you don't get away? I don't know if I could handle you or the children getting hurt, or worse."

"We will be fine. We are in God's hands. Don't forget that. Since you have to return to work at the prison, I will make sure Sam knows all the details. We will be out of the country within twenty-four hours. Don't worry, just pray."

Le hugged Linh. "Take care of yourself and the kids."

The guard reached out his hand to his trusting friend. With a hearty handshake, Sam said, "I don't know what my part in this is Le, but I do trust you. You have my word…the helicopter will be there at the designated time."

Le began to walk away, and then had another thought. "Sam, remember you and your staff need to be out of the country within twenty-four hours. If we are not at the pickup point at 10:00, then something went wrong. Don't look for us. Just get out. Hopefully, my family will be safe."

Le added, "By the way Sam, thank you for telling me about Jesus. If something does go wrong, at least we know where we will spend eternity."

Sam shot him a smile, giving him the "thumbs up" signal.

Le embraced his wife one last time and gave her a parting smile.

Now, Le had less than forty-eight hours to convince six imprisoned Americans to trust one of their Vietnamese guards. *Was it even possible?*

It was early evening when Le arrived back at the prison camp. The prisoners were in their cells receiving their nightly rations.

Le knew he had to convince every one of them to trust him and follow his plan. And it had to be soon—their window of opportunity was narrowing.

It was Thursday's night to tap. His chat was not about baseball, as usual. He told about a time in college when he wanted to cheat on a test. Instead, he took the test honestly and found out later he aced the exam. "That was an important lesson for me. I learned if I did the right thing, good would come."

That was Le's perfect opportunity to cut in. "Saturday here. Good could come to you…if you choose."

Instantly someone tapped. "Saturday, where were you last night? Why did you bring this up again?"

"You are going to get us another beating," someone else tapped.

There was silence.

Eventually, the conversation started again. "This is Monday. I have an idea where you were last night, Saturday, why you were not here. Explain yourself."

Le knew he must choose his words wisely. He tapped, "I have discovered a way all of us can be rescued."

"Rescued? Who would bother to rescue us after all these years?" one prisoner asked.

"It's Monday again. Saturday, I want to be free more than anything. I want to go home, but let's be realistic…how can that be possible?"

"You have to trust me. I know it is hard, but you must follow my lead."

"How do we do that?"

"I will let you know the time and place. However, you all must agree to the plan, or it will not work. Every single one of you has to be onboard."

"Can't you explain in detail what you're talking about?"

The comments kept coming, but no one knew whom they were from.

"Not tonight."

"Saturday, I don't like this feeling. I think it could be a trap or another way to torture us." The tapping became more vigorous than before.

"Right. This whole thing is strange. Who are you really?" another added.

"Monday here. Let Saturday speak."

"No! Ask him a question!"

"Yeah, ask him a question that only an American would know. Ask him who the President of the United States is."

"Even we don't know that."

The tapping continued, and each prisoner came to life.

"Ask him who won the 1930 World Series." Obviously it was a question from Thursday, the baseball lover.

"I don't even know that. Get real," another prisoner tapped, adding to the lively conversation.

Thursday asked another question. "Saturday, what was the date of our country's independence?"

The question confused Le. He stopped tapping. He had read about it, but did not remember the exact date.

Thursday tapped, "Saturday, did you hear me?"

There was complete silence. The conversation was over. No more tapping.

When Le got off duty that night, he immediately went to a computer on base and typed the words, "America's Independence." He memorized the date.

Now, he was ready for the next step.

The next day, Le spent his shift guarding Monday at the rice paddy.

Occasionally they glanced at each other, trying not to make the second guard suspicious.

Finally, the other guard walked a short distance away leaving them alone.

Le edged closer to Monday.

Unexpectedly, the guard turned around and returned, forcing Le to walk away.

As Le passed Monday, he mumbled, "July 4, 1776." The surprised look on Monday's face was one Le had never seen from any prisoner. *Could it be hope?*

Le nodded his head, smiled, then whispered loud enough for only Monday to hear, "John 8:36."

The prisoner slowly went back to working, his mind racing with the details of the recent events. Monday was unsure what to think.

Eventually, a big smile came to his face when he recalled John 8:36. *If the Son therefore shall make you free, ye shall be free indeed.*

He hoed faster. Then with an unmistakable smile to Le, he nodded his head, acknowledging that he understood. *Could this guard really be on their side? Was there a chance the end of the nightmare was in sight?* He was afraid to believe, yet in another way, he felt more alive than he had in years.

As he worked, he began to believe the Vietnamese guard was really going to help them escape. Even if it was a trap, he no longer cared. He was ready to end it, one way, or another.

That night it was Friday's turn to talk.

Le waited for the right time to enter the conversation. This was his last chance to convince the men he was on their side. He hoped Monday would take the lead and provide a good opening for him.

Friday tapped, "They beat me again today. I'm worn out, exhausted. I tried to get them to shoot me, but they just laughed. Then they smashed me with their rifles. Won't they ever quit?"

There was silence for a long time.

"Monday here. John 8:36."

There was another lengthy pause.

Le was about to step in when someone tapped, "Sunday here. *If the Son therefore shall make you free, ye shall be free indeed.*"

Monday replied, "That's what I thought it was. It's been such a long time since we talked about the Bible."

Friday tapped, "Who are you kidding? We are dead men…not free. No Bible verse will ever change that."

Le knew the time was right. "Saturday here." He tapped, *But they that wait upon the LORD shall renew their strength; they shall mount up with wings as eagles; they shall run, and not be weary; and they shall walk, and not faint.*

"Sunday here. I think that's Isaiah 40:31."

"This is Monday. What are you getting at, Saturday?"

"Think of me as being an instrument for God."

"Thursday here. That's pretty high and mighty of you."

Saturday continued. *"Be strong and of good courage, fear not, nor be afraid of them: for the LORD thy God, he it is that doth go with thee; he will not fail thee, nor forsake thee."*

Sunday questioned him. "Deuteronomy 31:6? I never knew you to quote scripture, Saturday. What are you getting at?"

Friday jumped in. "God left us years ago. What is this, some kind of church service?"

"Tuesday here. Saturday, I think you flipped out."

Immediately, Monday came to Le's defense. "No, he has not. He is perfectly sane. Let me ask everyone a question. We have all seen each other. We know who everyone is...except Saturday. Has anyone ever seen Saturday?" There was a pause. "Nobody has. Let me rephrase that. Has anyone ever seen the prisoner we know as Saturday?"

Nothing. Absolute quiet.

"It's Thursday. What are you getting at?"

"I think it's time for him to come clean. Who are you really, Saturday?" Monday tapped.

Le knew he had to be honest, right here, right now, or they would turn him off, and it would be the end.

The young guard tapped, "The real Saturday died forty years ago. Since then, "Saturday" has been twelve different Vietnamese guards. I am the twelfth. My real name is Le Huu Trang. I have been "Saturday" for four years. I have seen and felt your terrible plight."

He waited for a reply, but there was none.

He continued, tapping slower. "You have seen me many times. I offered you a drink when you were thirsty. I helped you when you fell. I bandaged your wounds when no one was looking. I was like an angel who came to comfort you. I cannot give back what you have lost, but I can give you hope for the future."

"Friday here. Do you mean you, 'Slant Eyes,' have been listening to our conversations since the beginning? You are crazy. If you really are one of those Commies, I will kill you the first chance I get."

"It's Thursday. Just listen to him, Friday."

Friday responded, "This could be a trap. They aren't going to help us. They want to kill us trying to escape."

"If they wanted to kill us, they don't need for us to try to escape. They would have already done it," Thursday replied.

"Monday here. I know who you are, Saturday. You have helped me many times, while others left me to die. You talk about freedom. How can we be free? We are in the middle of a jungle, miles from civilization. We are weak, almost like dead men walking. We cannot fight. We cannot run. We merely exist."

Le felt their pain and tried to encourage them. "For freedom, you can run, and fight, if need be. What do you have to lose?"

Friday answered, "Our lives for one."

"Wednesday here. Our lives? You call this living?"

"This is Saturday. Wouldn't you love to leave this place and go home and see your wife and family?"

"Who cares anymore? Our families have written us off, buried us long ago. All of America has forgotten us." Friday was his usual cynical self.

"I happen to know that is not true. Although, they have little hope of you returning, your memories still live in the hearts of many Americans," Le implored.

"Tuesday here. Americans! I have not heard that word for years. Does America still exist? Did it ever exist?"

Le followed through. "I assure you, America does exist. If you trust me, listen to what I say, and follow my instructions, you will see America sooner than you can imagine."

"Monday here. I'm in, Saturday. If it is a trap, then I will go down fighting. I simply can't go on like this any longer."

"Sunday here. I agree. When I entered the Army, I was a conscientious objector. Now, I will do anything for my…our freedom."

"Monday again. Are all the days of the week in?"

"Let's go for it," Tuesday tapped.

Wednesday quickly cut in. "I'm not sure what month or even year it is, but will we be home by Christmas?"

"You have a chance to be on American soil, probably within a week," Le tapped.

"Thursday here. How have the New York Yankees been doing, Saturday?"

"Winning, as usual. I have listened to you talk about baseball, so I Googled the Yankees."

Thursday asked, "What is 'Googled?'"

All was quiet. Le forgot that the prisoners had no idea how much the world's technology advanced since 1970. He added, "You will have plenty of time to learn about that when you get home."

"Home! Home is a word I haven't used for years," Thursday replied.

"Monday here. You are the last one to agree, Friday. Are you with us?"

"I'm in, but at the first sign of trouble, I'll start killing, and Saturday will be my first target."

"Okay. It's settled. Let's go! Saturday, what do we do next?" Monday asked.

"Like I said, follow my lead tomorrow. Right now, get your sleep. You'll need to be your strongest when we travel early in the morning."

Wednesday, too anxious to settle down, asked, "What are we going to do when we get out? I suspect our job skills are outdated."

"Friday here. I'm going home to my dairy farm."

"I don't think we have to worry about a job when we get back in the real world. That will be the least of our worries. Besides, in a few years we will be old enough to retire," Monday tapped.

"Good night men. Like Saturday said, we need our rest," Monday tapped.

The tapping stopped. The prisoners tried to settle down, but sleep would not come; their minds raced with possibilities. The men replayed the conversation in their minds. *Should we dare to hope?*

In the stillness of his cell, Le also reflected. He didn't want to confess to the soldiers that he only made forty-five dollars a month. His thoughts went crazy. *Is this worth it? Why couldn't I turn my back on them? It would only be a matter of time until they all died—most likely sooner than later.* He recalled what his friend Sam had taught him about love, freedom, and most importantly, Jesus. *What would God want me to do?*

Le recalled hearing about the wonders of America. *It must be an amazing place.* Sam talked frequently about his homeland and its freedoms. He explained how people are free to live where they choose. They can even own their home. When they want to travel, they are free to go where they want. A person can walk down the street with his head held high and not be afraid. People can work where they desire, and earn the kind of wage they need to raise their family. He realized how different America was from his homeland.

Quickly, he snapped back to reality. America would remain a dream to him, something he could never experience personally, but at least the prisoners had a chance of returning to that great country.

He must stay focused on the task at hand. His responsibility was to get these men on Sam's helicopter tomorrow. Then he would meet his family at the previously agreed rendezvous point. It saddened him that he may never see his parents and sisters again. He determined they would be all right—a long distance separated them from the demonic general.

After the prisoners quieted for the night, Le walked out of his small cell, and looked heavenward. The moon glowed full in the sky, and the stars seen through the jungle foliage seemed to sparkle with hope. He cried to his Heavenly Father, *God, You said You would never forsake us. I believe Your promise is true. I ask not for my sake only, but for these six innocent lives. I am clinging to Your promise. And God...please take care of my family.*

He went to his room on the base to get some needed rest.

Tomorrow promised to be a big day, an important one, not just for the prisoners, but also for their families.

If the United States is the country that Le has heard it is, it will be a day when all Americans stand united.

If everything goes according to plan, the soldiers who were considered dead would soon be coming home.

SEVEN

The Escape

Le slept soundly for a few hours. He was not certain why he could rest peacefully; perhaps it was because his family should be safe in Laos and soon on their way to Thailand. Maybe it was because he believed he was finally doing right in God's eyes, rather than following orders of evil men. Whatever the reason, he was grateful for the needed sleep.

While still dark, Le dressed. Reviewing the plan in his mind, he played out each scene, trying to envision anything that might go wrong. He knew he had only an eight hour window at best for the plan to succeed. It should take only two hours to arrive at the pickup point. He scouted the trail many times and searched for possible complications. He assured himself that unless an unexpected problem surfaced, all would be well.

He prayed the helicopter would arrive at the designated time. He prayed the men would trust him completely. What if any of the men decided it was too risky and tried to overtake him? That was a real possibility, and could be fatal for everyone.

He grabbed his rifle and canteen, tucking them under his arm. He walked to his bed. Under the mattress was a small, brown pouch. He picked it up gently, placing the strap around his neck. Stuffing the small bag inside his shirt, he patted it lightly.

In the pouch were valuables he had collected and stored for safekeeping. He bought some of them from other guards. A few items he took from General Yo, over the course of time. They were the general's trophies from "hunting expeditions." Le intended to return them to their rightful owners when the time was right.

He paused for a moment, looking around his modest room on the prison grounds. It had been his home away from home the last four years.

The stability and security he had known, not to mention his somewhat influential job, would soon be gone. He shivered at the thought. *What will I do? I am certain of only one thing...I know I am doing what God expects of me.*

With his heart pounding, he walked the short distance to the small mess hall. His coworkers were already eating. He sat with them, trying to appear calm as he ate his breakfast of sticky rice and a hard biscuit. He wondered if, or when, he would eat again; the idea made him slightly nauseated.

Le knew he had to blend in with the other guards, acting normal. Yet, inside he was anything but calm. He hoped no one noticed his trembling hands. He glanced over at his fellow guards, silently praying he could pull this off without killing any of them— he wished them no harm.

His only concern was saving the six Americans. Realistically, he knew that by the end of the day, blood would surely be shed.

Again, he prayed, asking God to give him the strength emotionally and physically to do what was necessary at the appropriate time.

He had never killed anyone. In fact, he had never abused the prisoners. The other guards asked him why he did not join in on the fun, and he simply shrugged his shoulders, explaining to them that he was the interpreter, nothing more. They seemed to accept his explanation.

The guards joking and laughing finished breakfast. They discussed some of the funny things the prisoners did. At least, they seemed funny to them. Le couldn't help but think it was a heartbreaking illustration of a depraved life.

The hour for freedom was drawing near.

The prisoners would be working about four miles away at an old airplane landing strip, now covered with debris. It was a rare occurrence, but for the first time in years, all six men would work together. That aided Le's plan. However, the backbreaking labor would be even more grueling than usual.

In recent weeks, Le noticed that General Yo seemed to be tiring of the prisoners. Perhaps they were getting to be an annoyance. The calloused, elderly tyrant was making life more grueling for them.

When the guards left the breakfast area, they grabbed a few provisions for the day, including a small amount of food for the prisoners.

Le filled a larger bag with more food than usual. The guards teased him about how hungry he must be. Little did they know, he took the extra for the prisoners' long, draining day.

The four guards piled into the vehicle, which would deliver them to the landing strip. It was an old U.S. Army ambulance, perfect for eight people in the back. Le sat in the back with one guard, while the other two took their places in the front cab.

As they stopped by the cells housing the prisoners, Le was keenly aware of the stillness. He breathed deeply, inhaling the fresh morning air. The tangerine sunrise was spectacular with shades of pink and orange splattered through the clouds. He looked up and felt the refreshing, warm, gentle breeze. It was calm, the start of a beautiful day—peaceful and surreal.

The guards unshackled the prisoners from their cells. They would work free from their usual restraints, but certainly not free from the watchful eyes of the captors. With no chains holding them, it would be in the POW's favor, allowing them to move around easier.

Le helped the men into the dilapidated ambulance. He nodded, and gave a hint of a smile to each prisoner.

They glared at him, still unsure of his motives.

Monday was the last one in. Le looked at him and whispered, "Look at the incredible sunrise. It's going to be a great day."

Monday did not say a word. He paused, and then stepped slowly into the vehicle. He stared at Le. *Dare I hope? Is this guard really here to help us? On the other hand, could this be another one of Yo's cruel, evil games? Soon, we will know.*

It was a rough, bumpy ride to the work site; the road rarely, if ever, had been used in the past thirty-five years. Ruts scored deep into the ground.

Dense jungle foliage grabbed the road from both sides causing a dark and eerie path. The sun's rays began to break through the jungle as if they would swallow it. Dew on the leaves danced as the sunlight glistened making thousands of tiny rainbows. The birds sweetly sang their songs of freedom and love.

The prisoners were unaware of the beautiful sounds and sights around them. Any beauty in the world ceased to exist long ago. Life became one endless day, followed by another. To them, this was just another day, but soon they would see it as their day to freedom—by either rescue or death. Either way, they would be free from the years of imprisonment, terror, and beatings. Today they were going home—home to their families, or home to their God.

As Le's mind raced, he recalled a time when he read a phrase penned on the side of an American soldier's helmet. "When I die, I'm going to heaven. I've already been to hell." Le often thought about those words. Being Vietnamese, he originally was offended by them. Lately when he studied the Vietnam War and learned what many Americans endured, especially these prisoners, he understood the meaning of those powerful words. They were not a direct insult against his country, but truth about the war itself.

Many times Le wondered what would have happened if South Vietnam had defeated the invaders of the North. *Would my country be free now?* Le found his mind drifting to what might have been, but quickly snapped out of it coming back to reality. *I must stay focused. Did I make any mistakes along the way? Did I forget any important details?*

The driver laughed, speeding crazily along the ruts in the road. He knew the bouncing hurt the prisoners. Their tired, aching bones caused them to cringe in pain with every hard jolt. He reveled in their misery.

One time he hit a bump with such force that those in the back toppled onto each other, landing in a heap. Sunday and Thursday fell onto a guard. Swearing, the grumbling guard roughly shoved them away. Quickly resuming his position, the angry guard struck both prisoners in the head with the butt of his rifle, almost knocking them out. Freeman's head bled profusely.

Le yelled to the driver to slow down, but then remembered he could not tip his hand by showing any compassion to the prisoners…not yet.

Finally, the ambulance arrived at its destination. It was just before seven in the morning.

Le felt confident things were going as planned.

The vehicle slammed to a stop near a rundown, deserted shack. It once served as a tower for a military airfield during the Vietnam Conflict. It was located less than twenty miles from the Laos border.

The two guards in the cab hopped out first. They noticed that nearby an old U.S. Army helicopter lay on its side, abandoned in the middle of the old landing strip—a remnant of what used to be. With piqued curiosity, the two guards walked over to get a closer look. They joked about how many Americans likely died when the chopper hit the ground.

Le jumped from the back of the ambulance. Looking around, he imagined what the airfield was like teeming with American soldiers, helicopters, and other military aircraft, four decades ago.

As the fourth guard started to get out, Le sprang into action. Without warning, he raised the butt of his rifle and slammed it into the back of the guard's neck. In an instant, Le mentally replayed the scene from moments before when the same guard hit Sunday and Thursday. "How do you like it?" Le sneered sarcastically. The guard's body fell limp as he collapsed to the ground.

The commotion caught the attention of the other two guards who were still gawking at the downed chopper.

Le noticed them watching and shouted in Vietnamese, "He tripped."

They sprinted over and bent down to help their injured coworker.

Without hesitation, Le struck one of them in the back of his head with the butt of his rifle. The remaining guard, confused, looked up at Le. Then unexpectedly, Le slammed the end of his rifle hard into his face. Blood gushed from his nose as he crumpled to the ground.

The three guards were now unresponsive, sprawled out on the cracked asphalt. Le did not know if any of them were dead, or if they were unconscious for a brief time. He only knew he had to act fast.

Without thinking, Le immediately raised his rifle toward the astonished prisoners who were staring at the unconscious guards.

Their natural response was to raise their hands in surrender.

Realizing his rifle was aimed at the prisoners who were still in the ambulance, Le quickly lowered it. He swung the strap over his shoulder, urgently dishing out orders to the captives. "Help me get them into the shack. You'll find some rope under the seat. Hurry!"

In his normal take-charge way, Sunday shouted, "I drove an ambulance just like this when I a medic...I wonder if it's the same one." He pushed the other men back and lifted the seat. The rope was in place, so he grabbed it hastily.

The Americans, even in their weakened conditions, operating on pure adrenaline piled out of the ambulance. They roughly dragged the guards into the nearby hut.

Le shouted, "Who ties the best knots?"

Friday replied, "I do. I used to calf-rope in the rodeo." He stepped forward, quickly securing the guards. He didn't need a reminder to tie the ropes tight. In fact, he tied them so tight that if the rifle butt to the head didn't kill them, his knots would surely stop the blood circulation. He had no pity on them. They had been extremely hard on him personally. It was payback time.

Le double checked the knots and stretched tape across their mouths. The longer it took for General Yo and his men to locate these guards, the better chance the prisoners had to escape successfully.

As Le turned, he stood face-to-face with three of the Americans who had grabbed the guards' rifles and were aiming them directly at him. They had been murmuring among themselves and still didn't trust this Vietnamese guard.

Le reasoned that the prisoners needed him too badly to kill him, so he stepped forward, quickly heading toward the truck. "We need to get going.

Time's a-wasting." He rushed past the former prisoners who continued directing their rifles at him.

Meanwhile, Monday stared at the words on a corroded, crooked sign, barely hanging from a rusty nail on the old hut. He bent over and grabbed a hat, which had fallen off one of the guards, and tossed it into the small rundown shack. Monday stepped back, shaking his head. "I can't believe it. I've been a prisoner all this time, only a few miles away from where I was stationed. This was my Army base. Unbelievable!"

Monday turned, and was stunned to see his fellow POWs had their weapons fixed on Le, the man who was trying desperately to help them escape. Taking charge, without batting an eye, Monday instinctively knew it was time to resume his role as Captain McCarter. Quickly sizing up the situation, he barked an order, "You heard the man...let's get going!"

McCarter jumped into the back of the ambulance while the three prisoners holding the weapons blankly stared at each other.

"No," Lomack snarled forcefully. "I say shoot him now and take the vehicle." Friday, always known for his quick temper and short fuse, reacted in his typical way as obscenities sputtered from his mouth.

Captain McCarter jumped out of the vehicle, stepping protectively in front of Le. Glaring at Friday, McCarter ordered, "Put the weapon down, soldier."

Lomack snapped back. "I see you haven't changed in all these years. You're not in charge anymore...this rifle and these bullets are clearly in charge."

Thursday, otherwise known as Freeman, intervened. "Lomack, put the rifle down. Think. Think of what you're doing." He stepped in front of the captain.

"Oh, I have thought about this. For forty long years, I've thought about this. I don't trust this Commie as far as I can throw him. It's a trap. I know it. I sense it's a VC trick, which will kill us all before the day is over."

"Think of what you're saying. They had forty years to kill us if they wanted to," Freeman bellowed.

"I say take the truck and head west," Lomack gestured toward the road.

Taking on his professional role as a counselor with his patient, Freeman pled with the distraught soldier. "Lomack, calm down and think. He is our only way out. We may die trying, but at least we tried. If we kill him, we will all certainly die. We have no idea where to go. We don't know what's out there." He pointed toward the dense jungle and continued. "There has been forty years of growth and industrialization. We have no idea what's going on. They may have flying cars or robots running around on this planet. We need this man's help. We can't do it alone."

Pfingston, in prison known as Tuesday, finally agreed, lowering his rifle. "Let's put the weapons down and get going."

Le challenged Lomack to end the foolish standoff. "If you're going to shoot me, then shoot me. We are wasting valuable time. We have a helicopter to catch and a psychotic general to escape from." Taking a chance, he hurried to the driver's side of the vehicle.

Lomack glanced around. Knowing he was outnumbered, he reluctantly agreed. "Alright, but I'm keeping this weapon on you at all times. One false move and you are history. I still don't trust you."

"Get in the truck now," McCarter ordered. His patience was growing thin.

Lomack glared at Captain McCarter, boldly confronting him. "You may think you are the ranking man here, but that doesn't make any difference to me. Rank died years ago. Now, we are equals," he shouted in the captain's face.

McCarter faced his comrades. "Rank may be out, but democracy is not. Who wants to shoot this man who is trying to help us?"

There was complete silence. No one budged.

"Who wants to go home?" The captain said, raising his hand.

Four other prisoners' hands immediately shot skyward. The remaining prisoner, Lomack, slowly raised his.

"Then it's settled. Load up. Men, we're going home!"

They piled into the old vehicle and were quickly on their way.

EIGHT

The Rough Road

Le felt the cold, steel barrel of Lomack's rifle pressing against his neck as they rattled down the abandoned road. Fortunately, he still had his weapons, if he needed them.

So far, everything was going as planned, except for Lomack's outburst.

They were slightly ahead of schedule, but they still had almost twenty miles to go on the rough road.

The mood was tense. Everyone knew the danger involved and was on edge. The uncertainty of the situation made all of them uncomfortable.

McCarter made his way to the front seat. Eyes fastened on Le, he began to question the guard. "Who…are…you?"

Le grinned. "I am Le Huu Trang. Just call me Le."

"Are you Special Forces or something?"

"No…I'm just a guard at your prison camp."

The captain shifted his gaze to the bumpy road ahead. "It's not my prison camp." He raised his voice. "None of this makes sense. I mean, how can you speak English so well? You have no accent."

"I don't know for sure. I think it just came natural. General Yo recruited me out of college. He wanted me to listen to the prisoners' conversations. I was unsure what that involved at the time. I really wanted to be an embassy interpreter, but what General Yo wants, he gets."

Captain McCarter cast a questioning look at him. "Why are you helping us?"

"My heart, I guess. I began realizing that what was taking place in the prison camp was morally and ethically wrong."

The other men hushed, moving closer to listen to the conversation.

A question came from the back. Le didn't know who asked it since he rarely heard their voices at the prison. The voice sounded hoarse and cracked, due to being inactive for years. "How is the war going?"

Le hesitated, struggling to find the right words. "Where do I begin? The war. Well...." He cleared his throat. "Well, the war here in Vietnam has been over for thirty-five years."

Another voice joined in. "Did we win?"

Thoughtfully, Le responded. "Well, yes and no." He gave the out of touch soldiers a brief history lesson. "Your nation signed the Paris Peace Treaty with North Vietnam in 1973 and the American GIs went home. All prisoners and bodies of American soldiers supposedly were returned to your homeland."

One of the men shouted angrily from the back. "Not all. What about us?"

Another added, "Yeah, why weren't we released? How could they forget about us?"

Le felt compassion for the men. He tried to explain. "You were being held by a vindictive, evil man named General Yo. A bomb from an American plane killed his entire family in North Vietnam in 1968."

Specialist Thomas Traber, also known as Wednesday, spoke. "We weren't even here in 1968."

"That didn't matter to Yo. He only wanted to see Americans suffer. Any Americans he captured, he punished. He made them endure horrendous suffering and torture, as you all experienced. Even after the Peace Treaty, he refused to release any prisoners, keeping them hidden on his personal property. He wouldn't even release the bodies of those that died, totally in opposition to the treaty. He had any dead Americans burned, eliminating all evidence of their existence."

Lomack finally entered the conversation. "How many Americans did that coldhearted monster kill or capture?"

"Counting you, thirty-two. Thirty-three, if you count me."

Lomack continued his line of questioning with his typical cynicism. "Counting you! You're not American, and you're too young to have served in the war."

Le responded patiently. "That's true. You see, I took on the identity of Yo's first prisoner—the one you knew me to be, Corporal Daniel Sparks. You referred to me as 'Saturday.'"

McCarter's head was spinning. *Was this really happening?* He paused. Finally, he asked, "Okay. So what happened to Corporal Sparks?"

"I'm not certain. I heard rumors that he died during an interrogation, but I also heard that he was killed trying to escape."

Finally calm, Lomack persisted, "If the war is over, why are you Commies still in South Vietnam?"

There was no response.

Lomack realized he could not be certain of anything, so he tread cautiously. "We…we are in South Vietnam, aren't we?"

"Yes, you are. This is all Yo's private property. It borders Laos." Waving out the window, he pointed in all directions. "The government awarded it to him after the war for his outstanding service." Le chuckled mockingly. "He's officially retired now, but he still wears the uniform and dishes out orders to his soldiers."

Lomack's voice began to escalate again. He repeated his question. "I said, what are you Communists doing here?"

Le took a deep breath. "In April of 1975, my country, South Vietnam, was taken over by North Vietnam."

Freeman probed further. "Then we lost the war in Vietnam?"

"That's what the world thinks. However, the fact is my people did…the South Vietnamese people lost the war. America's hands were tied because of the Peace Treaty and the unfavorable position, which many Americans had about the war." Le shook his head in disgust. "Politics, all politics!"

He continued. "Unfortunately, thousands of innocent people died when our villages were burned and destroyed by power hungry Communists. It was horrible for people like my parents, and grandparents, who only wanted to farm and live peacefully. Now they work hard every day simply to survive. My grandparents and all four of my parent's siblings were killed by the North Vietnamese."

No one knew what to say, feel, think, or believe.

Freeman cleared his throat. "What happened in the world in the last forty years?"

The guard contemplated the question. There was too much to say. From whose perspective—his own, the prisoners', or the world's? Le's mind searched for the right answers.

The world is more connected due to modern technology. In 1970, it took soldiers days, sometimes weeks to hear from their families. Cell phones and computers changed that! Instant communication throughout the world is available with a click of the mouse. Immediate news coverage, details shared with the public as they happen, was dramatically different from during the Vietnam War era.

How can anyone explain September 11, 2001, Desert Storm, and the Iraq War? Le's thoughts were jumbled.

The fact is some nations were getting closer to nuclear weapons. The threat of terrorism was not information he wanted to share at that time. *How can the men possibly understand terrorism?*

When they went to war, people were listening to record albums and eight track tapes. Today, thousands of songs are stored on a little piece of plastic, the size of a quarter—just one of the wireless wonders, and ingenious innovations available. *How can I explain any of that to the returning veterans? They missed nearly a half century of technology and transformation.*

Le pictured them like children in a large toy store with so much to see and learn. *Where do I begin?*

He chose to pay attention to the task at hand—finding freedom for the men.

The men patiently waited for a response.

"So much has happened in the last forty years that I don't know where to start. There will be plenty of time to talk later. Right now, let's just stay focused. We will be approaching the Laos border shortly."

As he considered the immediate situation, Le asked, "Does anyone know how to drive a clutch vehicle?" Even though it was decades since they had driven, most of the men nodded their heads. Le knew he needed to have the men prepared, in case he was not with them the entire trip. "If anything happens to me, stay on this path for as long as you can. In my left pocket is a GPS unit. The helicopter will locate you."

Le noticed the confusion on McCarter's face. "I'm sorry...let me explain what a GPS unit is. It stands for Global Positioning System; it's a navigational tool directed by satellites and will trace your exact location."

"Are we expecting company?" McCarter raised an eyebrow.

"Just being realistic; anything can happen. I do mean anything. I think I covered all my tracks, but no one should underestimate General Yo."

"I'd give anything to kill that man. Even my freedom," Lomack yelled.

Everyone thought about what he said.

With a hoarse voice, Williams, formerly Sunday, questioned, "Where are we going, and who is picking us up?"

"We are driving to the Laos border. There, a helicopter will be waiting for you." Le felt his stomach tighten.

"Who is picking us up?" Freeman persisted.

"A man called Sam. He is a good, Christian man, and the reason I am helping you. He formerly served in the United States Army Special Forces. He operated an orphanage here, but has recently been ordered to close it and get out of the country."

"You mean to tell me you're a Christian?" Williams gave him a weak smile.

Le looked Williams directly in the eyes. "Yes, I am. Thanks to Sam and his missionaries at the orphanage. Actually, everyone in my family is a believer in Jesus."

"No wonder you're helping us." McCarter nodded his head, finally understanding.

Williams continued. "Why was Sam asked to leave when he was helping the orphans?"

"For talking about Jesus," Le replied, maneuvering around a fallen tree in the road.

"Let me get this straight. He ran an orphanage, and was asked to leave because he was preaching the gospel." Williams could not believe what he heard.

"That's about it. Most Communist and Arab nations are like that these days."

"What about Russia?" Freeman inquired.

"Russia? As a nation it collapsed over twenty years ago."

The men's eyes widen. "No more Russia?"

"Well, there is a Russia. All of its satellite countries, Romania, Hungary, and others are free and govern themselves."

Freeman asked, "What about East Germany?"

"Germany is all one country, no longer divided. There is no Berlin Wall. It came down during Ronald Reagan's presidency."

Lomack immediately inquired, "Ronald Reagan, the actor? Are you saying an actor became President of the United States?"

"Yes...the one and only."

Lomack continued with his line of questioning. "What kind of president was he?"

"History will be good to him. He is considered by many to be the greatest president of modern times."

Lomack's expression lightened. "Wow! Who would have guessed?"

The men were intrigued by what they were hearing.

Changing the subject, McCarter asked, "What shall we call you?"

"Excuse me?" Le's response came quick.

"I mean, we can't call you Saturday or Sparks. You gave us your name, but I don't remember it. What should we call you?"

"Le would be fine."

"Okay, Mr. Le. What are you getting out of this? I mean...a person does not put his life on the line and possibly kill three fellow soldiers to help prisoners escape, and not want something in return. I repeat my question, what's in this for you?" Lomack coughed.

Lomack's inquiry prompted Le to question his actions. *Why am I doing this? Is it because of my newfound faith, or because I saw how wrong it was to imprison these innocent men? Perhaps it is because I want freedom for myself.*

Le felt it was an opportune moment to return a special token to the soldiers, a significant part of their past. "Men, there is something urgent that I need to do. I am sorry that it's taken forty years to get these back to you."

Reaching into his shirt pocket, he pulled out six sets of old dog tags, still on their chains. He handed them to Captain McCarter. "If you don't mind sir, please present these to the proper soldiers."

McCarter's expression changed. His hands trembled as he reached for them. Staring in unbelief at the tags, he recognized they were the same ones they wore forty years ago. For a few seconds, he was stunned, too shocked to move or speak.

The other prisoners didn't say anything but their expression told the story.

"Our dog tags. I can't believe it!" McCarter grinned.

Almost reverently, he read the name on each tag, proudly handing it to the rightful owner.

"Should we put them on?" Williams' voice cracked.

"I would. That's the only way the Americans will know who you are when you get to the embassy. When you arrive, they will probably fingerprint you to confirm your identity," Le responded.

"You mean this is real? We are really going home?" Pfingston shook his head in disbelief.

"Unless something goes wrong, you will be landing in the courtyard of the American Embassy in Thailand by sunset. First, they will look at you with skepticism...that will turn to astonishment, joy, and excitement." He smiled. "Men, tonight you should be able to take a hot bath and eat a nourishing meal. You will be able to sleep in a comfortable bed with clean sheets and a soft pillow for your head."

The men sat quietly subdued, clutching their dog tags, and trying to comprehend all they had heard.

Mindful of the time, Le glanced at his watch. "I hope that within a couple days you will be headed home to your families. I think the American government will want to get you to your loved ones as soon as possible."

The men stared at each other, afraid to hope because too much was at stake.

Suddenly, the silence was shattered when reality hit McCarter. He shouted excitedly, "Men, we're going home. We're really going home!"

The men hugged each other, chanting, "We're going home! We're free!"

The old ambulance swerved all over the rugged road. The excitement of the newly released prisoners made it difficult for Le to avoid the deep ruts and other debris on the abandoned trail.

Le knew they weren't out of danger yet, but had to smile. He also realized that some of them would face heartbreak when they arrived at home. Their future was uncertain.

For the next hour, the men bombarded Le with questions as the old military vehicle bumped along slowly.

The road was rough and pockmarked, but to the men it was beautiful—it was their road to freedom.

They were running on pure adrenaline. Le answered many questions, but as a Vietnamese, he could not answer some of them.

The exhausted travelers finally started to wear down.

Le knew they needed their strength. "Sit back and relax. Drink plenty of water. Go to sleep. Time will pass faster that way."

As much as they tried, rest was not possible. They had waited forty years for this moment.

They still needed to get to Laos undetected. As the inside of the vehicle finally quieted, Le took time to pray for continued safety to their destination, uninterrupted by Yo's henchmen.

NINE

The Evil Tyrant

Shadowy trees blew in the hot wind adding mystery to the deserted jungle road. The beautiful, deep green forest went unnoticed by the passengers.

It took longer than Le expected, but they were still ahead of schedule. In less than an hour, the chopper was due to arrive. Everything continued as planned…uneventful.

Le stopped for the men to take a much needed break as they neared the Laos border. The hazardous road, as well as fielding the many questions, made the trip stressful—he needed a break himself.

Everyone stumbled out of the vehicle. Most of the men were barely able to stand; all were suffering from aching bones and muscles.

"Hey Le, would you have a smoke? It's been a long time since we've had one," Lomack pleaded.

"Yeah, a cigarette would be great," added Traber.

Le shook his head in disapproval. "No way, men. Cigarette smoking is bad for your health…it causes cancer."

"Are you serious? Who cares?" Lomack chuckled, sarcastically.

"You heard the man," McCarter stated with authority. "He doesn't have any cigarettes. In addition, they're bad for you. End of subject."

Lomack swore under his breath, but no one responded.

The men sipped some water and ate the food Le brought. For the first time in many years, they enjoyed fresh fruit and drank clean water.

The silence of the jungle was creepy. A bird heard in the distance, and the wind rustling the leaves, added to the strangeness of the moment.

Suddenly, Le sensed something was amiss.

Captain McCarter noticed Le's apprehension. "What is it? You look scared. What's wrong?"

"I don't know. Something seems wrong. I can't put my finger on it."

"It seems pretty quiet to me," Williams confided.

"Too quiet," Le whispered. "Too quiet."

The soldiers stood and instinctively gathered close in a circle. They scanned the area, aiming their rifles towards the thick brush.

Suddenly the jungle came to life, startling the men. The sounds of the birds fluttering as they took flight added to the eeriness. Then, there was total silence.

"Get in the truck," Le quietly ordered. "Fast!"

The men scrambled into the vehicle.

Le started the engine and hastily took off. He clenched his teeth, gripping the steering wheel with both hands. They drove a short distance, barreling around a blind curve.

Le slammed on the brakes.

Blocking the road directly in front of them was a truck with a machine gun mounted over the cab.

Gunfire interrupted the quietness of the jungle.

There was no escape. The road to freedom was blocked—something had gone dreadfully wrong.

Two men hopped out of the unfamiliar vehicle, aiming their weapons at the startled Le.

"Can we fight?" McCarter whispered, his heart pounding.

"Not with that machine gun staring us down. It will tear us to pieces before we fire the first shot."

Le sized up the situation. "Everybody, get out the back of the truck. Keep your distance from each other. Captain, you, and I should step out slowly."

"Is this the border patrol?" Williams asked.

"No. It's General Yo's men." Le's shoulders slumped forward, his voice sounding defeated.

"I knew we couldn't trust this Commie," Lomack shouted. He leveled his rifle at Le.

"No!" Freeman yelled, shoving the weapon aside. "They'll kill us all if you shoot now."

Lomack glared at Freeman.

The Americans glared with watchful eyes as the backdoor of the intruding truck swung open. The fright of the moment intensified when General Yo emerged from the vehicle. His cocky, arrogant face proudly displayed his victory.

The soldier's nightmare became reality! A sinking sensation overwhelmed the men.

Yo eyed each of the prisoners with his vengeful grin.

Two of Yo's men stood in front of him with weapons aimed at Le and the captain. From the bed of the truck, another man pointed a mounted machine gun directly at the rest of the group.

The situation appeared hopeless.

At a standoff, the prisoners still had not dropped their weapons.

Yo took out a cigarette, lit it, and blew smoke rings into the air. He strutted closer to Le, staring at him defiantly. "I'm surprised at you, Le. You were one of my brightest students."

"How did you find us?" Le cast a questioning look at his enemy.

The general laughed aloud—his mocking, evil cackle. "Oh, the miracle of technology! We put a bug in your truck. We have been following you all morning, thanks to our GPS. It really was quite simple."

Le knew the escape was well planned and orchestrated precisely. His loud voice echoed through the forest. "How did you know?"

Yo slipped something from his pocket and waved it, taunting an angry Le.

With a cruel laugh, he handed it to one of his thugs. The coldhearted soldier hurriedly stomped over to dangle the item in front of Le.

Barely able to breathe, the former guard snatched it.

Yo mocked snidely, "It didn't take long to get information out of her. She did not want to see her youngest without a head."

Le's heart sank. In silence, he studied a photo of his adored wife and children. Bound and gagged, their bloody faces displayed terror. *How could this be happening? What went wrong?*

Le's blood boiled. He stepped forward to confront Yo.

McCarter grabbed his shoulders, holding him back, as the enemy's weapons swiveled immediately toward Le.

"How did you find out?" McCarter shouted.

"Well, listen to that. He speaks." The sarcastic general smirked, puffing his cigarette. "Le, I heard reports your wife had been working at that orphanage. They stated you were with her. Your house has been under surveillance for months. I knew you were going to do this before you knew it. Such is Christianity…helping fellow man. So predictable," he mocked. "I was the one that ordered the people at the orphanage to leave. I have also commanded your chopper to be shot down when it arrives."

Then it came again—his sadistic laugh.

Yo blew out a lengthy cloud of smoke. "It was obvious when your wife and children left yesterday that something was up. I had them detained, and I myself got the information out of them. It really didn't take much effort." He pointed toward the prisoners. "Le, your wife was not as strong as the six of them."

Discarding his cigarette butt, he crushed it under his boot.

Le needed air; he took a breath, but it didn't help. His head was spinning.

"They will be no problem to anyone again. You will never see your family in this life. Maybe your so-called Christian religion will allow you to see them when you are dead."

Yo bellowed, "I suggest you drop your guns or you will die here. I really don't care."

"Neither do we." Lomack roared, pointing his rifle toward Yo's head.

Infuriated, Yo hollered, "Your guns do not scare me!"

Lomack stepped forward and fired three shots. The noise of the gunfire was deafening.

General Yo did not fall…nothing happened!

"Go ahead. Try shooting them all." Yo laughed.

Two other prisoners fired their weapons.

Again, nothing happened. Every man remained standing.

"I was not sure when this would take place, so all I could do was set everything to my advantage. I had blanks put in all the guards' magazines. Even yours, Le."

Le grabbed his pistol from his side and released the magazine. It was true. It was filled with blanks.

"You are mad, insane," Le shouted.

"Not mad, just doing my job as a soldier…for the war…for the cause."

"Job! Job! This is not a job. There is no war. There is no conflict. There is no cause." Le's voice was loud and harsh. "These men should have been released thirty-seven years ago when the peace treaty was signed."

General Yo's face was red with rage; he was livid. "Peace Treaty. There is no treaty for those who killed my family. There never will be. That's a joke."

"Your family. Your family!" Lomack yelled. "That was over forty years ago. You are crazy."

"Yes, my family. Your people, you Americans, murdered my family."

Freeman tried to reason with the lunatic. "No! War killed your family. Innocent people die in war along with the guilty."

"It was not your war," Yo screamed in anger.

"Neither was it yours," McCarter shouted. "The people of South Vietnam just wanted to live in peace. How many innocent people died when you and your people invaded? How many millions suffered death for your political purposes?"

Williams interrupted, "How many are still suffering today because of your iron-fisted control."

Yo continued. "Those weak people do not know how to take care of themselves. They are subjects of a deeper, more meaningful cause."

"When will it end, Yo? When will it end?" McCarter quavered.

"It will never end as long as there are people like you and Le out there. You are too stupid to realize that Mao is the way. He is the only answer."

"Mao is dead!" Le yelled.

"This conversation is over." Yo was out of control with rage.

Le continued to argue. "Yes, you have suffered for the loss of your family, but these men did not do it…a bomb did it."

"A bomb dropped by men, just like them." Yo pointed to the POWs. His hatred oozed from every ounce of his being.

"No, the bomb was dropped because of war. Because people can't get along. Because of petty events, miscalculated risks, or misinterpreted thoughts. Do you think what you have done is any better?" Le's voice became more forceful.

"It's justice," Yo thundered.

"No, it's not. It borders on insanity. Do you think that once the Vietnamese government finds out that you have been holding American POWs, they will turn and look the other way? Your life will be worthless, Yo. Yes, they will probably kill these six men and destroy any evidence they ever existed, but you will go down, too. You know you will!"

"I did what any professional soldier would do," Yo retorted.

"You call keeping a man in a cage for forty years professional? I call it barbaric. You are a terrorist!" A shiver ran down Le's arms.

"No, they are the terrorists," Yo screamed, gesturing toward the prisoners.

"All I see are six shells of what used to be proud men. Look at them! They are men with families that did what their government told them to do. They have done nothing wrong. They are not the problem. No! You and others like you who refuse to listen to logic, peace, and God are the real problems."

"I am done talking."

Turning to his men, Yo forcefully ordered, "Take them back to the prison. All of them, including Le!"

The Communist soldiers looked at each other, unsure what to do. This was all new information to them. *Who was right? What did Le mean?*

Le noticed their hesitation, and yelled to them in Vietnamese. "Your lives will be worthless, too. Were you ordered to keep your jobs secret? Not to tell anyone about the prison? I know I was. And why? Because if the Vietnamese government found out what was going on, something would have to be done about it. Your best bet is to end this charade now.

Let us go. Turn yourself in. Tell the authorities what happened here. Turn against General Yo...or you will all end up dead."

Yo's soldiers looked at each other, uncertain how to react. They were unaware that the Vietnamese government did not know about the prison. *Did they make a mistake obeying the general? Should they risk listening to Le and walk away from Yo?*

General Yo glared at his men, sensed their hesitation, and feared they were not going to carry out his orders. "Cowards," he thundered. He pulled his pistol out of his holster, aiming it directly at Le's head. "Die!"

Lomack shouted, "No!" He jumped in front of Le as a shot echoed through the forest.

McCarter and the other POWs gasped in horror.

In a split second, one single shot ended the standoff.

Le stared at Lomack, the man who only hours ago threatened to kill him.

Lomack appeared confused, but he felt no pain. Fear overwhelmed him as he wondered where he had been shot. Perplexed, he looked at his comrades. *What happened?*

In unison, all eyes turned to the evil general, still standing with his pistol directed toward the ground. Suddenly, he slumped to his knees, staring at Le with a look of horror. Then he collapsed in the dirt, face first—motionless!

Without warning, three mysterious figures dressed in camouflage clothing emerged from the jungle.

A fourth person appeared from the trees, and a familiar voice commanded, "Danh tu."

The Vietnamese men obeyed the order, dropping their weapons.

A tall, black man dressed in Army fatigues, carrying a military rifle, stepped into the clearing.

"Sam!" Le shouted excitedly.

The American hurried over and put his hand on Le's shoulder. "Are you okay, my friend?"

Le nodded his head, still in disbelief. "How did you know?"

"I was worried that if you arrived early you might be detected. We landed ahead of schedule just a few hundred yards from here. While we were waiting, we heard gunfire. We knew something had gone wrong. We followed your GPS signal, and made the decision to fire before things got any worse."

Sam's gaze turned to Captain McCarter and the other prisoners. His hand slid off Le's shoulder and went limp. A tear came to his eye. "Oh, dear God, it's true."

Snapping to attention, Sam proudly saluted the six frail men. "With my highest respect gentlemen, I salute you. Thank you. God bless you."

Sam strode over to Specialist Anthony Williams. With trembling arms, he respectfully embraced him.

While Sam greeted the others, Le extended his hand to Lomack. "You were willing to give your life to save mine. Thank You."

"So were you, Le. You put your life on the line for us." Lomack grabbed his outstretched hand, shaking it vigorously.

Freeman smiled. He knew it was a vital step in his patient's healing process.

The emotional scene had left Sam shaken. Tears flowed down his cheeks as he hugged each of the men, unable to speak.

Sam paused to collect his thoughts. After a deep, steadying breath, he flashed a big grin and shouted with authority. "Okay, gentlemen. Let's go home! Let's go home!"

"Wait! There is one more thing I must do." Le walked closer to Yo's soldiers, still held at gunpoint by Sam's men. In their language, he begged, "Please tell me where my family is?"

They remained silent until Sam confronted them face-to-face. When they noticed him reaching for his pistol, they started talking at once. "We do not know. Yo captured them near the border and brought them back to the prison."

Le shouted in a loud, desperate voice, "Are they alive? Tell me…is my family alive?"

One hung his head, sadly. "I do not think so. Yo took them into the building, but later came out alone. He only had that picture. There was blood all over his uniform."

Another guard added. "There was a lot of screaming and crying when he was inside...and then it was quiet."

Le looked in the direction of the prison, and then at Sam. "I must go back. Even if they are dead, I must go find my family."

"I understand," Sam said, putting his hand on his friend's shoulder. "I would do the same thing for my family."

At that moment, the helicopter pilot's voice blared through Sam's headphones. "Sam, we have company. Three enemy choppers are heading our direction."

"How far away are they?"

"About fifteen minutes."

Sam looked at the three despondent Vietnamese soldiers and then at General Yo's lifeless body. "The war is over." He spoke in their language. "It is finished. Go home! Go home!"

Sam turned to his men and issued a series of orders. "Disable the vehicles and weapons. Make them walk home. I will take pictures of the evidence. We need to move quickly!"

As if rehearsed, the men sprang into action. Grabbing the weapons, they took out the magazines, smashing the guns across the vehicle. One of the men opened the hoods of Yo's truck, and the old ambulance, cutting the battery cables and plug wires, leaving the vehicles useless.

Sam took a small camera from his pocket and snapped pictures of the POWs, General Yo's body, and the three Vietnamese soldiers.

Another one of Sam's men sent Yo's soldiers home on foot, and then turned and signaled "thumbs up."

Sam shouted, "Now we're ready. Let's go home!"

Le glanced one last time at the body of General Yo as he walked around it.

Some of the prisoners kicked the dead tormenter in the head as they passed him.

Lomack kicked him and spit on the motionless body. "You took forty years of my life. May you rot in hell!"

The POWs trudged with Sam through the forest, growing more excited with each step. As they entered a clearing, they could not believe their eyes. Freedom was within their reach—in the form of a large helicopter!

For the first time in forty years, all six men were smiling.

Sam and his men put their arms around the prisoners, repeating the words, "You're going home, men! You're really going home!"

Sam's aides were formerly in the military. Two were Navy SEALs and the other was a U.S. Marine. They assisted in many rescues, but this was their ultimate mission. Something they would be proud of forever—a story they would tell their children and grandchildren for years to come. This is what they lived for!

The prisoners were finally on their way home!

After all, home is where you lay your head. Soon the returning soldiers would lay their heads at home in America, and experience freedom, real freedom, after forty years of indescribable torment.

As they reached the chopper, the soldiers' eyes were moist. The rotors roared, and the fumes permeated the air. The sound and the smell triggered memories of the prisoner's war days.

Sam's men helped them into the aircraft and strapped them into their seats.

Staring straight ahead, the survivors never looked out—their minds were miles away.

Finally, everyone except Sam and Le were aboard.

Sam put his hand on Le's shoulder, shouting above the deafening noise, "You have to come with us now. The men in the approaching choppers will kill you if you stay, and then you will be of no help to your family or anybody else."

Le glanced at Sam, then the prisoners. He looked back into the jungle. This was his country and life—the only one he had ever known. Somewhere out there were his wife and children. Alive or dead—he had to go back for them. "I have to get my family. They are probably dead, but I still must find them. They deserve that much."

"You can't do it by yourself. We will take the POWs to the embassy. We will go through official channels and get help for you. I promise, we will return to search for your family."

"The embassy—what can they do?" Le sighed.

"Think about it, Le. The Vietnamese government will soon hear about this. We have taken pictures. It can't remain a secret. I believe they will bend over backwards to help us. Right now, your life is worthless here. You have uncovered something big! The world will certainly stand up and take notice. Unless I am sadly mistaken, there will be a public outcry. You are a dead man in this country. Come. Let me deal with this, the right way, at the right time."

Just then, the pilot shouted, "Sam, we have to leave. Now!"

Le knew Sam was right. He and Linh agreed what they would do in this situation. They both knew what could happen and understood the risks. They had decided together to trust God and accept the consequences, whatever they were. Yet, Le felt the need to protect Linh. Their children were his responsibility. He couldn't shake the feeling that he had failed them.

However, he trusted Sam and believed he would keep his word.

The sound of the helicopter blades reminded Le of the urgency of the situation. Throwing his rifle on the ground, he hopped into the chopper, followed by a much relieved Sam.

The chopper rose quickly, flying low over the dense jungle.

Below, Le saw the abandoned ambulance and the body of General Yo. He felt no pity for him.

Le looked at the rescued men, confident he did what he had to do. All was quiet as the former guard watched the trees and brush beneath him disappear into the distance.

The soldiers stared straight ahead in complete silence…for a long time.

Unexpectedly, a grateful smile spread across Captain McCarter's face. Reaching his hand across the aisle, he placed it on Le's arm. Realizing the tremendous sacrifice this one-time "enemy" had made for him, he squeezed the young guard's arm. With misty eyes and heartfelt words, he mouthed the words, "Thank you! Thank you!"

At that moment, Le was convinced that no matter what happened to him or his family, it was worth the risk. It was the right thing to do.

TEN

The Embassy

The Vietnamese helicopters pursuing the Americans were no match for the first rate flying ability of Sam's pilot. As they crossed into Laos, Yo's helicopters finally retreated. With the general dead, the chase was over.

During the entire flight, the soldiers remained silent; the only sound was the familiar, monotonous drone of the chopper.

Sam spent a great deal of time talking on the radio. Occasionally, he would look back at the POWs who sat motionless, staring straight ahead. He could not imagine the thoughts racing through their minds.

Before long, the helicopter entered Thailand's air space. They stopped briefly to refuel at a site previously arranged by Sam.

Just before reaching Bangkok, two United States military helicopters joined them to escort them toward a large compound. They began their descent into the courtyard of the American Embassy.

Le studied Captain McCarter as he silently stared out the window. All of a sudden, his eyes filled with tears and an indescribable look came over his face.

The other five men glanced up, and then grabbing each other's hands began sobbing.

Le realized why the soldiers were weeping. They caught their first glimpse of a most welcome sight. Flying high in the bright sky over the compound was an enormous American flag. For the first time in forty years, the returning soldiers saw "Old Glory" waving freely in the breeze. Their emotions erupted as the love they felt for their country surfaced with tears of joy. It was a moment of ecstasy.

Unexpected tears trickled down Le's cheeks.

The two military helicopters hovered overhead as Sam's aircraft touched down.

When the chopper was safe on the ground, the other two landed close by. As the rotating blades came to a stop, the military personnel in the other helicopters jumped out. With weapons in hand, they surrounded Sam's chopper. No one moved a muscle.

Sam unbuckled his seat belt. "Wait here," he shouted, climbing out.

A small group of people streamed out of a nearby building—some dressed in military garb and others in civilian clothing.

Sam introduced himself, shaking the hand of the Ambassador to Thailand, Michael Wagner.

Sam pointed in the direction of the prisoners.

The stunned look on the ambassador's face showed disbelief. He turned to an aide. "Get some medical personnel out here…now!"

Wagner walked over and stared at the thin, frail men in Sam's helicopter. The freed captives continued to sit motionless, noticeably in shock, hands clasped tightly to each other.

Le was concerned their hearts would not be strong enough to handle all that was happening. *What were they thinking? They must be paralyzed with fear.*

Suddenly the embassy door swung open and a number of medical personnel rushed to the helicopter to assist the passengers.

A soldier clutching a laptop sprinted to the chopper door. Addressing the man closest to him, he asked, "Sir, what is your name?"

The prisoner stared straight ahead, unresponsive.

In an effort to assure him he was safe, Le reached over and patted Freeman's knee, nodding his head in an attempt to coax him into speaking.

After a lengthy pause, the prisoner's raspy voice responded slowly. "Specialist Robert M. Freeman, United States Army, US 16917813."

The young man with the computer typed in the information. A sudden moment of awareness jolted him. He turned the computer screen toward the ambassador, who looked at it, and gasped, "Oh, dear God."

With urgency in his voice, Wagner issued an order—"Take care of these men, now! Now, I said!"

Within seconds, the helicopter was bustling with medical aides.

After the quick preliminary check, the two Navy SEALs who helped with the rescue assisted the men out of the chopper and into wheelchairs.

As Le stepped out of the helicopter, he felt a sense of awe he had never experienced before. He could hardly believe he was in the presence of Americans. Their assistance and kindness defied everything that had been drilled into him by his superiors.

The ex-Vietnamese guard thought about the "land of the free and the home of the brave." *I wonder if my hope of visiting America someday could ever become a reality. Is it merely a dream?*

Sam stretched his arm around Le's shoulders as they watched the medical personnel care for the now former POWs.

Within minutes, medics wheeled the men toward the building.

Abruptly Captain McCarter motioned the man who was pushing his wheelchair to stop. The captain stood, wobbly on his feet, and turned around eyeing Le. He lifted his trembling hand slowly to his forehead, saluting his former guard. His face beamed.

Le snapped to attention and proudly returned the salute, grinning from ear to ear.

The medical personnel helped McCarter back in the wheelchair, then pushed him into the building.

"You are a hero to them, Le." Overcome with emotion, Sam could barely get the words out. Never in his life was he more grateful to be an American than at that moment.

Le's head was spinning.

He was thrilled that they pulled off the rescue successfully, but it came at a terrible price. He thought of his family. *I hope their suffering was not prolonged.* Le shuddered at the endless possibilities. He and his wife both knew the risks, but still the pain was immense—unbearable. His heart felt like it had shattered.

Le looked heavenward and silently prayed, *Dear God, I know you are with them, but I hope they didn't suffer.*

In his mind, he replayed the last time they were together. *Why did it have to end this way?*

Sam lowered his head, praying silently for his friend.

Then without a word, Sam put his hand on Le's shoulder in a show of support, and climbed back into the chopper.

The silence was shattered as the helicopter's engines roared, and the giant aircraft slowly began to rise. Within minutes, it was out of sight.

The last ten hours had definitely taken a toll on the soldiers. However, the last four decades had drained them—physically, emotionally, and even spiritually.

The worst of their ordeal was over. No longer would they sleep in rat-infested, filthy, cramped quarters, or slave all day in the grueling sun with little to drink and garbage to eat. There would be no more physical, verbal, or emotional abuse. The horror has ended.

Le stood in the courtyard, struggling to collect his thoughts.

A young woman, a United States Marine, hurried to him. She stepped in front of him, looking directly in his eyes, and shouted, "Sir? Sir?"

Le's mind was miles away trying to unscramble his emotions.

He was jolted to the present by her words.

Looking into the Marine's deep blue eyes, Le smiled warmly.

She returned the smile.

"Yes," he finally responded.

Realizing he felt misplaced, she touched his hand. "Sir, will you please come with me? We need to debrief you. Don't worry. You will not be harmed in any way."

Feeling the touch of her hand, he imagined Linh's delicate touch. Heartache encompassed him when he realized he would never feel the warmth of his wife's hand again.

Exhaustion overwhelmed him, but somehow he found the strength to follow the Marine into the building. In the last week, Le only had a few hours of sleep each night.

Sensing his fatigue, the Marine led him into a comfortable room.

On the small table were bottles of water and soft drinks. Half a dozen donuts were arranged neatly on a plate—the tantalizing smell caught his attention. He never had seen anything quite like it before—he thought they looked and smelled delicious.

"Help yourself to a snack. I'll be right back." The young woman spun around, and left the room.

Le was starved and thirsty. He sat at the table and guzzled a soda. Within minutes, he devoured five donuts.

As he was eating the last one, the Marine woman returned with two men—an American and a Vietnamese interpreter.

Le stood to greet them.

The American, Lieutenant Jason Rader, introduced himself. He looked at the empty plate, and then watched Le as he stuffed the last bite of donut in his mouth. "You like those, don't you?"

Le nodded, wiping the corners of his mouth with a napkin.

"I'll get you some fresh ones in the morning…those were a day old." Rader smiled.

Le didn't know how they could improve on taste, but was excited to know he could have more of the delicacies the next morning.

"Do you know much English?" Rader asked slowly and precisely.

"Yes. I was an English interpreter," Le replied with perfect diction.

"Have a seat. We might as well be comfortable while we talk." Lieutenant Rader dismissed the translator.

The three sat down at the small table. The Marine had a recording device and a laptop. "This is Corporal Quinn," the lieutenant said, pointing to the young woman. "She will be documenting your comments. I know you have been through a lot and are tired. However, I need to ask you a few questions. Samuel Jefferson told me the story of your family. I am truly sorry for your loss. On behalf of the United States Government, and the families of the liberated POWs, I want to express our deepest sympathy."

Unexpectedly, Rader stood, saluted Le, and offered his hand.

Le stood. Somewhat baffled, he stared at the officer's extended hand, finally grasping it. He glanced at the young Marine, who was smiling pleasantly indicating her approval.

Lieutenant Rader looked at his notepad, reviewing the questions he would ask.

Before he could begin, a bewildered Le interrupted. "Are you CIA?"

Surprised by the question, Rader replied, "No. I am Army Intelligence though. I want to assure you, I'm only here to ask a few questions. No one will harm you."

"What will happen to my friends?"

The lieutenant paused, uncertain how to answer the question. "Your friends, that's a nice way to put it. Your friends are fine. They are being well cared for. They had a much needed, warm shower. I heard they were enjoying it so much they refused to get out. Understandably so. I expect it's the first refreshing shower they have had in forty years."

Lieutenant Rader continued. "Soon they will have a complete medical exam. A team is now en route to the embassy. The physicians will examine them thoroughly and update their vaccinations."

He cleared his throat. "We will have to be careful not to overdo it. They are very weak. They'll eat bland food for a couple of days, until their bodies...actually, until their digestive system can tolerate other food. As I said, specialists from around the area are flying in to oversee their care. Their physical conditions will be monitored closely. After so many years on a depleted diet, their bodies will reject certain foods. Nutritionists will see they are fed the right foods at the right times."

"When will they go home? When will their families be notified that they are alive?" Le's voice sounded nervous, he seemed jittery.

The lieutenant was touched by the Vietnamese man's heartfelt words. "You really care about them, don't you?"

"Absolutely. In a way, I was a prisoner with them for over four years. I understand the men better than anyone else does. I know exactly what they went through. I did not endure their suffering physically, but I did mentally. Trust me...I know how much their families mean to them."

Shifting his gaze to the Marine, Le commented, "I know the names of their wives, parents, brothers and sisters, friends, dogs and cats, and even a couple cows."

The Americans chuckled lightening the tense mood, but Le remained subdued.

The lieutenant leaned on the table with his chin in his hand, uncertain how much to tell the Vietnamese guard. He knew the plans for the former prisoners were confidential, but somehow he sensed Le could be trusted. He earned the right to know. After all, he was clearly not the enemy.

"Okay. I will give you some details, but this is highly confidential—top secret. We have not had time to finalize it. This is the plan, but keep in mind, it may change somewhat." Leaning closer to Le, Rader disclosed, "The President of the United States has been informed and will be updated as things develop. Soon he will open a dialog with the Vietnamese government."

The lieutenant glanced at his watch. "The men will spend the night here in the safety of this compound. Late tomorrow morning, they will board a chopper to the Bangkok airport. From there, transferred by military jet to Japan, they will go through more medical and psychological tests and receive more injections. In their weakened condition, even catching a cold could be catastrophic."

He sat straighter in his chair. "Fingerprints on file will verify their identity. It will take time to get that done because we will have to dig into archived files to get fingerprint records. After positive identification, we will notify their families, which must be done delicately. Some of their parents will still be alive. The shock of hearing the news could be more than they can tolerate emotionally or physically, especially the elderly ones."

The lieutenant sipped his water. "It also goes the other way. Until the time comes to meet their families, the men will not obtain any information about their loved ones. We know they are anxious to learn about the families left behind. The truth is that it could be traumatizing in their fragile conditions. Some of them will receive bad news. Others may not recognize their loved ones. Forty years must seem like a lifetime to the men. The people and situations have changed drastically. There are endless possibilities. We will help as much as we can to ensure a smooth transition."

"When can they see their families?" Le persisted.

"If all goes well, in three days. That's not definite. With any luck, within seventy-two hours the men will be rested and strong enough to face the facts of what years of confinement did to their bodies, their families, and the changing world. You know this world is a lot different than it was in 1970. We weren't even born yet!" He smiled.

Glancing at the still edgy Vietnamese, Rader continued. "Now, on a different note…I need all the information you can give me. Don't leave anything out; give me every detail. Let's get started, please, at the beginning."

The lieutenant took another drink and then began the debriefing. "First, let me ask you an essential question. Did the Vietnamese government know about these POWs?"

Rader waited for Le's response. He wondered if the Vietnamese guard would answer the tough questions about his own country truthfully.

Le drew in a deep breath and exhaled slowly. "I do not think the Vietnamese government, on the whole, knew about them. I do believe some did. Somebody, somewhere, high in the government, must have known and gave Yo the help he needed to stay hidden for all those years."

"Yo, that would be General Yo? Sam gave me his name. The U.S. military is well aware of his atrocities. Okay, let's start at the beginning. Again, don't leave anything out. Tell me everything you know. When did you have your first contact with this General Yo? What do you know about him and his operation?"

The guard paused, searching his memory of the last four years.

"I met him the first day of my job, if you can call it that."

For the next three hours, Le explained the duties of his job and talked about the treatment of the prisoners. He told how they used the days of the week for their names. He described how they communicated through tapping. He revealed some of the memories the prisoners shared with each other. It was especially difficult when Le tearfully discussed his own wife and children.

The Marine and Army lieutenant listened thoughtfully, entranced by his story. Both of them expressed sorrow for his loss. At times, the Marine's eyes were misty as she typed everything Le recalled. *Could this man's incredible story be true?*

An aide delivered a meal to their table. As they ate their nourishing food, they continued the conversation.

Le finally talked about Sam and the rescue, General Yo's death, and the trip to the American Embassy.

When the interrogation was completed, Lieutenant Rader stood, extending his hand to Le.

Le shook his hand warmly, but was still concerned about his own future.

Rader clasped his hand for a moment, not saying a word. Finally, he nodded his head and blew out a lengthy breath. "Thank you for your bravery and everything you have done for America. I promise, you will not be forgotten."

The lieutenant faced the young Marine. "Corporal Quinn, please accompany Mr. Le to his room, and make sure he is comfortable."

"Yes, sir." She motioned for the exhausted man to follow. "Mr. Le, please come with me."

Walking behind the Marine, he couldn't help but think how strange it was to see a woman dressed in military apparel.

"I don't remember your name," he stated.

"Corporal Quinn."

"No, I mean your first name."

"Oh, it's Nancee…with two 'e's."

"Well, Nancee with two 'e's, it's nice to officially meet you."

She smiled warmly. Corporal Quinn led him down the connecting hallways and up a flight of stairs to his room. Unlocking the door for him, she stood back waiting for him to enter.

A confused Le kept staring at the lock on the door.

The corporal noticed his troubled expression and tried to put his mind at ease. "This is where you will spend the night. It is usually set aside for dignitaries and political leaders from the United States."

Le reluctantly stepped into the room. He looked around and noticed its tasteful décor. A huge bed with a lightweight green comforter and at least six pillows looked inviting. On each side of the bed were nightstands with lamps dimly lighting the room. A giant, flat screen television hung on the wall at the foot of the bed.

"We have laid some clean clothing out for you. We guessed at your size." Quinn walked over to another door and opened it. "This is your bathroom. There is a shower and a whirlpool. You can take a bath, shower, or both if you want. You can lie in the spa for hours if you choose. We want you to be comfortable."

"What time do I need to wake up?"

"I will wake you about seven. Your friends are already asleep. They will be monitored all night for any health problems."

Still apprehensive, there was a question he needed to ask, one that had been weighing heavily on his mind. "Am I…am I a prisoner?"

Her eyes lit up. "A prisoner? No! Definitely not! Everyone is talking about you and the brave things you did. You're a hero, Mr. Le. I'm sorry you thought that."

"I ask because I see the locked doors, and everyone is staring at me. I am confused about everything. What will happen to me? I'm…I'm a stranger here. I'm alone. I have many unanswered questions." He lowered his head.

She sensed Le's heartache and desperation. She took his hand, cupped her other hand over it, and took a deep breath. *How can I help him find peace? How can I encourage him during this difficult time?*

After a brief pause, Nancee added. "The locked door guarantees your privacy. People stare at you because you are a hero. Look at what you've done! They wonder why you would sacrifice your life, and the lives of your family, to save six old men, presumed dead for forty years. Everyone here has the highest respect for you, Le. You are not a prisoner. You are our honored guest and free to leave whenever you choose. Whatever you need, I am here to assist you. "

Le listened intently.

She continued. "However, there is something I must warn you about. We are uncertain what will happen if the Vietnamese government locates you. We're concerned about you. You are safe while in American hands…we will protect you. If you leave, we can't guarantee your safety."

He didn't comment, but he thought about her words.

She turned to leave, but stopped. "If you need anything, just dial zero on the phone. Somebody will be here to help in a jiffy. Have a good night's sleep, Mr. Le." She closed the door and was gone.

In the stillness of his room, he had a recurring thought. *What am I going to do now?* He kept thinking about Linh. *How can I live without her and my children?* His heart ached. *I feel so lost…and alone.*

A familiar Bible verse replayed in his mind. *Lo, I am with you always, even unto the ends of the earth.* He looked heavenward, asking for divine guidance.

After a few moments, a thought hit him. *Did Yo actually kill my family? Maybe, just maybe, they are alive. Is there a possibility they could be prisoners somewhere? What can I do? How can I find them? Could they be at the same prison camp where I worked? Should I return to Vietnam?* These questions burned in his mind, but he remembered the corporal's warning.

Removing the pouch from around his neck, he laid it gently between the pillows on the bed.

He heeded Corporal Quinn's advice and took a long hot shower. Following that, he sat in the hot tub for nearly an hour, mentally replaying the events of the very long day. *How could I have protected my family? What went wrong?*

As he slipped between the fresh smelling sheets, he thought about his friends. Tonight, they too were sleeping in a bed like this. How strange it must be to them. Many people crawl in their comfortable beds night after night, never realizing how blessed they are. Yet, millions wonder where they will lay their head or get their next meal.

Exhausted, he reached for the pouch. Holding it close, he fell into a deep sleep wondering and dreaming about his life.

ELEVEN

The First Day of Freedom

Children were laughing and playing. An angelic looking woman dressed in white, opened the door, gliding gracefully into the room. She turned, smiling at the children. That was when he saw her beautiful face—his Linh, with their dear children. He called to them, but they didn't hear him. He summoned her repeatedly, but still no response. He started to walk to her.

Suddenly he heard pounding, and then his wife's sweet voice. "Mr. Le, are you awake?"

The pounding continued. He didn't want to wake up. Startled and groggy, he sat up in bed and whispered, "That's not my Linh—it's the Marine."

"Yes?" he muttered, trying to sound alert.

"Are you awake?" the voice queried.

"Just a minute. I will be right there." Le stumbled out of bed, opening the door a crack.

Corporal Quinn's pleasant smile greeted him. After the time they spent together the day before, he felt that she was a friendly face in the middle of chaos. She helped him when everything was new and frightening. Her presence was refreshing.

"Good morning. It is nearly seven, and we have a busy day ahead of us. Would you like to eat breakfast in your room, or come down to the cafeteria with me?"

He replied eagerly, "Give me a few minutes, and I'll be ready to go."

"I'll be back in ten minutes."

Le closed the door.

This was a new day for him and his friends. It was their first full day of freedom, and he was anxious to see them. At least, he hoped to have the opportunity to visit with the men. He was not sure what the embassy officials had planned for him.

Le washed quickly, dressing in the clothes provided for him. He slipped on a new pair of jeans and a light blue denim shirt, which had the United States Marine emblem on it. Le had never worn jeans before. The first thing he noticed was how comfortable they were, unlike the military khakis he wore.

He smiled, admiring the Marine emblem on the front of his shirt. He often read about the Marines on the internet—the Few...the Proud...the Marines. He knew the Marine Corps was the smallest branch of the U.S. military, but a choice fighting force.

Looking in the mirror, he combed his hair, and was ready to face the uncertain day.

Le opened the door, where the young woman was waiting patiently. "My, don't you look dapper." She smiled.

He started to close the door, but suddenly remembered something, and stopped. "Just a minute." He hurried back into the room. Grabbing the small pouch, he put the strap around his neck, and stuffed it inside his shirt.

The corporal observed his activity with interest, but said nothing.

He noticed her blue eyes focused on the string around his neck. Le had an uneasy feeling. Obviously, she was curious about the pouch. *I hope they don't take it from me. It is my most valuable possession.* Trying to get her focus off the pouch, Le announced, "Okay, I'm ready. I'm really hungry."

They took an elevator to the cafeteria. The noise of the busy dining hall took Le by surprise. He caught a whiff of the assorted breakfast foods and realized he was ready for a nutritious meal.

Several dozen people had already gathered. A few were dressed in civilian clothing, but most were in military uniforms. People were talking and laughing as they stood in the food line. Others were sitting at tables, deep in discussions, enjoying their breakfast.

Le noticed people staring at him when he entered the room. They stopped what they were doing, and the room suddenly hushed.

Then it happened. It began with one person clapping...then two, then four people. Gradually, everyone in the cafeteria broke into a standing ovation.

A group came from the kitchen and joined in the spontaneous applause of gratitude.

Corporal Quinn smiled, whispering, "I told you, you're a hero... and nobody here is going to let you forget it."

As the young Vietnamese walked through the cafeteria, the applause continued. Some patted him on the back; others shook his hand. Le was overwhelmed!

One of the cooks handed him a tray, then ushered him and the Marine to the front of the line.

Another man dressed in white stepped next to him. "Sir, what can I bring you for breakfast? You name it."

Le thought for a second. "Can I get one of those round things with a hole in the center?"

The man put his hands on the former guard's shoulders, looking him straight in the eyes. "Hole in the center?" he asked. The confused cook glanced at the corporal for help.

"I believe he wants a donut," she said matter-of-factly.

"A donut! You want a donut," he laughed, now understanding what the Vietnamese hero meant.

Le repeated, "Yes, a donut. I think they are very good. I never had one before yesterday."

"Sir, for you, I'm going to get the freshest donut I can find." Walking briskly to the kitchen, he quickly disappeared.

Everything returned to normal.

Corporal Quinn guided Le through the food line. He helped himself to bacon, eggs, and a cup of coffee. The variety of food amazed him.

They found an empty table and were seated.

Le bowed his head, giving silent thanks to God for the food. He prayed also for the six men, their families, as well as his own family.

The corporal noticed him bow his head, and looked around to see if anyone was watching. Not wanting to appear rude, she slowly bowed her head.

They had just begun eating when the man in white came bursting from the kitchen with a dozen fresh donuts, setting them in front of Le.

His eyes lit up, looking at the neatly arranged pastries, and then back at the man who brought them. With a wide grin, Le responded gratefully, "Thank you."

"Anything you ever want, just ask for Sal. I'll personally get it for you." He strutted back to the kitchen.

"He's nice," Le commented.

The corporal raised one eyebrow. "Many people would disagree with you. He runs this mess hall with an iron fist, but his food is always topnotch. He has taken a special liking to you. His grandfather was a POW during the Korean War."

"I feel for him." Le reached for one of the donuts. He thought it was undeniably the best food he had ever eaten. In just minutes, he had downed three donuts and was starting on his fourth.

Quinn chuckled. "Those things will make you sick, if you eat too many."

Le grinned. "Really? They sure taste good." He gobbled the remnant of donut in his hand.

All of a sudden, there was a commotion. Le looked up to see Captain McCarter entering the cafeteria, followed by the rest of the returnees.

Everyone in the room jumped to their feet and a thunderous applause erupted.

Corporal Quinn also stood, and a huge smile spread across her face as she joined in the celebration.

Le stood up slowly. Staring at his new friends entering the room, he froze. He hardly recognized them. Oversized, clean clothes replaced the smelly, drab rags they wore for years. They had on tennis shoes. The men were all clean shaven, even their heads, probably the best way to do away with the mange and lice. They no longer smelled like the prison that held them captive for all those miserable years.

The soldiers had enjoyed their first full night of sleep in forty years. Apparently, it did them good; they seemed bright and cheerful.

With eyes focused straight ahead, they walked past Le.

He was confused and hurt when they didn't acknowledge him. *Surely, they could have said hello to me after what we have been through together. Maybe they didn't recognize me dressed like this.*

About a dozen men, some high-ranking officers, followed the soldiers. Medical personnel were present to oversee health issues that could occur.

Military escorts showed McCarter and his men to a large table.

The applause continued.

The men were uncertain how to react to the situation. Some of them had a slight smile, while others kept their heads down, humbly looking toward the floor.

The medical personnel motioned for them to sit.

The applause subsided when the men took their seats.

The lively conversations in the crowded dining room resumed.

Captain McCarter glanced up, and noticed Le who was still standing, staring at him. The captain rose and the room instantly hushed. McCarter strode slowly toward the former guard. When he reached Le, they stood face-to-face.

All eyes in the cafeteria fixed upon the scene as it unfolded.

Placing his arms around Le's neck, he pulled the young man close, holding him tightly. Tears flowed from the captain's eyes. Finally regaining his composure enough to speak, he uttered, "Thank you. Thank you."

Stirred by his action and words, Le faced his new friend, Corporal Quinn, who was watching through wet eyes.

Tears began trickling down Le's face.

The other men formed a line behind McCarter, waiting to acknowledge their former guard. The men he knew as Sunday, Tuesday, Wednesday, Thursday, and Friday took this opportunity to express their feelings. Some said nothing. Words were inadequate to convey their wide range of emotions.

Sunday conveyed a simple, "God bless you."

Le was unsure what to expect when Friday neared him. He remembered that just twenty-four hours before, Lomack wanted to kill him. Wearing glasses, he approached Le. For the first time in what seemed to be a lifetime, Lomack saw clearly—he saw the world in a different light. Through tears, he stared at Le. Raising his right hand, he placed it on Le's shoulder, but couldn't speak. He nodded his head. Then without warning, he grabbed the former guard's neck, embracing him. "Forgive me for the way I treated you. Please, forgive me!"

Le drew a slow, deep breath. "It's all forgiven. I understand where you were coming from."

A smile lit up the soldier's face, something Le never expected to see. Lomack returned to his table and sat down.

The entire room erupted in another hearty applause.

The hubbub finally died down and the men began to eat their first breakfast as free men. It had been prepared specifically to meet their needs. The nutritionist planned a bland breakfast, since their weakened systems demanded special care. They would have to adapt gradually to normal eating. Their breakfast consisted of a scrambled egg, oatmeal, a slice of dry toast, and weak, green tea.

Captain McCarter called over to Le, "How's the food?"

Impulsively Le shot back, "I love the donuts."

McCarter laughed, along with everyone else within earshot.

Le stared at his friends.

"What are you thinking about?" Corporal Quinn asked.

"I wonder what they are thinking. What are they feeling? Is it excitement, joy, relief, or apprehension?" He toyed with the food on his plate, and then glanced around the room searching for some way to express his feelings. "I would like to know if any of the people in here know what real sacrifice is. Sure, they are away from friends and loved ones for a while, but they are in a clean room with good food, watching flat screen TVs. It's a far cry from where those six men have been the last forty years."

With a glimmer of a smile, Le added. "It's hard to believe that in a couple hours they will be on their way to Japan, and then home to America. Me? Where will I be? What will I do?"

The corporal looked at him, bewildered. "Nobody told you, did they?"

"Told me what?" His dark eyes widened.

"You'll be with them. Last night your six friends decided they were not going anywhere without you. You are one of them! They know you can't return to Vietnam. Where would you go? What would you do? You're going with them to live free in America."

Le was confused. *Surely, it has to be a mistake. It would be a privilege to visit America. Yet, she did not say I was going to visit…she said, I was going to live in the greatest country on earth. Live in America*! His heart pounded so hard with excitement he thought everyone could hear it.

He glanced at McCarter and their eyes met. A smile erupted on their faces, both men realizing their prayers were being answered.

At the same time, he felt empty because he would not be sharing the experience with his family. The moment was bittersweet. Things were happening quickly, and he had not even had a chance to mourn his tragic loss.

TWELVE

The Journey Begins

In spite of Le's heavy heart, at times he felt a deep inner peace. Even though he had many unanswered questions, he felt God's presence in an unexplainable way.

Other times, the darkness engulfed him as if he was drowning in a sea of despair, unable to swim.

One thing was certain, God had a plan for his life, and it would be revealed in His time. He had to trust God, similar to the way the prisoners needed to trust him.

Following breakfast, Corporal Quinn escorted Le back to his room.

Standing at the doorway, she briefed him on the latest details of his upcoming trip. "The chopper will be leaving at precisely ten. You and the former prisoners will be chauffeured to the nearby airport. From there, you will fly together to Japan aboard a military transport plane."

Le nodded, but wasn't sure how much he really was taking in. There was so much! He was grateful he would be with the other men.

"The world does not know about you and your friends yet. Nothing will be released to the media until fingerprints confirm the identities of the former POWs. Then their families will be notified." A smile tipped her lips. "However, from everything we can gather, they are really who they say they are!"

She looked into Le's sad eyes. Her heart broke for her new Vietnamese friend. His love for his family was evident every time he spoke of them.

"I see how much you love your family. I can only hope that someday I can be lucky enough to find a man that loves me that much."

"I am the lucky one." His eyes were soft with memories.

She touched his hand gently. "I'll come back to get you in an hour. Please be ready."

Le nodded his head, signifying he understood.

With that, the Marine was gone.

In the stillness of his room, loneliness engulfed him. He collapsed onto his bed, weeping.

He raised his arms, crying, *Oh God...How can I go on without them? My whole world has come crashing down and I've never felt so alone! Help me find comfort in my memories.*

Fear rippled through Le. He sobbed aloud, "*I did the right thing. I did the right thing. The expression of appreciation in the cafeteria proved it...so why do I feel miserable? Why do I feel like my heart could quit beating at any moment?*

How much time passed... he wasn't sure.

Finally, he composed himself, and sat upright, looking at his watch. It was almost nine.

He collected his few personal items and placed them in the carry on bag provided by the Embassy. It contained a change of clothing, a shaver, toothbrush, toothpaste, deodorant, and a comb.

He eyed a Bible on the desk; his was back home, hidden from the Communists. As a new believer, he memorized many verses of scripture, he was now grateful that he did.

Sam once told him, "When your heart is broken, and you need an answer, read God's Word. A verse will come to your rescue and calm your hurting heart when you need it most."

He had a few extra minutes. Le picked up the Gideon Bible and began to read. A verse jumped out at him. He read the words of Jesus. *Lo, I am with you always*. He realized God had been with him all along. Always means now, as well as past, and future. This assurance gave him the inner peace he needed. *Thank You, Lord for being with me always!*

He continued reading the scripture while he waited.

Corporal Quinn arrived promptly as scheduled.

He noticed she was always prompt and he appreciated that.

Picking up the pouch, he carefully placed it around his neck, gently putting it under his shirt.

Grabbing his few possessions, he hurried to the door. He glanced around the room one final time.

The corporal greeted him with her usual smile.

As they made their way down the hall to the elevator, they chatted about their lives.

"Nancee, may I ask where you are from? How did you end up in the United States Marine Corps?"

"I'm from a city in Arizona called Flagstaff."

"Oh yes, I've heard of that. You have skiing there?"

"Yes, we do. Have you ever skied?"

"Me? Oh no, there aren't very many places to ski in Vietnam." He laughed.

"What did you do there for fun, Mr. Le?"

"Fun…what do you mean by fun?"

"You know, like play baseball, bowl, swim, horseback riding—things like that."

"All my life, I simply tried to survive. I spent most of my time learning to do something beneficial. My parents wanted me to amount to something, to live a worthwhile life. They forced me to study all the time. I guess you could say, I had the gift of learning." He chuckled. "That's what I did for fun. I read everything I could find. I spent days at a time reading and learning on the internet."

"Learning what?" she asked.

He glanced at her. "Mostly, your language…English is a very difficult language."

"So I've been told," she agreed.

Determined to probe her past, Le continued. "You didn't answer my question."

"And your question was…what is a nice girl like me doing in the Marines, right?"

They both laughed.

She cleared her throat. "Well, to make a long story short, my grandfather was a Marine, and my father is a Marine. He always wanted a son to carry on the family tradition." She stopped and faced Le. Spreading out her arms, she laughed. "So here I am, my father's son."

"Wow! We never had soldiers like you in the Vietnamese army."

"Do you disapprove?" she asked, while they resumed walking.

"Disapprove of you, or the fact that you are a Marine?"

"Both," she teased.

"Well, I certainly do not disapprove of you. You have been very helpful to me. I appreciate you. As for you being a soldier, I can't really say. We were taught in our army that men are powerful, and women are weak and need to be kept in their proper place."

"What do you think?" She emphasized "you."

"What do I think?" he repeated, unsure how to respond. "First off, it's really none of my business. Second, well…second is, that I personally would find it hard to fight with a woman beside me because I would feel I should protect her." As soon as he said it, he stopped.

Corporal Quinn searched his eyes. "You're thinking about your wife and family, aren't you?"

"Yes, I wonder what I could have done to change the way it all turned out. Could I have protected them somehow?"

The Marine's eyes clouded and her look became solemn. "Le, I'm sure when the time comes and the announcement is made about the former prisoners, the U.S. Government will question the Vietnamese government and demand answers about your family."

"You can demand any information you want. You don't understand…they will deny everything." His voice grew agitated. "They will even refute that my family or I ever existed, but it will not bring them back. Maybe I should have stayed there to fight for Linh and the children." He looked around. "I feel helpless. I can't do anything here. It's all very confusing."

"Do you pray about it?" she asked boldly. "I noticed that you pray before you eat, and I saw a Bible on your bed. You must be a religious man."

"Are you a Christian?" Le asked.

"Me?" She paused. "Define Christian."

Before Le could respond, she started down a somewhat unfamiliar path. "I was raised in a military family…power was everything." Her mind was searching for the right words. She looked directly in Le's eyes and said, "I was taught you pray in foxholes, but that's as far as it goes. I'm not sure what I believe."

Le cast a questioning look.

She persisted. "You never answered my question."

"You mean about praying?"

She nodded.

"Yes, of course I pray. That does not alter the fact that my family is dead, savagely murdered by a madman."

Scraping up courage, she added, "You don't know that for sure."

"True, but I do know how Yo operates. I saw it firsthand."

"Listen to me, Le. My country will get to the bottom of this. The Vietnamese government officials will face up to these horrific war crimes…they will have to."

No further words were spoken. They walked in silence, each deep in thought.

Just as they reached for the outside door, it flew open, startling them.

Lieutenant Rader greeted them. "There you are. Do you have everything?"

Business-like, Corporal Quinn answered, "Yes, sir. My gear is already on the chopper. Mr. Le has his belongings with him."

"It's time to get going. You both will be on the second chopper with two of the POWs and their escorts." Rader turned and was gone.

"You are coming with me?" Le asked the Marine, surprised.

"Yes. I've been designated to escort you all the way to America."

He was relieved. She had been a good friend to him, and he felt comfortable with her.

"May I ask you one more thing?" Nancee probed as they reached the door of the helicopter.

"Sure."

"What's in that bag that you keep close to you? Why do you guard it so carefully?"

Le felt the pouch, holding it tightly to his chest, but did not reply.

Smiling, she added, "Family mementos?"

"I guess you could say that. In fact…that is an understatement."

They climbed into the chopper. Le took a seat directly across from his Marine friend.

Freeman and Lomack were already aboard.

He greeted the soldiers cheerfully, "Good morning."

Freeman's heart swelled. "That would be putting it mildly."

"What do you mean?" Le asked.

"Good!" Lomack spoke loudly as the helicopter's blades whirled. "Good morning. No, it's not just a good morning…this is probably the best morning of our lives."

"From here on, gentlemen, hopefully, each morning will only get better," Corporal Quinn replied with a smile.

Le leaned slightly toward the corporal, whispering, "May I ask a favor of you?"

"Sure," she readily replied.

"This." He motioned to the pouch under his shirt. "This is what I live for now. This little bag means everything to me." He leaned closer.

She leaned toward him, making sure no one else could hear. She sensed the importance of what he wanted to tell her.

"I planned originally to give this to Monday, I mean, Captain McCarter. Now, since I am going to America, I believe it is my responsibility. Although, I'm worried it might be taken away from me when I get there."

Startled, she sat up straight. She realized that whatever was in that pouch must be extremely significant to him. "It won't be," she reassured him. "I'll see to that. We are in this together, my friend."

Le thanked her. The relief he felt was evident.

They watched the ground disappear beneath them as the helicopter rose. The crowded, little homes below grew smaller. Le realized this would probably be the last time he would see this part of the world—the only life he had ever known. He would never be able to return to his native country. His face reflected a change in his demeanor, a look of hopelessness and despair replaced his smile.

Unexpectedly, a hand touched his knee. Surprised, he looked up and saw Specialist Robert Freeman. The action, a simple reminder that he was not alone. No words were needed between the two.

A smile brightened Le's face. He realized how many people cared about him, and it gave him a renewed sense of peace and comfort. A new life awaited him, and he would not face the future alone.

He closed his eyes, and thanked God for his new friends…and new life.

They landed at the airport near a military transport plane that awaited them. As they disembarked the helicopter, Le grabbed his small bag.

The corporal reached for her duffel bag, but Le snatched it first.

"I can do that," she said, quite forcefully, trying to retrieve the luggage from his grasp.

"Lead the way, Miss. Lead the way." He stared straight ahead.

She decided not to persist, realizing it was a cultural tradition in his country to assist women. She thanked him…reluctantly.

They headed to the waiting airplane.

After they had gone a few steps, a Military Policeman (MP) halted them, demanding to search the Vietnamese passenger.

"He's with me," Quinn spoke protectively.

"Sorry, corporal. Our orders are to search anyone who is not in military uniform. It's the policy…no exceptions."

"Do you know who this is, soldier?"

"No, but actually I don't care if he's the King of Thailand. He's not in military uniform; therefore, I have orders to search him."

"Is there a problem, soldier?" A voice boomed from behind them.

The MP snapped to attention.

Captain McCarter stepped forward. Dressed in his Army fatigues, officer's hat, and bars, he stared at the young soldier, brow tight, without a hint of a smile.

"No, sir. I just need to search this man."

McCarter looked sternly at the MP, then at Le. He immediately stepped between them. "No, you don't. You see, he's with me, and he's not going to be harassed. Do you understand?"

"I have my orders, sir," the MP shouted.

"Now you have new orders, understand, soldier?"

Standing at attention, the MP bellowed, "Yes, sir!"

McCarter continued as if nothing happened. "Mr. Le, would you and the young lady kindly accompany me onto the plane?"

"We would love to," Le replied, following McCarter, and avoiding eye contact with the MP.

Although the event unnerved him, he felt reassured by McCarter's intervention. Le thanked the captain for his assistance.

"Le, I will go to my grave defending you."

McCarter peered at the strap around Le's neck, which was obviously hiding a treasure, something of great meaning. "Maybe one day you can tell me the importance of what you hold so close to your heart."

Le glanced back at him, clutched the pouch, and nodded his head. "One day...yes, one day."

As the former prisoners took their seats on the plane, the other passengers who were there to assist the soldiers watched curiously. They could only imagine what hardships the men endured during their grueling captivity.

However, many eyes focused on the young Vietnamese guard. *Who is he? Why would this man risk his life for six forgotten American POWs?*

Many questions remained unanswered.

THIRTEEN

The Land of the Free

Lomack's thin frail fingers clutched the armrests so tightly that his knuckles turned white. Nervously, he stared ahead, his heart racing as the plane began its ascent. Fear threatened to overtake him.

Forty years of captivity left the men emotionally numb. They didn't know how to react to the unfamiliar sights and sounds in the aircraft.

McCarter, since he was a former pilot, was more relaxed than the other men on the flight to Japan. Glancing around at the new surroundings, he was intrigued with the differences from the planes he remembered.

When they finally reached cruising altitude, the former prisoners began to unwind.

The returnees were fascinated as they observed the latest technology. A few of them inquired about the laptops some individuals were using. Some were curious about the tiny earpieces many wore.

One passenger, whose dress and demeanor indicated he might be important, was talking on a cell phone. Traber laughed, pointing, "Look, that phone is not attached to anything. It looks like that thing Captain Kurtz used on that sci-fi show."

One of the aides nearby wisely corrected him. "I believe that would be Captain Kirk."

"Beam me up, Scotty," Freeman joked loud enough for all to hear.

Everyone on board laughed. The mood on the plane lightened. Laughter had been unfamiliar to these men the past four decades. There had not been anything to evoke laughter. The joyous sound encouraged the other passengers.

When the men left America's shores in 1970, the world was different. Now returning to their native land, what surprises are in store for them? How will they adjust to the bewildering changes they may face?

Descending to the Tokyo airport, the men's eyes were wide with wonder. Looking out the windows, they noticed massive skyscrapers and a sprawling, bustling city.

Physicians on board continued to observe them closely—on the alert for any abnormal behavior.

The Army would shield the men from the outside world for a brief period.

Before the news of their escape was released to the public, family members would be notified. The plan was for the soldiers to be en route to the United States at that time.

The world's media would demand access to the former prisoners as soon as they learned about them. To prevent a leak before the designated time, security measures were in place. A premature release of information could be disastrous for the families, who for years believed their soldiers were dead.

The plane came to a stop at a secluded area of the airport, away from a crowd of anxious reporters who were trying to sniff out leads for a big story.

Six black limousines pulled alongside. The men boarded the limos, which whisked them away to a specially prepared facility in a high tech military hospital. Skilled physicians awaited their arrival. The medical team's sole purpose would be to care for the needs of these very special returning soldiers.

For eight hours, the men underwent a multitude of tests, shots, MRI scans, X-rays, and eye and ear exams. To the returnees, it seemed endless.

After a few hours, the men grew weary of all the probing and injections, but no one complained. Compared to the torture they had endured, it was nothing! The men knew they were about to go home and needed to be ready physically and emotionally.

Each of the soldiers spent individual time with psychiatrists and counselors who evaluated their mental health.

The physicians were doing everything possible to make a smooth transition for their return to society. The professionals realized they could only partially prepare them for their homecoming. No one could predict what the men would experience when reunited with their loved ones.

The day was grueling. However, the medical team pushed on. The goal was to return the men to their families as quickly as possible, so they wasted no time performing the necessary exams.

Le received many of the same treatments, especially the shots. At the end of the day, he told Corporal Quinn, "I feel like a human pincushion.

I'm tired of all the probing, injections, and especially the endless questions. What more can I tell them?"

Le was drilled with certain questions repeatedly. For clarity, they were asked in both Vietnamese and English, "Why did you risk your life for these men?" Another asked, "How will you react if they find the bodies of your family?" He was even asked the tough question, "Will you be willing to renounce your country to become an American citizen?"

Much was at stake for Le, for America, and ultimately for the world.

The whirlwind of events confused the Vietnamese guard. A quiet room away from the fanfare sounded good to him as the day wore on.

Finally, they boarded the limos, heading to the hotel designated for them. Le sat next to Corporal Quinn. Though bewildered by the strange surroundings, he felt safe with her.

As the Marine escorted Le to his room, she reminded him she would be next door. "Just bang on the wall if you need my help. Next stop…America!"

In a parting remark, she whispered, "Take care of those mementos." Without another word, she slipped away.

Le closed the door. He took the pouch from his neck, placing it carefully in the drawer of the nightstand next to his bed.

Removing the Gideon Bible from the drawer, he laid it on top of the stand.

Worn out and fully dressed, he collapsed on the bed thinking about all the events of the day and wondering what tomorrow would bring. In minutes, perhaps seconds, he was in a deep sleep.

Fingerprints authenticated the identities of the men! Any lingering doubts were gone. Six men…presumed dead…were going home. Alive!

Word spread fast among the men—they would jet to the United States on a new 747, which was on its way to Tokyo. They would head to America the following afternoon and spend their first night on American soil in Los Angeles. The next morning, the heroes would fly to Washington, D.C. where they would reunite with their families.

Visits to their closest relatives by their congressional representatives, along with military and medical personnel, were already taking place across the United States. Many family members were now elderly with multiple health issues. Those breaking the news to them would be delicate and use utmost caution.

The persistent ringing of the phone awakened Le. A pleasant female voice greeted him, "Good Morning, Mr. Le. This is Nancee. It is 0500 hours. We are due to eat in fifteen minutes. I haven't heard your shower, so I figured you were still sleeping."

Le jumped out of bed, shouting into the receiver. "I will be ready. I'm sorry. I will hurry." It was the fastest shower of his life. He dressed quickly, and then ran over to the nightstand to grab the pouch. Picking it up, he noticed the Bible. He uttered softly, *Thank You Lord, for Your guidance today.*

The corporal met him with her usual warm smile as he opened the door.

Due to high security, the hotel restaurant was only open to their group. After the soldiers ate their breakfast, they were hustled to a secure location in the hotel.

For the next six hours, some of the men were fitted with glasses and hearing aids.

Medics shared their test results with them. The men were weak, but in overall good health.

At 1400 hours, the men hurried into the elevator, which would take them to the underground parking garage.

Security was tight.

There seemed to be a strange, unexplainable feeling in the air. Something was not quite right as they piled into the limousine...and most of the men sensed it.

Dozens of motorcycle police quickly surrounded them.

The men's personal escorts ordered them to sit back and relax. The dark windows of the limo allowed privacy.

When the police were satisfied it was safe, they escorted them out of the garage and into the hustle and bustle of afternoon traffic.

Within minutes, reality hit them. Thousands of people were screaming and cheering in a cordoned-off area.

Dozens of police officers were trying to maintain order, keeping the crowd under control.

The news was out! Hundreds of cameras were flashing.

The United States military had gone to extreme measures to protect the identity of the POWs, yet somehow word leaked out.

The massive crowd indicated that their homecoming was something bigger than any of the POWs could have imagined.

Lining the streets, many uniformed American soldiers saluted the returning soldiers as they passed. Children waved flags enthusiastically. Parents held small ones on their shoulders so they could catch a glimpse of the caravan of heroes. Many people held "Welcome Home" signs.

Le watched the shocked expressions on his new friends. Their faces displayed happiness, astonishment, and confusion created by the fanfare. *With this greeting in Japan, what would it be like in America?*

Forty years ago, there were protesters, violence, bloodshed, and death in the streets of the United States due to opposition to the war these soldiers fought. What a difference!

At the Tokyo Airport, the limos pulled up next to an impressive new 747. Emblazoned on the aircraft were the words, "United States of America." The American flag stood out brightly on the tail. On the side of the plane was the Presidential Seal. It was the newly commissioned presidential plane!

"Wow, is that what I think it is?" Freeman inquired.

"The presidential plane? Air Force One?" Pfingston asked. "I wonder if the president is on board."

"It's only called 'Air Force One' if he is aboard," Freeman countered.

"Or she," Trader added.

"A woman president…that would be a surprise," Williams noted.

"I saw pictures of the president…it's still a man." McCarter said the words matter-of-factly.

Corporal Quinn joined the lively conversation. "The president is not aboard. I understand he wanted to be, but with all the rush, he could not adjust his schedule. The leaders of Japan, Germany, England, and France were at the capitol for meetings, but he ordered his new plane to bring you home. Gentlemen, you have the honor of flying home on the most distinguished airplane in the world…and you deserve it. You are true life heroes who endured the unthinkable, the reprehensible, and are finally coming home…in style!"

Once aboard the splendid aircraft, the pilot greeted them. "Welcome aboard men. My name is Captain Roland Shelton. I will be taking you home. On behalf of the President of the United States, my crew and I…Thank you for your service. Please make yourself comfortable."

The soldiers looked around in awe. There were three levels with over four thousand square feet of floor space. The medical suite could function as an operating room. There were two large food galleys, which could easily serve everyone on the flight simultaneously.

Dozens of people were on board to make the soldiers' trip home pleasant and comfortable.

Each soldier sat in a soft, high back seat. As they buckled their seatbelts, a personal television dropped down in front of them. The screen lit up and a well dressed man appeared. With a broad smile, the man introduced himself. "Good morning, gentlemen. My name is Nathan Alexander, and I am the President of the United States. It is my privilege to welcome you home."

The men stared at the screen as the president read each name, slowly, and precisely. "Captain James McCarter... Specialist Thomas Traber... Specialist Anthony Williams... Specialist Robert Freeman... Specialist Ronald Lomack... Sergeant Brent Pfingston. Welcome home, men! America excitedly awaits your return."

He continued, "I trust you are being treated well. We cannot give you back the forty years you have lost. All we can do now is to make the rest of your life the finest we can. We, the American people, owe you an immeasurable debt of gratitude. I look forward to meeting you personally. You are six of the bravest men the world will ever know. If there is anything you need, feel free to request it. The staff on board is available to assist you."

The president cleared his throat and with fervor explained, "We have planned a celebration in Washington, D.C. to welcome you home. The outpouring of love shown by the American people will amaze you. Right now, thousands are on their way to our nation's capitol to give you the reception you richly deserve. Your families and friends are among them."

Staring at the screen, each man was deep in thought, wondering how it would affect him personally.

President Alexander continued. "Forty years of alienation from your loved ones is incomprehensible. You realize that more than anyone does. I must warn you that some of your family members are no longer with us. For your loss, you have my condolences. I regret that an earlier rescue was not possible."

With added emphasis, he said, "Those who are responsible for your imprisonment and brutal treatment will be held accountable. Trust me on that. I assure you, we will do everything in our power to prevent this from happening to any American in the future. As a fellow Vietnam veteran, and president of this great country, you have my word."

The men's hearts were racing. They tried to comprehend what they were hearing, but they were being bombarded with so much information, they couldn't absorb it all.

President Alexander added, "Gentlemen, there is one more very important matter. I understand we have a special guest among us. Mr. Le Huu Trang, thank you for making this homecoming possible. Your sacrifice is one of honor. I thank you sincerely, and the American people thank you. You are also a hero."

Lomack looked at Le, nodding his head in agreement.

"Sit back gentlemen and enjoy the ride. It is a privilege to provide special transportation for your trip home. Consider this your 'Freedom Bird.' It is the least we can do. Again, thank you. God bless you."

He was gone and the screens displayed an American flag waving in the breeze.

The men looked at each other. No one knew what to say, each absorbed in his own thoughts. *Could this really be happening after all these years?*

Le studied the men and their reactions. He dreamed of this moment, and it was here. The men's faces expressed unbounded joy, and why not? They were finally going home.

After a short time of silence, an unexpected burst of excitement erupted among the returning soldiers. The truth finally gripped them!

Even in their weakened condition, they somehow found the strength to unfasten their seat belts and break out dancing in the aisles, chanting, "We're going home! We're going home!"

Williams grabbed Le to join the celebration. Even the reserved Le joined in the tide of emotion.

Everyone else on board watched with delight, even the medical personnel smiled at the display of exhilaration. They had never seen anything like it!

Before long, everyone on the plane participated in the clapping, cheering, and dancing. Many had wet eyes. All of them had hearts filled with gratitude. The tearful celebration continued for the next several minutes.

The men finally settled down, returning to their seats.

The air was electric with anticipation!

When the plane took off, the soldiers watched out the windows as Tokyo faded into the distance.

Ahead, was the place the former prisoners thought they would never see again…the United States of America.

The trip back to the States seemed to take forever.

The men's anticipation was beyond comprehension. A multitude of thoughts flooded their minds as they wondered what the future held. No one could predict; they could only hope!

An aide gave each man an MP3 player with music to help pass the time during the lengthy flight. At first, they just looked at the gadget, unsure what to do with it. A few of the aides demonstrated them, but the men who had been out of civilization for decades were still confused.

Freeman examined the music player and blurted, "How can such a small thing hold thousands of songs? It doesn't make sense. Look at this little thing!"

The aide sitting next to him replied, chuckling. "It's the wonders of technology…don't even try to figure it out!"

The ocean below was expansive and inspiring. Their memories of such beauty had faded through the long years.

With delight, the flight attendants served anything the soldiers requested. A couple of the men had dental problems and needed to be careful what they ate. Their stomachs were still fragile and getting used to regular foods and drinks—alcoholic and carbonated beverages were out of the question.

Ice was a special treat. Cold water was the most popular drink—they thought it strange that it came from a bottle, and stranger still, when they were told that people paid money for it.

Someone said, "Water in a bottle…whoever heard of that? Who would buy water?" Before the words were out, the soldiers mind's retreated to their captivity. Each grew silent drawing into their past world of horror. *I would have given anything through the years, for even one sip of fresh, clean water.*

The other passengers respected their time of reflection and remained quiet.

After a time, one-by-one they snapped out of it, gradually emerging into the hope of the future.

The men were fascinated with the attractive features of the female flight attendants, especially their long hair.

Thomas Traber reached out and gently stroked the hair of one of the women.

She smiled at him.

He pulled back immediately, like a frightened child. "I'm sorry," he stammered. "It's been so long since I've seen a beautiful woman…and your hair is so soft."

"You don't have to say you're sorry. I'm the one who should apologize." She bent down, giving him a heartfelt hug.

A dam of emotions broke, and his tears flowed freely as she knelt, nestling his head close to her.

Her tears mingled with his. She could not imagine how much he and his comrades had suffered. "In just a few hours you'll be reunited with your family," she reassured him.

His voice sounded shaky. "They won't tell us who is dead, or who is alive. We don't know what to expect. We're scared to death."

"I know, I know." After a short time, the caring flight attendant released the soldier, and stood. Radiating concern, she tried to comprehend the dilemma of these brave men.

"Thank you. I needed that," Thomas responded.

Education about the past and present would help ease the men's entry into society. During the long flight, they viewed film clips of America's history during their years in captivity.

The videos, shown on the personal screens, contained valuable information: the eight presidents of the lost years, the advancements in the space program, the progression of technology, and the latest information in the entertainment and sports world.

Clips of new movies were popular with the returning soldiers. The special effects amazed them, and they asked for certain scenes to be played repeatedly. Some of the soldiers asked, "How did they do that?" They were unaware of modern computer generated graphics.

The scanty clothing on the girls surprised the men. The foul language left them shaking their heads in disbelief. Tattoos and earrings in both men and women shocked them. Whenever they noticed a man with an earring, they laughed.

Each soldier saw forty years of historical highlights pertaining to his hometown, and state. Authorities knew they would be wondering about events at home.

Sports updates on baseball, football, basketball, tennis, and car racing were of special interest to the returnees.

Watching an interview with a sports celebrity, Freeman shouted, "Why is he wearing his baseball cap backwards?"

The most excitement came when they heard about a baseball game in St. Louis on September 8, 1998. A man named, Mark McGuire, smashed a homerun, which broke the record Roger Maris set in 1961—the same homerun that Robert Freeman witnessed as a young boy. A shocked Freeman watched with interest, not believing that anyone could ever top Maris' record. Disappointed, he hung his head. "I thought it would never be done."

In racing, Pfingston noticed that Indy was no longer king; stock car racing replaced it. He could not believe his ears.

On the screens, movie stars welcomed them home, as did well known singers and songwriters. Sports personalities also wished the returnees well.

The men laughed and cried when updated on the last four decades. The startling changes were hard to comprehend.

The intercom interrupted the droning of the airplane. "This is your captain speaking. If you look out your window, you will see a sight that you have waited forty years to view. Gentlemen...it's America!"

In the distance was a small, dark silhouette of something not yet discernible.

As the plane neared the coastline, they could make out the lights of Los Angeles brightening the horizon.

Standing in awe, they watched the huge city come into clear view.

America! Home! They were almost home!

The plane began to circle the "City of Angels."

Below, thousands of lights flashed repeatedly. "Why are all the lights blinking?" Lomack asked.

One of the flight attendants next to him glanced out the window. "That's for you. That's all for you. Los Angeles is welcoming you men home."

They buckled their seatbelts in preparation for landing, staring out the windows the entire time.

Their heads reeled with an array of emotions.

Finally, the plane began to descend.

The excitement in the men's eyes was evident; the anticipation was almost more than they could bear.

The plane landed and slowly taxied to a stop.

Expectation was high as the men waited patiently to disembark.

Each one thanked the crew for the flight home.

The attendants gave each man a long, tearful hug.

The captain emerged from his cockpit to greet the returnees. "Gentlemen, you can now breathe the fresh air of freedom!"

The doors slowly opened.

Nervously, the former POWs stepped into the warm California air.

Spectators on the ground stood at attention when Captain James McCarter descended the stairs of the plane, stepping on American soil for the first time in four decades.

His comrades followed.

Cameras snapped. Official photos, taken by a select group of military photographers, would not be released until after the returnees connected with their families.

A man in a suit and tie reached out to shake McCarter's hand. Without glancing up, the captain's shaky voice declared to those gathering around him, "I'm sorry. The greeting will have to wait."

He turned to his fellow former POWs, the only ones who truly understood what they were feeling, what they had endured. McCarter blinked his eyes open, and for a moment, the group only stared at each other.

The small crowd silenced, watching and waiting in anticipation.

McCarter's eyes were clear and intense. He struggled to get the words out. "Gentlemen, there is something we must do."

Maybe it was instinct…perhaps it was their natural reaction. Whatever it was, without McCarter saying another word, they all knew what to do.

Spontaneously, the six soldiers formed a circle, clasped each other's hands, and carefully lowered to their knees. Together they kissed the hard, black asphalt, the ground of their homeland, the United States of America.

On bended knee, Williams prayed. *Lord, we thank You for Your love. Thank You for remaining with us during the years of captivity. We recall the promise in Your Word that those who wait upon the Lord will renew their strength, and will mount up with wings as eagles; they will run and not be weary, walk and not faint.* Choked up, he continued. *Renew our strength. May we live the remaining days of our lives like eagles…free. Free as You created us to be. Thank You, Lord.*

The men responded with a hearty, *Amen.*

The nearby medical aides helped the weakened men to their feet.

The Vice President of the United States, the Governor of California, and the Mayor of Los Angeles were the first to welcome them.

Famous entertainers, they did not recognize, thanked them for their gallant service. The celebrities were all anxious to welcome back the six heroic survivors.

While the soldiers appreciated the pleasantries, they only had one thing on their minds—their families! They could not wait to embrace them…to meet them face-to-face.

The only secret now was Le. Nobody knew about his role. He stood in the background watching the events unfold, trying to stay out of the limelight.

The men protectively kept the former Vietnamese guard in their sight at all times. At the right time, his significance would be revealed.

The men were escorted to limos and whisked to a local hotel where penthouse suites were reserved.

For the next ten hours, security precautions demanded the men remain in their rooms. Secrecy was still vital.

In the morning, they would travel to Washington D.C. for an early afternoon welcome home event.

They continued to be under close medical supervision. The physicians were pleased how well the men were adapting to the new environment. None of them had adverse reactions to the medical treatment, diet, or stress. The doctors could not explain it. One of them termed it, "Miraculous."

At times, the returnees looked out the windows of the hotel where thousands of people were gathering. Some of them were chanting, "Welcome home. Welcome home."

The city was bustling with honking horns. Helicopters hovered overhead. Cameras and video recorders were everywhere. Many were desperately trying to get the first coveted photo of the freed POWs.

The humble men catapulted to celebrity status overnight, but they only wanted one thing…to return to the families they once knew.

Most family members were on their way to the nation's capitol.

Out of respect to the men and their families, the returning prisoners' names had not been released to the public.

However, excited friends and family leaked a couple identities. Persistent investigative procedures by the media narrowed the search. The news reports showed high school pictures of Pfingston and Traber.

The other four POWs remained unidentified, but the names of their hometowns were announced. It would only be a matter of time until the investigative reporters unraveled the personal details, releasing all the privileged information. It was a race against the clock.

Many cities around America planned celebrations at schools and sporting events.

Churches were having special praise services thanking God for the survival and arrival of the unsung heroes.

News specials about the Vietnam Conflict aired on television. The names of thousands still missing POWs and MIAs scrolled across the bottom of the screens. America's media brought reminders of those still missing to the forefront of daily reports.

The entire world watched the events as they unraveled.

With permission, Captain McCarter stopped by Le's room and the two of them talked for close to an hour.

"Le, I feel something is not right. I believe something happened in America and we are not being told about it—something big. I have seen decals and posters, which said, 'Remember 9-11.' I asked the doctors what it meant, and they seemed to skirt the issue. They told me that it was actually 9-1-1, an emergency phone number to call police and fire units. Then I realized I was saying it wrong, it was 9-11. I know the officials are trying to protect us, but please, will you tell me about it?"

He had hoped no one would ever ask him about that fateful day in American history. *How would I possibly explain it? There is no explanation.*

The Vietnamese guard thought about McCarter's request. He felt himself tense up as the leader of the group watched, waiting for a reply. Finally, he decided to divulge the information about what happened on September 11, 2001. To the best of his knowledge, he told the details of the day that changed America forever.

McCarter's eyes clouded when he heard about the death toll.

Then Le attempted to explain the world's war on terror.

McCarter was shocked, but listened politely.

When he finished, McCarter agreed not to tell the others. After all, this should be a time of happiness, not sorrow.

When the captain left, Le thought of those who perished on that day. The events affected him in his country, as well as most of the world. *I can't even imagine what a day of unimaginable horror that was.*

Le clutched the pouch, still protected under his shirt. He contemplated the contents. The idea was never far from his mind. He knew what he had to do with it. *Will I be permitted to carry out my plan? Will I be able to cope emotionally? I will have to be strong... I will face rejection, most likely.*

Opening the pouch, Le retrieved a small item. Holding it in his hand, he closed his eyes, quietly uttering a prayer. *God, please prepare me for this endeavor.*

FOURTEEN

The Anticipation

Stars twinkled in the still-dark, early morning Los Angeles sky.

The guests had been escorted secretly to the hotel roof, where the helicopter waited to deliver Le and the six men to the airport.

The chaos from the excited citizens and extremely heavy commuter traffic made a limousine drive impossible, so they boarded the chopper for the short flight to the airport.

The reporters in helicopters hoped to catch the breaking story. A number of newshounds were trying to get the first pictures, even to the point of breaking the law. The invaluable photos could make them a fortune.

Military helicopters escorted the news choppers away from the area.

The delay irritated a couple of the returnees; they complained because it slowed down the process of getting home.

At last, the area cleared and the helicopters landed safely.

The magnificent presidential aircraft stood ready, waiting for its honored passengers.

They quickly boarded the plane for their flight to Washington.

Euphoria mounted; the anticipation of the men was at a peak. The hype over their return astonished the heroes.

The giant plane lifted into the clouds, heading east to the nation's capitol.

Time seemed to stand still during the flight. The freed men stared out the windows. A cloud of uncertainty plagued them. Each man had mixed emotions—excitement and joy, as well as fear and dread of the unknown. More than anything, they were grateful to God and Le for making this day a reality.

They had been briefed on the details of the upcoming hours, although, much did not sink in. The entire idea was more than their minds could comprehend, too overwhelming.

The men enjoyed a healthy breakfast and spent quiet moments looking at places of interest below.

At times, the plane would alter its route to show the men sights they had not seen in years, if ever. The plane descended lower over the Grand Canyon to allow the men to take in its majestic beauty.

The snow-capped Rocky Mountains were another spectacular sight; such beauty was put on hold during their imprisonment.

McCarter especially was enthralled with the mountains. He recalled his experiences with his family, piloting them over the towering peaks. Memories of special times flooded his memory. He smiled thinking of Wendy, and his heart beat faster.

The plane was scheduled to arrive about noon. They were served an early lunch as they neared their destination, although most were too nervous to eat more than a few bites.

As they neared the East Coast, one of the flight attendants stepped to the microphone. Moisture filled her eyes. "Gentlemen, if you look out your windows you will see the great city of New York. We're ahead of schedule, so we gained special permission to fly over the 'Big Apple.' We have been notified that the entire city is honking horns and flashing lights to welcome you home. The pilot thought it appropriate for you to view the 'Statue of Liberty.'"

Speechless, the men stared out the windows. There she stood, as big and beautiful as ever—the "Lady of the Harbor" welcoming home the brave, and now free soldiers.

In the stillness of the moment, Williams commented about New York's picturesque skyline. "It hasn't changed a bit."

Concentrating on the sight below, Freeman added thoughtfully, "Yes, it has. Something is different. I remember two huge skyscrapers under construction when I left for the Army. I don't see them. Where are they? What happened to them?"

Captain McCarter glanced at Le with sad eyes. He already knew the answer, but hoped the others wouldn't discover the truth until they were stronger.

The flight attendants looked at each other, wondering how to explain what happened to the twin towers on September 11, 2001.

Reluctantly, one answered, "That's a story in itself." She paused a moment as the men stared at her waiting for a response. "I guess you'll find out soon enough anyway."

She stared past them to the open skies, and blurted out the words. "Terrorists hijacked two passenger jets and crashed them into the twin towers. The buildings collapsed."

"Terrorists? What do you mean?" Williams raised a questioning brow.

"Collapsed? The whole buildings are gone?" Freeman inquired.

"How could that happen? How does a huge building like that collapse?" Williams asked.

"It just did," she recounted. She was struggling about how much to say. "It was a terrible time in American history…the worst imaginable."

Freeman asked the inevitable question. "Was anyone killed?"

McCarter felt compelled to intervene. He faced the nervous flight attendant. "Thank you ma'am, but I'll take it from here."

He cleared his throat. "I questioned Le about this last night. I'll share what I learned." He closed his eyes, not wanting to admit the tragic truth. "About three thousand people perished on that dreadful day."

"Three thousand people!" Williams repeated. "That's impossible!"

The soldiers looked at each other, bewildered. Then it hit them—the only news disclosed to them so far was good news. They wondered what else happened on American soil while they were captives.

"Did we catch the ones that did it?" Williams persisted.

"They all died in the planes." McCarter continued, "There's more…a third plane crashed into the Pentagon."

"The Pentagon? The military headquarters? Are you serious?" Freeman's voice escalated.

McCarter nodded sadly. "I understand that the men who did it were Islamic terrorists."

The news of the dreadful attacks was taking its toll on the men, leaving them visibly agitated. Some were shaking; others were listless, staring blankly into space.

The medical team tried to protect them from bad news, unsure whether their weakened bodies and strained minds could take the pressure. However, this incident happened before the medics could intervene.

Still wanting details, Williams would not let it drop. "What kind of planes did they use?"

One of the nearby physicians suggested they change the subject. "You'll hear all the details later. Right now, let's focus on your homecoming."

"One last question," Freeman persisted. "I would assume these terrorists were not Americans. Did we make their countries pay for their horrific deeds, or did we just turn our backs like we did in Vietnam?"

He asked an important question, and certainly deserved an answer. Le and McCarter knew the answer, but they watched and waited to see what the response would be.

Corporal Quinn had been listening attentively. She interjected, "Yes, we waged a war on terrorism." She opted not to tell the soldiers the war was ongoing.

The plane became strangely silent, each person deep in thought.

They continued their flight, and soon began their descent to Washington D.C.

Finally, the pilot's voice boomed over the speakers, breaking the silence. "Gentlemen, thank you for flying with us. It has been an honor to bring you home. I have been a pilot for many years, for many dignitaries. However, this flight with you heroes has been my highest privilege. My father fought in Vietnam. He is a proud Marine and will join the crowd to welcome you home."

He paused for a moment and then continued. "It is going to be a busy day. Thousands of Americans have come to greet you. Don't be alarmed...be honored. I have asked Marissa, the head flight attendant, to inform you of the day's scheduled events."

Marissa spoke clearly. "Gentlemen, there will be a massive crowd here today to welcome you home...six brave heroes!"

"Seven," Lomack blurted, eyes fixed on Le.

"I stand corrected...seven heroes." She smiled at Le.

"First, we will land at Andrews Air Force Base, where the President of the United States will greet you. Your relatives will watch you land, but you will not meet them at that time. You will go through the usual welcome by the president and other dignitaries. Next, a limo will take you to an airplane hangar where your families will be anxiously awaiting your arrival. You will have approximately one hour to visit with them.

"After briefly visiting with your families, you'll be chauffeured to the foot of the Capitol for the ceremony. That's where you will be introduced to the world. At that time, you may offer comments, if you wish. At the end of the day, an aide will take you to the Vietnam Veterans Memorial, built in honor of those who fought and died in that war. You will undoubtedly find that a memorable experience. I assure you, this will be a day you will remember forever."

Marissa hesitated. "After that time of remembrance, you will truly be free men. You can live the life you dreamed of for the last forty years. I'm sorry that you lost that time. Again, I want to say on behalf of the pilot and the entire crew, thank you, and welcome home."

The men stared out the windows in silence while the plane landed. As it taxied down the runway, they could only imagine their families watching with anticipation. There could be no comparison as to who was most excited. Yes, the men had endured hardship beyond comprehension, but their loved ones—parents, siblings, wives, and children had gone through tremendous heartache as well.

None of the men knew who would be there to greet them. The doctors thought it best for them to find out in person, rather than tell them bad news of a loved one who passed away, or remarried, believing their soldier to be dead.

Unexpectedly, Le walked over to James and sat in the empty seat next to him. A subtle smile appeared as he reached into his shirt pocket, pulling something out. Clutching it in his hand, he reached over to the apprehensive soldier who watched him curiously.

McCarter opened his hand, and Le laid the item in it. He could not believe what was in his palm. It was a gold ring. He picked it up and read the inscription on the inside. "Love forever, Wendy."

Le returned to his seat, respecting his friend's privacy.

Tears filled McCarter's eyes as he stared at the ring—his wedding ring from Wendy.

James made eye contact with Le, his smile expressing his gratitude. Nothing was said…nothing needed to be.

When the plane came to a standstill, there was an eerie silence. The men acted composed, but their hearts were pounding. They walked slowly to the door of the plane.

As they deplaned, the flight attendants gave each returning soldier a heartfelt hug and a quick kiss on the cheek.

"Oh, great! I'm going to be meeting my wife after forty years away, and I'm going to have lipstick on my collar." Captain McCarter chuckled as a couple of the men broke out singing an old Connie Francis' song, *Lipstick on your collar, going to tell on you.*

Everyone laughed, and the door flew open.

Standing near the plane was a group of about fifty people in front of a long line of stretch limos. A red carpet stretched to the foot of the plane's stairs.

Captain McCarter was the first to exit. Immediately, he noticed the cool temperature, something he had not experienced in Vietnam.

Forecasters predicted snow in Washington by evening.

The returning men would shake hundreds of hands and meet many important people on this special day. However, their focus was on the airplane hangar where their families waited. They knew the eyes of their loved ones were gazing at them from a distance, and wondered what they were thinking.

The soldiers were directed to the crowd on the tarmac. From the earlier videos, they recognized the man in front of the gathering was the President of the United States. Standing next to the president was a man neatly dressed in full military uniform.

The six frail soldiers stood at attention, saluting the leader of the free world.

President Alexander returned the salute, and then warmly shook their hands. Choked up, he spoke. "Gentlemen, welcome home. On behalf of all American citizens and free people in the world, I say again, welcome home." The president was uncharacteristically at a loss for words.

He took a deep breath. "In moments, you will be reunited with loved ones you left behind forty years ago. I can't imagine the depths of your emotions. You must be bursting with excitement, yet fearful of the unknown. You do not know what the next few hours will hold, let alone the next few days, or years. I assure you, America will be there to aid in your transition to civilian life."

President Alexander gestured to the man standing beside him. "Now, I would like to introduce you to the Chaplain of the Army, Brigadier General Norman Kingman."

The cross on the officer's lapel was the first thing Captain McCarter noticed.

It was unclear how much the soldiers were absorbing. Their demeanor was difficult to discern as their eyes kept searching for a sign of a loved one, anyone they recognized.

General Kingman stepped forward, saluting the soldiers. Speaking in his usual straightforward manner, he said, "This is indeed a privilege, gentlemen. President Alexander and I think it appropriate to pray with you before you visit your family members. Is that alright with you?"

Captain McCarter, stepping forward, replied with certainty, "Sir, we would be honored."

The frazzled soldiers bowed their heads, along with the President of the United States, as the chaplain prayed. *Lord, thank You for bringing these men home safely. They have been gone a long time and suffered much. Enable them to adjust to the changes they will encounter. Please calm their nerves and give them physical stamina to endure what they are about to face. Help them to enjoy this day. We ask You to grant calmness and peace when they meet their families. Give them and their loved ones patience and understanding. Thank You for the young Vietnamese guard who made this possible. We thank You for Your abiding love and care. We ask this in the name of Jesus. Amen.*

Slowly, they all raised their heads.

Captain McCarter noticed Le standing a short distance away. He signaled for him to come closer. "Mr. President, this is the man who engineered our rescue, Le Huu Trang."

President Alexander's face brightened, and he greeted Le with a firm handshake. "It is my privilege to meet you."

Le responded, "the honor is mine, sir."

The president faced the soldiers. "I know you men are excited, and I will not delay you any longer. I will not be joining you in your reunions…this is your special moment and should be private."

The president and chaplain raised their right hand to their brows, once again saluting the brave heroes. The men knew normal protocol called for the lower rank to salute first. Humbled by this extraordinary act, the soldiers snapped to attention, and saluted the President of the United States, and the Army Chaplain.

Professional photographers were taking pictures and videos. However, the pictures were for these men and their families, not for the public. The journalists would have their chance soon enough.

Le followed the men to a single limo. Approaching the vehicle, he suddenly remembered Nancee. He looked toward the crowd and noticed her standing in the front, her face beaming. Le paced over to her, "Are you coming with us?"

"No," she said shaking her head. "This is your time. My job is complete."

"Will I ever see you again?"

"Maybe I will see you tonight at the White House. Following the banquet, I head back to Thailand."

Le looked into her compassionate eyes, recalling the kindness and support she had given him the last few days. "Thank You."

"For what?" she asked.

"For being so helpful to me. You were my friend when I needed one. I don't know if I could have done this without you. Thank you."

"It was my pleasure," she replied.

He realized he was delaying the men from seeing their loved ones, so he rushed off. He entered the limo, and watched her waving as the vehicle drove off. When she was out of sight, he turned his attention back to the men.

He noticed each man staring straight ahead, motionless. There was soft music playing in the background. No one recognized the song, but it was a peaceful melody.

Within minutes, their hopes and dreams of the last forty years were about to become reality. *What would they find? Who would be there to greet them?*

FIFTEEN

The Reunions

The authorities were still concerned with protecting the men's privacy, so they arranged a location for the reunions that would be away from the swelling crowd. The limo drove into the hangar at the end of the runway, which housed the presidential plane.

Cheerful, well dressed teenagers from a local high school's National Honor Society greeted each man as he stepped out of the vehicle. Each returnee had a couple of youth assigned to him—a boy and a girl. The teens welcomed their special veteran by name, standing beside him.

They each took a soldier's arm, escorting him to a large room. The hangar had been divided into six visiting areas with comfortable chairs and tables.

A crowd of people stood nearby holding signs and banners welcoming home the heroes. American flags of every size waved briskly. The onlookers were strangers to the returning soldiers. Some small children sat on the shoulders of adults, seeking a closer look at the historical event unfolding before them. As the men neared the group, they noticed many of the unfamiliar faces had tears in their eyes. These were their loved ones, unrecognized…but not for long.

Many years ago, the soldiers had funerals. Since their bodies were never recovered, they were listed as missing in action—MIA. Consequently, there was never full closure for the heartbroken families. Some of the parents, spouses, and siblings however, kept a faint glimmer of hope that their soldier would return someday.

Le would stay inconspicuous, but always within sight, while the men met with their loved ones. He knew this would be an emotional time for all. He did not want to intrude on their intimate moments. Yet, his heart was racing also.

Le watched Specialist Anthony Williams approach a cluster of cheering people. Signs read, "Welcome home, Tony. We love you."

As "Sunday" neared the group, he suddenly stopped in his tracks. The noisy distractions surrounding him went unheard when his eyes fixed on the man who stood unsteadily in front of him—his eighty-year-old father. His white haired dad was thin and frail, but a loving smile radiated across his face.

Standing only a few feet away, Anthony was unable to hold back a river of tears. Almost collapsing, the teenagers steadied him. When he fell into his dad's arms, both father and son were weeping. "Dad," he cried.

"My son, is it really you? Welcome home. I can't believe this moment has finally come. Thank God you are here!"

They embraced with such force they could feel the pain from old age and years of abuse, but at that moment neither man cared about the pain from the past—only the joy of the present, and the hope of the future.

Anthony learned that his mother died of cancer eleven years earlier. Two of his siblings also passed away.

Greeting him were his remaining sisters with their husbands, and several nieces and nephews.

The homecoming was incredible. Since he had been "dead" himself for those long torturous years, there were no tears to cry for those who had died during his absence. On this momentous occasion, Anthony would only shed tears of joy.

Williams looked around the group of well wishers, past his father and sisters, and spotted a woman with a small family standing quietly to the side. Her beauty immediately told him who she was—his wife, Abigail. As he approached her, she lowered her head slightly. The look on her face hinted how much things had changed. He was uncertain what to do.

She made the first move, walking closer to him. She threw her arms around him and exclaimed, "Welcome home, Tony." It was a long embrace, but not passionate.

His dad joined them. Speaking softly, he said, "Son, she waited five years for your return. The Army said you were missing in action, and presumed dead. Her life had to continue. Your son needed a man to guide him, a father. Finally, she remarried."

Abigail released his neck and looked at him through tears. "Tony, may I introduce you to your son and his family?"

Studying his son, he noticed a striking resemblance to himself, the way he used to look. The muscular young man stood with his wife, next to Abigail. With them were three children—ten, sixteen, and twenty-years-old.

"I was going to name him after you, but I knew you would like the name I chose. I named him after the character in that silly book you read so often...Logan."

Anthony looked at his son. "Logan. Yes, I remember *Logan's Run*."

"It was made into a movie," Abigail said nervously, trying to make light of a difficult situation.

Anthony stared at his adult son, whom he had never seen or held as a child. Unsure what to do, he reached out his hand.

The young man shook his hand and said, "Welcome home, sir. It is an honor to meet you."

Tears blurred the soldier's eyes as he struggled to keep his conflicted feelings under control.

Williams wanted desperately to hear his son call him "Dad," but realized that was asking too much. Someone else had raised his boy, and apparently did a good job. He was his father by blood, but another man was his dad.

"Son, meet your grandchildren," Anthony's father pointed to three handsome young men.

The awkwardness of the situation was obvious. No one could have prepared for it. Each grandchild reacted differently, dealing with the situation in his own way. His oldest grandson stepped forward to shake his hand. The other grandchildren greeted him with a nod.

After meeting his family, he was introduced to some good friends from his past. Sadly, he felt more comfortable with them than with some of his own family.

He glanced one more time at his relatives; they were a reminder of how much life he missed. He knew it would take time for everyone to get to know him.

Fortunately, he had plenty of time.

Sergeant Brent Pfingston, formerly known as "Tuesday," was amazed how different the world looked to him. Fancy cars, electronic gizmos—like those on Star Trek many years ago, were now reality.

His young escorts took him to the area where his family awaited. Brent saw his name on dozens of signs held by well wishers.

The long years had taken a harsh toll on him. Fortunately, he had not seen himself in a mirror during his captivity. Even with his new glasses, none of his family looked familiar. He could only imagine how different he looked to them.

Each of the visitors wore a nametag for identification.

He discovered his five sisters first. Each of them hugged him and joyfully welcomed him back to America.

After a bit of light talk, he found the courage to ask about his Mom and Dad. Since they were not there, he expected the worst. His sister reported that both of his parents had perished in a house fire twenty years earlier.

Another sister added, "Until the day they died, they never gave up on you being alive. They were very active in the POW/MIA movement. They started a chapter in Minneapolis, which they personally financed until the day they passed away. They always believed this day would come, I wish they were here to share your homecoming."

His siblings gave him time to come to grips with the sad news, and then he met his many nieces and nephews. He knew he would not remember all their names. It was evident many of them did not know who he was.

He sensed apathy in some of today's youth. They seemed more interested in the press coverage than the actual reason they were in Washington D.C.

The revealing clothing the girls wore seemed outlandish to him. The foul language many people used shocked him. He would have had his mouth washed out with soap if he spoke to anyone that way. The lack of respect some youth showed disappointed him.

He realized a new chapter in his life would begin today. It would not be a continuation of the old, but the beginning of a new life. A huge challenge was ahead…was he ready? Were any of these brave men prepared for the future?

The teens escorted Specialist Thomas Traber to his designated area where a large banner read, "Welcome Home, Thomas."

"Wednesday" spotted two women standing with an elderly lady in a wheelchair. He recognized his two sisters immediately. They ran excitedly to the returning veteran, threw their arms around his neck, and gave him a loving, welcome home hug.

His eyes then focused on the woman sitting hunched over in the wheelchair. Instinctively, he knew the gray haired, frail woman was his dear mother.

The mood changed when he saw her. A cloud of sorrow replaced joy. He knelt down and took his mother's hand, looking deeply into her shallow, empty eyes.

"She had her hip replaced just a couple of weeks ago after she fell and broke it," one of the sisters explained in a sorrowful tone. "We thought about not bringing her, but the doctors felt it might be good for her, and for you."

The other sister sighed. "Thomas, she's had Alzheimer's for about eight years. She does not remember anything or recognize anyone. Dad took care of her until he died four years ago."

Standing, he looked directly into his sister's distressed eyes. Choked up, he asked, "Dad's dead?"

His sister, with tears streaming down her cheeks, nodded. She barely could get out the words, "I'm sorry."

Staring at his sister and then back at his mother, Thomas asked softly, "What is Alzheimer's?"

He listened carefully as one of his sisters explained the debilitating disease. "The term Alzheimer's became familiar while you were away. What used to be senility or dementia now has a specific name. Mom suffered memory lapses, confusion, and had a decline of mental ability. She no longer recognizes anyone and is unable to communicate verbally."

The heartbroken GI looked down at his mother, compassion written all over his face. Fighting the tears, he knelt beside her wheelchair, and whispered gently in her ear, "Hello, Mom." He cupped her thin, frail hands with his. "I'm finally home, Mom. I am sorry I was not here when Dad died. I wish I could have been. I love you, Mom." He did not know what more to say. He stayed on his knees next to his mother, his eyes focused on hers.

"She doesn't understand you, Thomas," his oldest sister whispered. "Mom has not spoken for over two years now."

The medical team accompanying the soldiers throughout the trip monitored them closely during each event, giving special attention during the reunions. They also kept an eye on each of the family members. A heart attack could occur in either the returning soldiers or the older family members. They were there for any medical emergency. An ambulance and a medical helicopter waited outside the airport hangar.

The physician with Thomas had been watching his reunion carefully. The doctor noticed something unusual happening with his mother and leaned over the wheelchair to observe her more closely. The doctor said to Thomas, still on his knees next to his mother, "Look carefully at her eyes."

His mother's eyes were noticeably red. Slowly, they flooded with tears. Then one word came out of her mouth, crisp and clear—the first word she had spoken in nearly two years. "Thomas!"

Astonished, the doctor stepped back. He stared at the elderly woman and then back at Thomas. "Some things happen that doctors can't explain. I can't explain this, except that it's a miracle. Thomas, your mother recognizes you. She knows who you are!"

The soldier could no longer hold back the tears as he tenderly embraced his fragile mother. His sisters, kneeling next to him, held him tearfully.

No one observing this scene could ever forget the sight. It was the love of a family, still held together after forty long years of separation.

Finally, his sisters introduced him to their husbands, nieces, nephews, and the many good friends he left behind.

He asked about the little Kansas town he once lived in and was surprised that it was no longer a small town but a bustling city.

He realized how much times had changed.

Specialist Robert Freeman's parents were there to greet him. Both had remarried while he was gone. In fact, his father married three more times. At least for now, they were together for this special occasion.

"Thursday" was grateful to find his parents in good health. He greeted his mother with a hug, and shook hands with his father.

Compared to some of his friends, his was a small reunion. Robert was an only child; neither parent had any additional children.

A few childhood friends from Cooperstown came to welcome him home.

His father handed him a small box. Robert opened it, grinning. He reached in and carefully removed the glass case. Inside, was the baseball Roger Maris had signed and given to him so many years before. Speechless, he looked at his father, smiling with approval.

Robert looked over at his fellow comrades and saw the commotion and excitement in the large crowds at their reunions. His gathering was almost nonexistent when compared to his fellow soldiers. There were no signs or banners. Yet, he was not disappointed—nothing could sadden him. He was free!

He pulled the baseball close to his chest and then did something completely out of character. He looked heavenward, uttering the words, "Thank You, God."

He realized this was the first day of the rest of his life and he would make the most of it!

Ronald Lomack's reunion was of special interest to Freeman. For the entire confinement, he tried to help his patient, "Friday," who was traumatized when a landmine exploded killing his comrades. Freeman wondered if he succeeded in helping his friend.

It warmed the soldier's heart to see Lomack's parents hugging their son enthusiastically, welcoming him home. Freeman wondered what the rest of Lomack's life would be like.

Two of Lomack's brothers were also there for him. David now operated the family farm. Gary moved to California to get away from small town life and have more excitement. Lomack was also introduced to his many nieces and nephews.

After a few moments of chatter, David shared heartbreaking news with the returning soldier. "Thirty years ago on graduation night, a car crash killed our youngest brother, Ben. The school curse continued—the driver was intoxicated. Five young men in his class of fourteen died needlessly, including our brother."

Lomack listened somberly, trying to take it all in.

Gary continued the painful story. "Our parents were devastated over their son's death. Times on the farm were tough. They were on the verge of bankruptcy. During that time in America, many family farms failed. When our parents needed help with the farm, David responded to the challenge."

David added, "I married my high school sweetheart, Susie Templeton. Do you remember Susie?" He put his arm around his wife's shoulders, pulling her close. "We built a big house on the farm property. We had five children, but unfortunately, they all left for big city life. I need your help operating the farm. There is a job waiting for you at home," David pleaded.

Ronald smiled. "I'd like that. More than anything, I looked forward to returning to the farm."

All eight classmates from his graduating class of 1969 showed up to welcome Ron home. It was sort of a class reunion.

Nearby, the young people with Captain McCarter escorted him to his visitors.

One face in the crowd grabbed his attention. His eyes met hers. Wendy was as gorgeous as he remembered. She had taken the time to have her hair fixed exactly as it was when they said their tearful goodbyes in 1970. She even had on a dress similar to the one she wore that day. He instantly recognized the scent of her perfume, the same brand she wore many years before. It was as if time stood still.

He stood motionless, unsure how to react. *Should I hug her or shake her hand?* Thoughts raced through his head. *Surely, she has remarried and has other children. Who could blame her? Of course, she assumed me dead.* He tried to prepare himself emotionally for whatever news she would tell him.

McCarter noticed a man and a woman standing with her. They gently held her arms, supporting her trembling body.

The woman made the first move. She let loose of the two people supporting her, and ran to the returnee, throwing her arms around him. Squeezing his neck hard, she repeated tearfully, "James…James...James."

Without warning, she planted a long kiss on his lips.

She left him breathless, unable to speak.

Not wanting to let go of him, she stepped back only a few inches. Holding up her left hand, she showed him the diamond ring he put on her finger that night in the park when he proposed to her. To his surprise, she had waited for him—she never remarried, or even removed her wedding ring.

He raised his left hand, showing his wedding ring, which Le gave him minutes before. It fit loosely on his middle finger because of his significant weight loss.

She clung tightly to his neck, smiling through her tears.

He shifted his focus to the younger man and woman with her.

McCarter whispered softly, "Is this my son and daughter?"

"Yes, these are our children—Kaylie and Braden."

Without hesitation, they embraced their long lost father. Time did not erase the tender memories they had of their daddy. Their warm welcome was evidence of the love James showered on them as children.

His wife's demeanor changed, obviously, something was troubling her.

"What is it? There's more…I can tell by the look on your face?"

She took a deep breath. "I wish my parents were here to celebrate this day, but they passed away." She hung her head. "And James, you're right, there is more. I'm sorry, but your mother also died…three years ago."

"What about Dad?" His voice cracked.

Wendy smiled, stepping aside.

James could not believe his eyes! He glanced over to see a frail man sobbing uncontrollably. His father! He rushed to his dad to embrace him.

They held each other tight, neither one willing to let go.

"Son…Son," the elderly man repeated. "It's really you…after all these years!"

"Dad, I thought you were dead." James' mind flashed back to the letter he received from Wendy on the day of his capture telling about his father's critical illness.

Wendy stepped in, "The doctors couldn't explain his recovery. They believed he was going to die. Once given the news that you were missing in action, your father suddenly began to improve…miraculously. God assured me you were still alive. That is how I knew you would return, and why I never married again. Your father's recovery reminded me that our God is a God of miracles…and I believed that another miracle would one day take place…today it has!" James' heart was racing, tears coursing down his cheeks.

When he was finally composed enough to speak, he asked, "How did you manage without me?"

"With the help of God, and our parents, we kept going. I took over your insurance company. Now, our son operates the business."

"I always knew you were amazing, that's why I fell in love with you. I still love you!"

"I never stopped loving you…I knew you'd come back to us," Wendy sobbed.

For the moment, it was just the two of them holding each other in reassurance of their mutual love.

A thrilled James met his six grandchildren as Kaylie and Braden introduced them one-by-one.

The heartwarming scene, when he met his three-day-old great grandson, touched all observers.

The baby was born the same day they received the news that their grandfather was alive—the news that altered all their lives forever.

Plans changed that day for the new parents—Braden's son and daughter-in-law. They had intended to name the newborn, Nathan, after the President of the United States.

Braden handed the infant to the tearful great grandfather. Proudly, he stated, "I'm honored to introduce you to my grandson, 'James.' He's named after you, Dad."

The great grandfather's joy was undeniable. As he held the newborn, he realized how blessed he was.

Le watched from a short distance, noticing the tears streaming from his friend's eyes. He marveled at the love this family showed one another. He thought of his own family and his heart broke.

Others stood nearby waiting to greet this returning hero, but had to wait their turn.

Finally looking up, James shifted his attention to a well dressed man in the crowd who stood slightly lopsided. He did not have an inkling who the man was, or why he was there.

Kaylie noticed his reaction. She approached the man, and taking him by the hand, led him to her father. "Daddy, this is Bobby. You may not remember him. When I was a little girl, I gave a man in a wheelchair a dollar. You got him a job at a cabinet shop. Do you remember?"

James was stunned. So much had already happened... and now this!

Grabbing his hand, the returnee exclaimed, "I remember. A fellow vet. Oh, how well I remember!"

"Sir," Bobby said boldly, "Welcome home. I want you to know how...what you did in my life. I mean...." He struggled to maintain his composure.

He felt a soft hand take his. Reassuringly, Kaylie smiled at him, and then looked back at her father.

"That act of kindness...." Streams of tears ran down Bobby's cheeks as he related his story to James. "That act of kindness you and your daughter showed me years ago changed my life. Thanks to you, after getting that job, I pulled my life together. I worked hard and returned to school, earning a business degree. I opened a hamburger franchise. Now, I own ten others throughout the state."

James grinned. He asked a question, which surprised the old veteran. "Did you ever get to see your daughter again?"

A smile lit up Bobby's face. "You do remember! I can't believe it. Yes. A few years after you got me the job, I received a call from her. We had a wonderful visit. Her mother remarried, but I had visitation rights. In fact, I did something I never thought I would be able to do. With a lot of rehabilitation and hard work, I walked her down the aisle on her wedding day."

His voice cracked. "My grandchildren visit me frequently. I even married a beautiful woman, and we had three more children. I owe it all to you. You believed in me, when no one else did.

Thank you Captain McCarter…and welcome home." He stepped back, and saluted the soldier. "Thank you for serving our country."

James returned the salute proudly.

The sight was indescribable as the two veterans embraced.

James' homecoming was perfect. He could not have asked for anything more.

Suddenly, through the tears, James' eyes widened. Standing behind Bobby was a tall man with golden colored hair. Dressed in a suit and tie, he held a book in his hand.

"Goldie?" James scratchy voice called, "Is that you?"

"In the flesh," the man shot back.

James rushed to hug his old Army friend with a speed that surprised the onlookers. Again, tears flowed as the two embraced. In fact, there was not a dry eye anywhere.

Finally, James stepped back, eyeing his friend, Goldie.

James spoke first. "I thought many times about you when…when…." It was difficult for him to talk about his painful ordeal as a POW. After a lengthy pause, all he could manage to get out was, "What have you done with your life, Buddy?"

Goldie responded. "James, my friend, you saved my life not once, but twice.

James tilted his head, looking puzzled.

"The first time you saved my life was when you gave me your seat in your helicopter. The second time came a couple years later when I met your wife and family. You were presumed dead. I stopped by to meet them. James, I saw the same thing in them that I saw in you. I knew I wanted that for my life, so I started going to church." Goldie held up the book in his hand—it was a Bible. "This book changed my life. I gave my heart to God, and before I knew it, I became a preacher. I have been preaching ever since. I am pastor of a church in Dallas where I have served God for thirty-three years."

James put his hand on Goldie's shoulder and they continued to chat.

Goldie spoke fast, knowing time was short. "I want you to know I have prayed for you every day since you were missing in action. I mean every day, Deacon. On my desk in my office is a picture of the two of us in front of your chopper, taken the day before you disappeared. Every morning, I looked at the photo and prayed for you. You are an answer to prayer, my friend. I realize now, it should have been me in that prison camp."

"I prayed for you many times, too. In fact, my fellow prison mate, Sunday, I mean Anthony, prayed for you also. Without him and his faith, I don't think I would have made it. I guess you could say we helped each other through it all."

The hour sped by.

The two friends said goodbye, promising to keep in touch.

James reached for Wendy's hand, holding it tight. He felt his heart rate speed up.

Her eyes danced with delight.

There were a number of other friends and relatives at James' remarkable homecoming.

He wished his mother could have been there. However, later he mentioned to Le that he missed his mother, but at least she knew he was alive. When Le questioned what he meant, all he said was, "I'm not with her…." and then added, "…yet!"

Le knew what he meant. James' mother was in heaven, and since her son was not there, he must still be alive.

An official announced it was time to move on to the next event.

It was time for the world to meet and thank these six brave heroes.

There were still medical concerns, which would need to be addressed in the future. The years of abuse had left emotional and physical scars. The medical staff was already planning physical therapy, mental health counseling, and further medical treatment.

Most of the men were clutching the hands of their loved ones, but everyone knew further memories and stories would have to wait.

The men and their immediate families were escorted to the waiting limos.

As they climbed into the vehicles, Le was instructed to go with Freeman, because he had a smaller family present.

Le followed, uneasy. He wondered what he was doing there. It was the returning prisoners' day, so he would continue to maintain a low profile.

However, each man still kept a protective eye on his rescuer.

The cars moved away from the hangar toward the Capitol.

Soon, the world would view for the first time the six men making history.

A sea of people lined the streets waving American flags, as the limos with darkened windows made its way down Pennsylvania Avenue.

The returnees' tears dried up during captivity, but now there seemed to be no end to them.

The streets were roped off for the occasion.

The caravan crept slowly, allowing the men to view the throngs of people cheering and waving.

The massive crowds erupted in cheers as the procession passed. After so many years of silence, the cacophony of sound was beautiful to their ears.

Soon, they arrived at their destination—the United States Capitol Building.

Never in their life had they seen such an extraordinary outpouring of support and appreciation. Every direction they looked, flags were waving. Signs and banners with messages such as, "Welcome Home Heroes," or "America Thanks You," were in abundance. The men were awestruck. Words could not adequately describe the scene.

Yet, nothing would compare to what was ahead of them.

SIXTEEN

The Homecoming

The heroes hardly noticed the plunging temperature when they stepped out of the vehicles at the Capitol.

The music heard in the distance only added to the soldiers' exhilaration. The U.S. Army Band was playing lively patriotic music.

The overwhelmed men followed a parade of people the short distance to a stage.

The authorities believed it necessary to keep the families in sight of the honorees during the ceremony. Therefore, the soldiers' loved ones were escorted to a roped-off section in the front.

As the men neared the side entrance to the platform, many well wishers rushed over to them, all hoping to be among the first to meet them and be a part of this important, historical event.

An energetic woman welcomed each of them with a hearty hug. She spoke rapidly, in a take-charge way. "Gentlemen, let me thank you right now before we get started. My name is Ellen Burns, and I am the stage director...sort of. My job is to ensure that everything runs smoothly today."

She paused briefly to take a quick breath. "I cannot imagine what you must be feeling right now. However, I can relate to the emotions your families are experiencing. My father was a POW in Vietnam. Fortunately, he was released when the war was over. He told me to thank you. I certainly do the same. Thank You." She clutched each man's hands warmly.

Ellen continued, bubbly, "Now, before you go out there, let me explain a few things so you know what's going on. U.S. Army, Chief of Chaplains, General Norman Kingman, has a short presentation and prayer before the president speaks. The president will introduce you to the nation, actually to the world. Let me warn you of something, which will astound you. Hundreds of thousands of people have gathered here today. That's right men. It has been just a little more than forty-eight hours since the details of your release hit the news. Americans have traveled from all over the country just to welcome you home. People have come from other countries, too."

Ellen pulled her hood up on her coat, noticing the drop in temperature. "This event has created worldwide excitement. It is unbelievable, I know. Reporters from almost every major newspaper and television network are here. People are viewing today's ceremony on live television around the world. The six of you are bigger than any movie star or sports figure. You are the biggest celebrities in the world right now. Isn't that exciting?" By now, Ellen was so on edge she could hardly stand still.

The men looked at each other in disbelief. Each had thoughts racing through his mind as he tried to comprehend the enormity of the occasion. *Apparently, not everyone has forgotten us! Could this really be happening after all those miserable years of confinement and torture?*

Confused, Pfingston asked, "Why would so many people want to come and see us?"

"You are heroes, sir. All of you."

"We're not heroes, ma'am. We are...we are POWs. Captured prisoners," Freeman stated with conviction.

As the music grew louder, so did Ellen's voice. She spoke passionately. "Sir, let me try to explain something. Since your capture, America has changed more than you can imagine. We have experienced wars. We have seen this country go from 'Leave it to Beaver' to reality TV. We went from genuine sport heroes to athletes using steroids in order to set world records. Many of our heroes today are people who at one time in America would have been thought of as...how should I say it...well, sort of unsavory characters. Our children used to play baseball in the street, but now they sit in front of a computer playing video games for hours every day."

She continued. "Our nation needs this special time. We need valiant men like you. America needs real life heroes. You may not consider yourselves heroes, but everyone else does. That is why they are here. You are patriots worthy of praise! Gentlemen, please accept the honor...if not for yourself, do it for the country you love."

The men knew it was futile to argue the point, so they listened trying to retain as much as they could.

Ellen glanced at her watch. "Gentlemen, about the ceremony...each of you will be called individually. If you don't want to say anything, don't feel obligated. Oh yes, one more thing. Your friends and families are seated in the front rows. You will be able to see them, and I trust you may draw strength from them."

She turned to walk away and then had an afterthought. "I hope we can get through the ceremony before the storm hits. We are expecting about four inches of snow tonight. Welcome home soldiers, welcome home."

Lomack turned to Le, "Snow! We haven't seen snow in forever. Have you ever seen it, Le?"

Le smiled, shaking his head.

The men were seated in a row of chairs offstage to rest. Physicians stood nearby, occasionally asking an ex-prisoner how he felt. They were also concerned about the effect of the cold and damp weather in their weakened condition.

The prisoners did not know how they felt—they were numb. Every emotion imaginable flooded their minds.

The music came to a stop, and the excited crowd began to settle down.

General Kingman, U.S. Army Chief of Chaplains, a decorated soldier from the Gulf War, stepped to the microphone. He could read clearly from the teleprompters on each side of the podium.

Giant screens throughout the mall projected the historic event.

"We gather today to honor six brave men. Those of us who have had the privilege of serving in the military understand the personal sacrifice many of our brothers and sisters have made defending this country. At this time, I would like to ask everyone to stand as we sing our national anthem."

At the back of the stage, a giant American flag lowered, slowly. The audience gasped at the breathtaking sight. The talking stopped as hundreds of thousands of Americans stood and proudly placed their hand over their heart. Appropriately, the U.S. Army Band played, *The Star Spangled Banner.*

The freed men stood tall, with gleaming faces, gratefully singing the well known melody. Tears were streaming down the faces of multitudes, including the former prisoners.

General Kingman returned to the microphone, issuing an invitation for all to join him in the *Pledge of Allegiance.* The scene was indescribable as people all over the National Mall recited the oath of loyalty to the flag and to the Republic of the United States of America.

When it was finished, a thunderous applause engulfed the Washington mall.

Eventually, General Kingman raised his hand to quiet the enormous crowd.

The nervous men took their seats.

The general's gaze was intent, and he prayed silently that his words would pierce the heart of many who had grown calloused over the course of time.

Kingman addressed the gathering. "Today we honor six returning Prisoners of War. However, we must never forget the thousands of soldiers who still have not returned. This day is for them, too."

His voice revealed his passion. "During the past forty years, while these men cowered in filthy cells, we enjoyed freedom to work, play, eat, worship, and love. These six men, as well as countless others, have not experienced those freedoms. In captivity, their meals consisted of a couple handfuls of rice a day. If they received meat...well, I'll let your imagination guess what it was."

In the audience, many shook their heads, murmuring comments of disgust.

The chaplain pointed to a small, round table with a chair. "In front of me is a table—not just any table. It occupies a place of dignity and honor at the front of this platform. Notice that it is set for one, symbolizing the fact that some members of our armed forces are missing from our ranks. A family member is absent. Perhaps your soldier never returned. People refer to them as POWs—Prisoners of War, and MIAs—Missing in Action. We call them comrades."

He somberly continued, stepping closer to the table. "They are unable to be with their loved ones today, so we join together to pay our humble tribute to them and bear witness of their continued absence. This table set for one is small, symbolizing the frailty of one prisoner alone against his or her oppressors." The chaplain pointed to the table. "The tablecloth is white, symbolic of the purity of their intentions when they responded to their country's call to arms."

Pointing to the flag, he continued. "On the front of the table is an American flag. It represents this great nation and the principles on which it was founded."

The chaplain held up a small vase. "The single red rose in the vase signifies the blood, which many have sacrificed to ensure the freedom of our beloved United States of America. This rose also reminds us of the family and friends of our missing comrades who keep the faith while awaiting their return."

The audience was spellbound. Many had tears stinging their eyes.

"The yellow ribbon on the vase represents the ribbons worn on the lapels of the thousands who demand, with unyielding determination, a proper accounting of our comrades who are not among us tonight."

The chaplain lifted a small plate. "The slice of lemon on this plate reminds us of their bitter fate."

Sprinkling salt on the same plate, the general continued. "The salt reminds us of the countless fallen tears of families as they wait."

The chaplain lowered the plate and picked up a small black book. "This Bible represents strength gained through faith to sustain those lost from our country, which was founded as one nation under God."

He took a deep breath, holding an upside down glass. "This glass is inverted—they cannot toast with us tonight."

Directing the crowd's attention to the single candle on the table, he said, "The candle is reminiscent of the light of hope, which lives in our hearts to illuminate their way home, away from their captors, to the open arms of a grateful nation."

All eyes turned to a chair as the chaplain motioned toward it. "The chair is empty—they are not here."

The chaplain stepped back as a lone bugler walked to the microphone to play the haunting notes of *Taps*.

The audience was moved deeply, listening to the famous melody.

After a moment of silence, the chaplain spoke. "Let us pray to the Supreme Commander, so that all of our comrades will soon return. Let us never forget their sacrifices. May God forever watch over them and protect them and their families."

He bowed his head reverently.

Everyone stood. Throughout the massive crowd, men removed their hats. People of all races, ages, and religions lowered their heads. Many closed their eyes and came together in unity as one nation before God Almighty.

Heavenly Father, we come to You today thanking You for bringing these courageous men home. We can only imagine what they have gone through during their captivity. However, You know, because You were with them every step of the way. You helped them through each dark night when they could only dream of being free. You enabled them to endure the pain and healed their broken bodies after frequent beatings. You were with them in recent days as they made their daring escape to freedom. Lord, they were always in Your hands. I look out across this vast sea of people who came to celebrate the return home of these six brave souls, and realize there may be more POWs who have not yet escaped the clutches of tyranny. For them we pray. We ask that You protect them as You did the men we honor today. Lord, bring them home. Bring them home to their families and loved ones. Bring them home to this great nation, the home of the brave and the free. Amen.

Silence reigned over the attentive crowd. Tears trickled down the cheeks of many. Others stood quietly contemplating the events that brought them together.

Some family members of POWs began to have a glimmer of hope for their missing soldiers.

"Mr. President." The chaplain stepped aside and the president appeared on the platform, nearing the podium.

Everyone stood and a booming applause billowed from the crowd.

Ellen glanced at the stage, and then back at the honored guests. "Okay. Get ready. This is your moment gentlemen."

Finally, the crowd quieted. The people in the front, mostly family and honored guests, sat anxiously in their chairs. Anticipation was high awaiting their leader's words.

President Nathan Alexander began his address. "My fellow Americans and honored guests. We gather this afternoon to welcome home and honor six men who for the last forty years were prisoners of war. Forty long years! That is two generations. We cannot imagine what these six men have endured during their captivity. I've had the privilege to meet them. They are thin and frail, but ready to begin their new lives."

The men listened, thoughts racing through their minds. They still were not able to comprehend all the publicity and fanfare associated with their arrival home.

"The past seventy-nine hours have been a whirlwind experience for them. Their *Quest for Freedom* was perilous. They began their trek in a Vietnam prison camp, and traversed through Laos and Thailand. They traveled over rough, almost impassible roads, and through dangerous jungles. They were in a life threatening gun battle. The obstacles they faced were many. Finally, they flew thousands of miles to get to America's shore. You may wonder why. Why?" His voice grew louder. "For freedom!"

The crowd was ecstatic.

"As Americans, there is one thing each of us should cherish." The president's voice grew more forceful. "Freedom is a blessing we should treasure, but often take for granted."

Many in the crowd nodded in affirmation.

"I was informed that when these brave men first saw the American flag at the United States Embassy in Thailand, they began to weep. Even after four long decades in a prison camp, they remained patriotic. They still loved our great country. Why? Why after all those years when they saw the American flag did they weep?"

The president's voice cracked. He paused briefly and pointed to the American flag. "Because of what it represents. It stands for the one thing, which millions of people for two-hundred thirty-four years have been seeking in this nation. Men, women, and children have been coming to this wonderful country to find what these men yearned for. Throughout the world, it has been denied to millions of people. It is what my own grandfather sought when he emigrated from Germany in 1917. In one word...freedom. Freedom!"

The audience broke out in a deafening applause, which lasted for several minutes.

"I look at this tremendous reception for these six Vietnam War veterans, and recall the difference in my homecoming July, 1971. The welcome many of my fellow Vietnam veterans and I received was a stark contrast to today. The veterans who came home then did not deserve to be dishonored with protests, violence, hate, and ridicule after serving their country. In a sense, today's homecoming ceremony is for every Vietnam War veteran—from the one who is a successful business owner, to the one who lives on the street with no place to call home. I hope and pray it will be a time of healing for all of us, so that we can finally put all the bitter memories behind us. After all, we did our duty as Americans when our country called us."

The audience went wild, waving flags, whistling, and cheering.

The men sat silent, awed by the president's words and the crowd's reaction.

Finally, the mall quieted enough that President Alexander could continue. "On a more somber note, I have information that the remains of twenty-seven other brave soldiers are also returning home. Unfortunately, their return is not a joyous one. In the next few weeks, twenty-seven families will be notified in person that their loved ones made the supreme sacrifice in the Vietnam War. To the families of these fallen comrades, I pray you will finally have closure. As your president, I offer my sympathy and that of a grateful nation."

He continued, "I am reminded of what a great president said to a family in another unpopular war—the Civil War. The mother had lost five sons. Five sons...I cannot even imagine a loss of such magnitude. Abraham Lincoln wrote to the grieving mother the following words: 'I feel how weak and fruitless must be any words of mine, which should attempt to beguile you from the grief of a loss so overwhelming. But I cannot refrain from tendering to you the consolation that may be found in the thanks of the Republic they died to save. I pray that our Heavenly Father may assuage the anguish of your bereavement, and leave you only the cherished memory of the loved and lost, and the solemn pride that must be yours, to have laid so costly a sacrifice upon the altar of freedom.'"

Sniffling and quiet sobs rippled through the audience.

"Freedom! There is that significant word again. In all wars, there are casualties. Freedom is not free…it never has been, nor ever will be. It is purchased with the blood, sweat, and tears of many brave men and women."

The president scanned the immense gathering, and then focused directly on the honored guests sitting in the front rows. "The forefathers of this great country sacrificed much. Our Constitution and our Declaration of Independence go to great lengths to protect it. Today, that privilege is restricted in many countries throughout the world where there is no freedom to worship, choose their own leader, or protest things that they believe are wrong. Freedom is costly! Our forefathers can testify to that."

He held up an envelope. "These twenty-seven names can be included for their sacrifice; they too, were brave men who gave their lives for the cause of liberty."

He paused briefly. "Why would anyone fight and die for this cause? A few days after the famous Battle of Gettysburg, where eight thousand Americans died, President Lincoln uttered these immortal words, engraved on monuments throughout America. 'That we here highly resolve that these dead shall not have died in vain—that this nation, under God, shall have a new birth of freedom—and that government of the people, by the people, for the people, shall not perish from the earth.' Citizens of America and people of the world, these twenty-seven soldiers, and others who died in prison camps did not die in vain."

The ovation started slowly as people contemplated what their leader said. As the truth of his remarks settled, the applause swelled to a deafening roar.

After several moments, the president added, "As an American, and the leader of the free world, I have the great honor of introducing six of America's bravest men. They came from all walks of life. Each one had hopes and dreams that were shattered the day of his capture. I am certain that every day for the last forty years this band of brothers dreamed of freedom. I would expect that near the end of their captivity they never expected to see it. America, here they are. Welcome them home!"

The crowd roared with delight.

President Alexander waited patiently for the crowd to hush.

Several minutes later, he read the names of the brave heroes: "Captain James McCarter, Specialist Anthony Williams, Sergeant Brett Pfingston,

Specialist Robert Freeman, Specialist Ronald Lomack, and Specialist Thomas Traber."

People jumped to their feet, hollering, whistling, and cheering. The thunderous ovation echoed throughout the National Mall as the President of the United States recognized the six liberated heroes.

The nation's leader motioned for them to join him on the stage.

SEVENTEEN

The Ceremony

The men, dressed smartly in new military uniforms, stood subdued.

They were apprehensive as they stared at the vast crowd.

No one could predict how the former POWs would react to the stress of the day. The years of quiet isolation in captivity affected them in various ways.

They remained in place, afraid to move.

Nearby aides gently coaxed them toward the president.

Reluctantly, Captain McCarter led his men to the front of the platform.

Le watched in the background, enjoying the poignant scene. As they inched toward their president, he observed the men he had grown to respect and admire. *I am honored to be their friend,* he thought.

"Sir…" Ellen whispered, "…you need to be with them."

"No," Le replied. "This is about them, not me."

"That's where you are wrong. It's about freedom, as the president said. Without you, this moment would not have occurred. You made it all possible."

Le barely heard Ellen's words, not wanting to miss a moment of the festivities.

Captain McCarter glanced back at Le, and without hesitation made his way over to him. An insistent McCarter put his arm around his friend's neck and whispered, "Come, Le Huu Trang. I want America to meet you."

Confidently, Le and James strode side-by-side to join the waiting president.

The six worn American soldiers and the young Vietnamese guard stood beside the President of the United States. History was being forged as a hurting nation came together in unity, with one purpose. It was an unforgettable sight.

As far as the eye could see, people of all ages, ethnic groups, and religions waved American flags and cheered.

The men did not believe they were heroic. They believed the true heroes were the men and women who came back to the protests and ugliness of a split nation; the true heroes were the soldiers who did not make it back alive, or were still missing.

At last, the crowd settled and the men sat down in a row of chairs behind the president. Soon each man would have his deserved moment in the spotlight.

"Specialist Thomas Traber, please step forward," the Commander-in-Chief ordered.

Traber stepped to the front. Raised in a small town and out of touch with the world for years, he was noticeably jittery. Yet he marched forward, stood at attention, and smartly saluted the president.

The president returned the salute.

President Alexander shook the trembling soldier's hand firmly.

Camera shutters clicked from every direction as news photographers and spectators alike captured the historic event.

"Specialist Traber, I am deeply honored to pin these stripes on you. Thank you for your years of service. As President of the United States, I officially promote you to the rank of Sergeant First Class. With these stripes, you will have all the benefits that accompany that rank."

An aide handed the president a plaque from a nearby table. "Sergeant, I proudly present to you an honorable discharge from the United States Army. You will receive a pension and back pay for the time you were held a prisoner of war as the rank of Sergeant First Class."

A smile replaced Traber's serious look when he grasped the significance of the leader's words.

"It is my privilege to present to you the Prisoner of War Medal." President Alexander held the medal high for the spectators to see. "This medal may be presented to any person who was a prisoner of war after April 5, 1917—the start of World War I. President Ronald Reagan signed the proclamation into law in 1985. It is awarded to any person who was taken prisoner or held captive, while engaged in action against an enemy force of the United States. The prisoner's conduct during captivity must have been honorable."

He turned to face the men seated near the back of the stage. "Gentlemen, I have it on good authority that your behavior during captivity was honorable."

The president pinned the medal on the new sergeant.

Selecting an official document from the table, he read the inscription to the hushed crowd. "Specialist Thomas M. Traber, United States Army. On September 21, 1970, while on a mission in Vietnam to pick up injured comrades, the helicopter on which he served as a gunner was shot down by enemy fire. Subsequently, he was captured and spent forty years in a prisoner of war camp, where he did not break under harsh treatment and continued torture. His gallantry and indomitable spirit, while a POW, are in keeping with the highest traditions of military service and reflect great credit upon himself, his unit, and the United States Army."

President Alexander handed the certificate to the humbled soldier. "Sergeant Traber, I am honored to present you another significant medal. By special order of the United States Congress and as Commander-in-Chief of the Armed Forces, I proudly present you the Medal of Honor."

Sergeant Traber glanced over at his fellow prisoners, noticing their dazed looks.

President Alexander held up the nation's highest military decoration. "This is the only military medal that can be worn around the neck. The Medal of Honor can only be awarded to a member of the United States Armed Forces who has distinguished himself conspicuously by risking his life above, and beyond the call of duty, while engaged in military action against an enemy of the United States. The deed performed must be one of personal bravery and self sacrifice." He placed the medal over the neck of a very proud and emotional Sergeant Traber.

The men hardly could take their eyes off their family members, who were proudly smiling and cheering for them.

President Alexander stepped back, "Sergeant Traber, as President of the United States and a retired Colonel of the United States Marine Corps, I salute you as a Medal of Honor recipient." The president saluted the sergeant.

As people all over the world watched, Sergeant Traber returned the salute.

"Is there anything you would like to say to the American people?"

He shook his head. "No sir. Captain McCarter will be our spokesman."

Traber again saluted the president and returned to his chair.

Sergeant Brett Pfingston, Specialist Robert Freeman, and Specialist Ronald Lomack were also honored. Each had his own moment of glory when he received the same medals as Sergeant Traber and promotion to Sergeant First Class.

The president continued the award presentations.

Specialist Williams stepped forward when the president called his name.

President Alexander read the inscription on a document. "Specialist Anthony C. Williams, United States Army Medic, August 3, 1970, while on a campaign to search and destroy enemy combatants in the villages of

South Vietnam, pulled three wounded men to safety while receiving enemy fire. In the process, Specialist Williams received a wound to the head that knocked him unconscious. He regained consciousness, and with the help of a fellow soldier fled into the jungle. After three days on the run, North Vietnamese troops captured them. Subsequently, he spent forty years in a prisoner of war camp where he was brutally beaten and tortured. Williams never succumbed to the numerous beatings he received, remaining faithful to his fellow POWs, and his country."

The President of the United States pinned the Purple Heart on Williams. Like the other men, he received the Prisoner of War Medal and the Medal of Honor.

They saluted each other.

Williams returned to his seat by his comrades.

President Alexander asked Captain James McCarter to come to the podium. McCarter, in his confident style marched forward, proudly saluting the President of the United States.

"As Commander-in-Chief, I am honored to promote you to the rank of Colonel." The rank was pinned on him, and the delighted crowd cheered.

Colonel McCarter glanced at his wife, Wendy. Smiling broadly, he pointed to his new rank. He could see tears streaming down her grateful face.

"Colonel James McCarter, as President of the United States, on behalf of the United States Congress and the American people, I thank you for your service to the United States of America. I present you the Prisoner of War Medal."

President Alexander picked up another medal. "For your gallantry in action against an enemy force, and for your bravery in saving the lives of Captain Richard Jenson, and Specialist Anthony Williams, I am honored to present you the 'Silver Star' for gallantry in action."

James stood at attention as the president pinned the medal on his uniform.

When the noise of the energetic crowd died down, the president continued. "Captain James McCarter, Helicopter Pilot for the United States Army. While on a mission in Vietnam on August 3, 1970, bravely and heroically, without regard to his life, forced his helicopter down among enemy fire to pick up survivors of three disabled units. Captain McCarter's helicopter was loaded to full capacity. Captain McCarter noticed a fellow pilot, Captain Richard Jenson, seriously wounded. He sacrificially gave up his pilot's seat to his injured comrade. While running through the smoke-filled battlefield, Captain McCarter encountered resistance. Firing his pistol, he downed an enemy patrol, which was attacking the fleeing helicopter piloted by Captain Jenson."

The president continued. "He found Specialist Anthony Williams, unconscious from a bullet wound to the head. Discovering the soldier was alive, Captain McCarter took time to aid Specialist Williams. The two ran into the jungle to escape enemy forces. He bandaged Specialist Williams wounds, saving him from probable death. Captain McCarter assisted Williams the next two days as they trekked through the jungle. Enemy forces captured them on August 6, 1970. Captain McCarter and Specialist Anthony Williams were taken to a prisoner of war camp, where they were tortured repeatedly over the course of forty years. Due to the help of a Vietnamese Guard and Captain McCarter's strong leadership, the remaining prisoners finally escaped the clutches of their captors. Captain McCarter's leadership, while a POW, inspired his fellow captives and was instrumental in their eventual escape. His extraordinary heroism, at the risk of his own life, is one of gallantry and to be commended."

President Alexander reached for the medal. "Colonel McCarter, with honor I award you this medal, the highest decoration any soldier can receive—the Medal of Honor." James leaned forward, so the president could put the distinguished medal around his neck.

Again, the crowd roared its approval.

James eyed Wendy, her glowing smile and sparkling eyes just as he remembered. He found comfort in her presence. She was as beautiful as the day he married her many years ago.

Perhaps it was divine intervention, but a strange sight briefly interrupted the ceremony. Over all the noise, a faint honking echoed in the distance. It was unnoticed by most people.

First, Colonel McCarter looked upward. Then the other five men lifted their eyes to view a flock of geese flying overhead. They stared at the formation, mesmerized by a sight they had not witnessed for years. No one uttered a word.

A simple scene—birds flying free, captured their attention. Most people would not understand how meaningful that display was to the men who had lived in terror, filth, loneliness, and hunger for forty years.

The crowd quieted, undoubtedly wondering what the men were thinking. What could be so meaningful that it stopped the ceremony?

An aide, walking up to the president, whispered something in his ear, and handed him a paper. The president read it, standing thoughtfully for a moment, and then glanced at Le.

The nation's leader stepped to the microphone, "It is often little things of beauty, which we take for granted." He gestured toward the winged visitors. "Perhaps each of us should do as these soldiers are doing and take a moment to observe our feathered friends. Let us remember this impressive sight, and allow it to serve as a reminder to appreciate the unexpected occurrences in life, which happen every day."

Everyone was gazing skyward. Parents pointed out the fascinating formation to their children. For a brief time, the focus of the gathered spectators was on the wedge of geese, which soon disappeared in the distance as the skies again quieted.

Drawing the significant interruption to a close, the president returned to the planned activities. "Colonel, would you like to say something now, or should I present the next award?"

President Alexander handed Colonel McCarter the paper he received from his aide.

McCarter silently read the note and a huge smile spread across his face. He returned the paper to the president and stepped close to the microphone, still grinning. "Mr. President, would you please present the next award? After that, I would like to address the people of the United States and the world."

The president readily agreed. "Then, so be it."

He glanced at the Vietnamese guest, announcing his name—"Le Huu Trang!"

A startled Le peered at the president, heart racing. *What is wrong?*

The president continued. "Will you please step forward?"

Le strode forward, uncertain if he should salute or shake hands. As he neared the leader of the free world, he was stunned to see the crowd standing, cheering, and applauding him enthusiastically. He caught a glimpse of the former prisoners of war, now his friends, who were clapping wildly, smiles on their faces.

He tried to comprehend what was happening. Life had become a sudden and complete whirlwind overnight. Just a few days ago, he was a prison guard for the Vietnamese government. Now he's standing in front of the President of the United States with a countless mass of spectators.

He did what was natural for a military man. He stood at attention and saluted the president, who returned the salute.

"Le Huu Trang, as President of the United States of America, I present a unique award to you. I understand that your name means 'decorated' or 'honored.' How fitting." An aide handed the president a medal. "This is the highest award our country can bestow upon a civilian. You certainly deserve it. It is the Medal of Freedom." He placed it carefully around Le's neck.

The president shook his hand as thousands of cameras captured the presentation. The throng applauded heartily.

When the crowd stilled, President Alexander continued. "Mr. Le, Colonel McCarter believes your life would be in danger if you were to return to Vietnam. He mentioned that you often talk about our great country and the privilege of being an American citizen. Let me ask you this question. Would you like to become an American citizen?"

Le's eyes shone a little brighter as he thought about the question. He shot a glance at his friend James, and the other five comrades who were smiling.

I wish Sam were here, he thought.

He looked back at President Alexander and with certainty replied, "More than anything, sir. I would be honored to become an American citizen."

"Then let me ask you this. Do you realize that in so doing you will have to renounce your citizenship with Vietnam?"

He hesitated. "Yes sir. I would be willing to do that."

"Mr. Le Huu Trang, please raise your right hand and repeat this oath of allegiance after me."

Le lifted his right hand, standing at attention, with eyes directed at President Alexander. He repeated the president's words.

"I hereby declare, on oath, that I absolutely and entirely renounce and abjure all allegiance and fidelity to any foreign prince, potentate, state, or sovereignty of whom or which I have heretofore been a subject or citizen; that I will support and defend the Constitution and laws of the United States of America against all enemies, foreign and domestic; that I will bear true faith and allegiance to the same; that I will bear arms on behalf of the United States when required by the law; that I will perform noncombatant service in the Armed Forces of the United States when required by the law; that I will perform work of national importance under civilian direction when required by the law; and that I take this obligation freely without any mental reservation or purpose of evasion; so help me God."

The president read from a document, smiling at a nervous Le. "'October, 4, 2010, Le Huu Trang is hereby granted American citizenship.' I have signed this proclamation on behalf of the American people. It bears the official seal of the United States of America. Mr. Le Huu Trang, this recognizes you as an American citizen, a special privilege you richly deserve."

Humbly, the former Vietnamese guard replied, "Thank you, sir. For years I dreamed of being an American citizen, now my dream has come true."

"Mr. Le, responsibilities come with citizenship. You have the responsibility to vote, honor, and defend our flag. You will even be privileged to pay taxes."

A faint chuckle rose from the audience at the mention of taxes.

The incredible moment was bittersweet. He felt joy and heartbreak at the same time. How he wished his family could share in this momentous occasion. It comforted Le to know his family was in heaven, smiling down on him. At least he knew, someday they would be reunited for eternity.

President Alexander turned to Colonel James McCarter and asked, "Would you like to present the next award to Mr. Le?"

"I would be honored, sir."

James stepped in front of Le. Looking directly into the younger man's eyes he spoke sincerely. To the onlookers, it was one good friend talking to another.

"Le my friend, what you did for us went far beyond bravery. It was selfless. At great personal risk, you saw a wrong, and believed you could, and should make it right. You engineered our *Quest for Freedom*. We thank you sincerely for being courageous enough to do the right thing. We thank you for bringing us home."

The colonel grinned at the president.

"Le, this took a lot of doing, but it was worth it." Colonel McCarter's voice cracked, and his eyes moistened. Unable to speak further, he looked behind the former guard, nodding his head, and motioned Le to turn around.

From the back of the stage, Le's mother, father, wife and three children sprinted toward him.

Unable to move, he stood in total disbelief. *Could this really be happening?*

Holding them tight, it all became real. As they embraced one another, tears flowed. In fact, there were probably not many dry eyes watching the reunion.

It was a dramatic scene of inexpressible joy.

The family was unaware of everyone and everything around them as they clung to each other, rejoicing in the unbelievable moment. At last, Le composed himself enough to glance at the president, and then back at his friend, Colonel McCarter…the man he had known in prison as "Monday."

Le exhaled loudly, and then questioned the colonel. "How? When?" He could not find the words to frame his thoughts.

Colonel McCarter sensed what Le wanted to express. "You asked many times about Sam...what he was doing, and if you would see him again. Well, you can thank your friend Sam for this... I mean, personally."

Right on cue, Sam bounded from the back of the stage, his face beaming with his well known smile.

Le released his grip on his family, and embraced his good friend Sam— the one who helped make this reunion possible.

President Alexander stepped to the microphone with another surprise announcement. It was time to disclose the contents of the paper he received earlier. "The Vietnamese government sent a statement saying it will abide by all the treaties they have signed. They have issued a proclamation to assure there are no other POWs. There will be an immediate investigation into this entire affair. The United Nations is welcome to oversee the investigation. In addition, there will be an extensive search of Vietnam for any other POWs, or the remains of any. They will be returned immediately when located. As a goodwill gesture and an apology, the Vietnamese government released the family of Le Huu Trang."

The president spoke directly to Le, who was clinging to his wife. "Mr. Le, not only have you saved six American lives, but you have opened an essential, stronger dialog with the Vietnamese government, which I trust we can take to heart. I believe, thanks to you, our relations with them will improve."

The crowd roared with approval.

When they finally silenced, he added, "I also express appreciation to Mr. Samuel Jefferson. Without him, this day would not have been possible. As an American, he operated an orphanage in Vietnam. He established friendships with Le and his wife, Linh. Just a week ago, the escape plan went into effect. There was no military backing, nor United States assistance. These two men, Le and Sam, developed and executed the entire escape by themselves."

President Alexander cleared his throat. "Sam shared Le's vision—the urgent desire to do the right thing. Because of their perseverance, the six men we are honoring today are going to live out their lives in freedom. Mr. Samuel Jefferson will be an honored guest at our banquet tonight. Now, I have the privilege of awarding Sam the Medal of Freedom to express our nation's appreciation."

Shocked, Sam stood before the crowd unable to believe what was happening. Unexpected tears pooled in his eyes and he tried to blink them away.

The tribute became real to Sam when President Alexander placed the award around his neck.

As the celebration continued, Le introduced his family to the six men he had grown to love and respect, and to the President of the United States.

The audience finally settled, watching Colonel McCarter step to the microphone. "Mr. President and fellow Americans. It is hard to believe that only four days ago my comrades and I had given up all hope of freedom. An evil tyrant held us prisoners. We were each confined to a small, dingy cell, no bigger than a refrigerator box. Every day we received dirty rice, drank polluted water, and worked twelve or more hours a day. We had no shoes for our sore, calloused feet, or hats to shield us from the scorching sun. There was no protection from the mosquitoes, flies, cockroaches, and rats."

Colonel McCarter glanced at his wife. Wendy sniffled, but gave him a slight smile for moral support.

"Through our years of confinement, we seldom conversed with each other. Vocal communication was strictly forbidden. If we disobeyed and the guards caught us talking, the consequences were horrific. Some of our comrades died from the punishment."

Colonel McCarter drew a deep breath. "We started out with about thirty or thirty-five men, I do not recall exactly. We were moved to different locations several times, but the conditions were always brutal."

He shook his head, recalling the bitter memories. "We never knew what day of the week it was, let alone what month, or year, for that matter. Each tedious day was the same as the previous one."

The colonel's face displayed a tortured frown. "I believe it was about twelve years ago, although I'm not certain, we planned an escape. We knew we might never make it to freedom, but we had to try. I think there were thirteen of us at the time. We planned the escape using a unique system we had developed similar to Morse code. We tapped on the wall with our feet or hands, whatever we could use to communicate with each other."

He turned to his comrades for support, taking another deep breath. "The escape plan turned out to be a trap. We never understood why the attempt failed. The guards beat us for days afterward. They took great joy in our suffering. Some of our fellow inmates were beaten to death."

Colonel McCarter's rough voice ceased. He could not continue. The emotional toll was too much, so he stepped away from the microphone.

Suddenly, a voice behind him boomed. "We're with you, Brother."

Colonel McCarter turned to look directly at his spiritual partner, Sergeant Anthony Williams.

The encouraging words from his friend were all it took for the colonel to regain the strength to continue. "There were only seven of us left. For safety reasons, we code-named each of us a different day of the week. We had an idea who each of us was, but were quite confident General Yo didn't. Never did we suspect that the seventh day was actually a Vietnamese prison guard...we called him, 'Saturday.'"

The speech was straining his already weakened voice. "A few years ago, a new prison guard showed up on the scene. He was not brutal, like the rest of them. He didn't hit or kick us. Occasionally, he even smiled at us. You must understand, we trusted no one, especially after the failed escape attempt."

Colonel McCarter paused, clearing his throat. "It was not until a few months ago, I began to notice this guard was different than the others. You see, we had forty years of hatred and bitterness pent up inside us. Therefore, for a while we did not even notice his kindness. We did not hear the gentle words he spoke when the other guards were not around. Now as I reflect, I remember times when he smiled at me, or extended a helping hand when I fell."

Colonel McCarter glanced at Le, who still held his family close. "Once, when I was really down and hurting, I walked by that guard and heard him say, 'I'm sorry, GI.' I could not believe it! Those three words stuck with me.

"Soon after, he shared his bottle of water with me. I will never forget the taste of that cool, fresh water. Oh, it was good! What shocked me most was when I realized I had almost finished the entire bottle. I knew a beating would follow. I cautiously handed the bottle back, watching the guard raise it to his mouth, sipping the last few drops. He didn't whip me! No punishment!" Choked up, Colonel McCarter looked directly into Le's teary eyes. "Instead, he said...he said...'It's a great day to be alive.'" He paused. "I remember thinking, who is this man? What does he want? Could this be a trap?"

"Over the next few days, the guard showed me something about myself. He shared scripture from the Bible. I began to see that Le was a soldier for righteousness. His kindness reminded me that I was missing something in my life. Something I had at one time, but let slip away. That was God. I'm ashamed to admit that I...we, all of us, had given up hope in America, in ourselves, and even in God." He looked down, remorsefully shaking his head.

"Since returning to America, I realize that although some had forgotten us, many had not. The outpouring of love and support you have shown today has overwhelmed us. We never expected a welcome like this."

Looking into the vast crowd, he continued. "I see those black flags out there." He pointed to a number of POW/MIA flags in the audience; veterans dressed in camouflage clothing, some in wheelchairs, carried most of them.

"You sir, what is your name?" He directed his question to a rough-bearded man carrying a large black flag. He wore a shirt that read, "POWs never have a nice day."

The veteran snapped to attention, bellowing, "Sergeant Dennis Shelby, United States Marine Corps—Vietnam '67 to '69, sir."

"Sergeant Dennis Shelby, I thank you…we thank you." He gestured to his comrades. "We thank you for never giving up, Sergeant Shelby."

Colonel McCarter's passionate speech kept the onlookers spellbound.

"Last night before I went to bed, I asked Le what 9/11 was. My curiosity was aroused when I saw it on a bumper sticker. Le reluctantly explained to me what happened. He told me of the planes hitting the buildings, and Americans jumping out of the flaming inferno to certain death. Then, the horrible collapse of the twin towers! I can only imagine what Americans felt that fateful day…what the world felt. I would think that something of that magnitude would have pulled our nation together. Le believed it did for a while, but from what he could gather, it was temporary and many Americans became complacent soon after. Maybe it is because of what my fellow soldiers and I went through, but I will never forget it, and I was not even there. So many lives were lost needlessly that September morning in New York. I pray nothing like that ever happens again in America, or even in the world! I also hope and pray another American soldier never becomes a prisoner of war."

The crowd responded with enthusiastic applause of affirmation.

"You may wonder if we ever gave up. Yes, we did…each of us did. It saddens me to say, we gave up on America. But, you know what I realized? Some of you continued to be steadfast. People like Sergeant Shelby never gave up. Neither did God…He never forgot us, nor did He forsake us. No, quite the contrary. He brought an angel in a Vietnamese guard uniform to help us. Who would have guessed?"

The colonel smiled at Le; admiration was evident by his remarks.

"Many times in recent hours, I asked Le why he helped us. Why would he sacrifice his life and the lives of his family for six forgotten American prisoners? His reply was always the same, 'It was the right thing to do.'"

Colonel McCarter's voice slowly intensified. "Today America, I challenge you. Do the right thing, every day. Do the right thing."

He beckoned his comrades to join him.

Together, the former POWs locked their arms, and in front of the vast gathering, tapped the floor rhythmically with their feet.

Afterwards, McCarter stepped to the microphone. "That was the code we used for communicating with each other during the years of confinement. I'm sure you wonder what we tapped." His voice cracked. "We said what every American should affirm daily…God bless America."

Instantly, the crowd began to chant, "God bless America."

After several minutes, when the throng quieted, the Colonel concluded. "We thank you for your warm reception. God bless you and God bless America!"

Colonel James McCarter and his band of liberated POWs waved to the audience, and walked off the stage while the ovation continued.

Spontaneously the crowd broke out singing, *God Bless America.* Those present and those viewing on TV will never forget the sights and sounds of the incredible scene.

Le stood with his arm around Linh. He could hardly believe he was in America, and for the first time in his life was free…really free! The most exciting part was sharing the experience with his family.

Le noticed each of his loved ones had a look of fear, uncertainty. Beyond the joy of the moment were understandable concerns about their future—monumental concerns!

All Le could do at that time was reassure them with a confident, loving smile.

Somehow, he knew things would be all right. God reunited his family. He guided them through perilous times protecting them the entire way; He must have a plan for them.

As the reality of their situation began to sink in, Le started to laugh and a peace enveloped him. He was thrilled beyond words as he remembered God's promised presence.

Colonel McCarter and his comrades returned to the stage and welcomed Le's family.

President Alexander joined in the greetings.

All the men were exuberant, except Lomack, who was noticeably disturbed.

Freeman and McCarter noticed his sadness. Lomack was staring at the medal he received only minutes before. When his friends neared him, Lomack noticed their concern and remarked, "I keep thinking how I got here. Each of you deserves these medals, but me…me, I flipped out forty years ago. I might have been court-martialed, given a medical, or perhaps even a dishonorable discharge for my actions. I don't deserve this honor." He looked down, dejected, ashamed.

"Ron," Freeman pleaded. "You can't look at it that way. None of us knows what we would have done in your place. You spent forty years in a POW camp where you were tortured excessively. You never cracked. In fact, you challenged your captors. You did not break."

Hesitantly, Lomack nodded his head in agreement. Yet deep in his heart, he still felt unworthy.

It started to snow gently as the event began to wind down. Smiling, Le looked up allowing some snowflakes to melt on his face. Snow was something he had never experienced before. He thought it was another amazing thing about an already incredible day!

Le noticed Sam standing alone offstage, and knew Sam was instrumental in the reunion of his family. He rushed over to him. "How can I ever thank you for bringing my family back?"

"No thanks are needed. I gave you my word, and I did what I had to do. You said so yourself…it was the right thing to do."

"Yes. I did say that, didn't I?" Le smiled. "How did you find them?"

"I contacted a friend in the Vietnamese government. The U.S. authorities had already notified them, and they were working on the situation. They permitted me to participate in the storming of the prison compound. We found your wife, children, and parents locked in cells with about twenty-five other missing people. They released your family immediately, no questions asked."

Sam continued, "My chopper flew to the site. We left with the Vietnamese government's blessing. A few of the other prisoners were missing dignitaries held by Yo. They were in captivity because they found out about him and were going to turn him in. Yo is despised in Vietnam. If he were not already dead, he would be now."

Le shook his head, speechless.

Sam added, "There is more good news—that horrible prison is no more."

"I'm glad it's over. What a relief!"

"It sure is."

Le's gaze fell to the floor. "Sam, what do I do now?"

"Concerning what?"

"My future. How do I support my family?" Le waited for an answer, anything to help.

"Le, the sky is the limit. Tell your story. Write a book. Make a movie. Go on a lecture tour of universities, anywhere in the free world."

Le considered the ideas. "Write a book. Yes, I could do that."

EIGHTEEN

The Wall

The guests arrived at the White House for the banquet in honor of the newly acclaimed heroes. The staff ushered them into the State Dining Room.

The soldiers, who only days ago were imprisoned in filthy, repulsive conditions, gazed around the banquet room—it was luxury at its finest. The décor and furnishings were magnificent. Priceless art decorated the walls. Tables were set with fine china, crystal, and linens, as they would be at a dinner for a visiting head of state. A tuxedo-clad live orchestra played softly in the background.

The guests, including the soldiers and their immediate families, were dressed in formal attire. The returnees tried to focus on the occasion, but the extravagance around them captured their attention, distracting them.

Before dinner, the men mingled with one another as they delved into the delicious hors d'oeuvres. Their appetites were improving, and they were permitted to eat more foods to help regain their strength and stamina.

The soldiers proudly showed each other and their loved ones their new ranks and medals while they mingled. Many dignitaries also expressed interest.

Le and his family received well-deserved attention from his friends, other guests, and staff. His parents appeared to be adapting to the cultural changes. They were laughing, and enjoying all the attention they received. Conversing with some of the Americans who knew their language proved to be a special treat.

The former Vietnamese guard tried to absorb the scene around him. He still couldn't wrap his head around it. *I can't believe I am dining in the White House with VIPs, even the President of the United States and the First Lady. It all seems surreal.*

Le's blessings were abundant. His family was alive and celebrating with him. He was with new friends who genuinely cared about him, and the tables were filled with more food and drink than he had seen in his entire life!

Suddenly a strange sensation swept over him, as if someone was watching him. Glancing across the room, he was delighted to see Corporal Nancee Quinn, beautifully attired in her stunning, red dress. A wide smile crossed his face as he walked over to greet her.

"Hi," she said softly. Her big blue eyes and captivating smile made him feel comfortable and secure, which was the effect she typically had on him.

"Hi. I'm glad you could make it."

"I wouldn't have missed this for the world," she replied earnestly.

They glanced around the room at the guests; most of them were strangers to Le.

"Some party," she commented.

"Yes, but you sure have a lot of strange food in America. Fortunately, there are some familiar dishes from my country. I guess I should get use to saying the country I was born in…America is my home now." He was thrilled that he was going to live in the greatest country on earth!

Le reached for her hand. "Come, Nancee. I'm anxious for you to meet my wife." Together they walked over to his wife who was engaged in conversation with some other guests.

"This is my wife, Linh. Honey, this is Nancee. She accompanied me all the way to America and was a remarkable help to me. She motivated me and helped me get through the confusing transition. I don't know if I could have done it without her. She has become a good friend."

The women greeted each other with a hug.

"Thank you for taking care of him," Linh remarked genuinely. "I was so worried about him, and I know he was concerned about us. I prayed that someone would be there to help him and you were the answer to my prayers. Thank you, Nancee."

"It was my pleasure. He often talked about you and the children. He prayed for your safety. Le is a kind and gentle man and you are fortunate to have him."

Le summoned their children to introduce them to his new American friend. They individually thanked her for helping their daddy.

"You have beautiful children, so polite." Nancee offered. "You are blessed."

"I sure am," Le readily agreed, reaching for his wife's hand.

After a few minutes of small talk, Le noticed the beverage table was unoccupied. "Would you like some punch?"

"I'd love some," Nancee answered.

Le faced Linh. "I'll be back in a moment."

He walked over to the serving table with the Marine, and poured her a glass of refreshing punch. They stood away from the crowd chatting comfortably, like old friends.

"You have a lovely family, Le. Are they doing okay?" she asked, sipping her punch.

"Yes, they are doing well. Linh has a few burns inflicted by Yo. My youngest has a badly cut finger, but they will heal. Now that we're together, they'll be fine."

Concerned, Nancee inquired, "Le, what are your plans for the future?"

"I sure wish I knew. I am unsure what the future holds, but excited about some possibilities. I am not certain how I will support my family. Sam suggested I write a book, or go on a lecture tour, but I don't know how to do that."

"Hmmm…lecture tour. Yes, that's a great idea and could be quite lucrative."

"How would that work?"

"Perhaps you could speak at schools, universities, and public events. You could probably get an agent to set up speaking engagements."

"Are there many opportunities?"

Nancee smiled. "For you… thousands of them."

"How much do they pay? As a guard, I made forty-five dollars a month. Can I make more than that?"

Nancee chuckled. "Oh my, yes. I've heard of people making fifty-thousand dollars or more to speak at an event. You may be surprised at the opportunities that come your way. Speaking at churches might be a possibility, too. They don't usually pay like that, though! There's no limit to where you can go, what you can do, or how much money you can make."

Le was shocked, but thrilled and hopeful at the prospects. He realized he and his family would be all right. This was the beginning of an adventure…a new life. They would be stepping into a world of exciting tomorrows.

Sipping his punch, he glanced at his family and then back at Nancee. *How can I thank her for the kindness she showed me during my time of fear and uncertainty? I guess it is not necessary—after all, she also did the right thing.*

Le would see Nancee again a few more times in his life. She invited his family to her wedding two years later. It was a spectacular military ceremony, just like her father desired. She married a Christian, who was also a Marine.

The banquet was exquisite.

The chefs prepared a superb five-course dinner, which the men and their families enjoyed.

As they dined, Le glanced around the room. He noticed Sam and McCarter involved in a lively conversation. Then he caught a glimpse of the other free men getting reacquainted with their families. He looked at his wife and children…all he could do was smile. *Thank You God…You made it all happen!*

After the banquet, chauffeurs drove the men to the Vietnam Veterans Memorial. Le and his family accompanied them in a separate limo.

By the time they arrived at their destination, it was snowing heavily. Maintenance had cleared the freshly fallen snow from the area around the Wall.

Visitors, reporters, and photographers were kept at a distance. It was vital for the six men to visit the site in private, and pay tribute to the men whose names were engraved on the Wall. This was not a time for media, or even family members. No one could understand how sacred this time was for the men.

Le knew his friends needed this time together, free from the watching world and activity of the past hours.

Walking down the path to the memorial, each man's emotions ran high.

The two black granite walls were striking with light gray lettering. It was larger than they imagined, spanning two hundred and forty-six feet, and standing ten feet at the highest point.

The men stared solemnly at the 58,261 names listed on the Wall. Grief overwhelmed them. It was amazing they had any tears left after their eventful day. Somehow, more tears coursed down their faces as six brave soldiers wept for those who paid the supreme sacrifice.

They paid particular attention to twelve hundred names listed as MIAs and POWs. Among them were many familiar names, twenty-seven were men they knew very well—fellow prisoners.

Colonel McCarter pointed to Corporal Daniel Sparks' name. Too emotionally drained to speak, they could only stare at the etching. For forty years, Sparks was one of them, in name only. Yet seeing his name was a reminder of how real Corporal Sparks had once been.

It was especially poignant when they saw their own names listed on the spectacular memorial. It left them breathless, deeply stirred.

After a lengthy time of reflection and memories, they were exhausted. Emotionally drained, they were ready to leave.

The worn out soldiers and their families would part in different directions. That would be strange for them.

Although this had been their dream for the last forty years, now that the time was here to separate, the men were filled with fear and apprehension. There would be no more tapping, except in their recurring nightmares. There would be no more isolation in the darkness of night. There would be no more torture, mental or physical, from their evil captors.

The one thing they hadn't counted on was how difficult it would be to separate from the prison guard who rescued them…there would be no more Le!

They walked back to the limousines quietly…thoughtfully.

It was time to say goodbye to each other and to Le. The handshaking, hugging, and the farewells were difficult and the tears wouldn't stop. The men were anxious to go home with their families, yet fearful of the unknown. They had been through so much together. They were the only ones who understood what happened in the course of those long years. During that time, their survival depended on each other, even if only through the tapping in a dark cell.

No one expected the goodbyes to be this difficult. Could they survive without each other? Could they survive without Le?

There would be many obstacles to overcome in their lives, but they would do it. After all, they would be exchanging the darkness of imprisonment for the light of freedom, and the kind protection of Le for the unending protection of liberty.

Finally, the inevitable moment came when they parted.

Le watched as the last limo disappeared into the darkness, tires kicking up the new fallen snow. Consumed with loneliness, he felt totally lost. Fatigue enveloped him.

He stood motionless for a second, then turned and noticed his family standing in the falling snow, waiting patiently by the limo. He fought the impulse to break down and weep. He drew a slow, cleansing breath and looked heavenward. *I will miss my friends greatly. Even though I have been with them for only four years, it feels like forty. I have been one of them, both physically and emotionally. God be with them!*

Le's family stayed in Washington, D.C. for three weeks while being processed for American citizenship. The luxurious five-star hotel provided comfort they never knew existed. They toured the city and enjoyed the sights Le had learned about on the internet. It was a beneficial time of transition for them.

A major university in Colorado offered Le a position teaching his native language. He readily accepted the offer. He would live near the mountains and be close to his good friend, James McCarter. The job would give him summers off, enabling him to go on lecture tours.

Just as Sam and Nancee predicted, speaking offers were abundant—churches, schools, universities, and public rallies. Because of his role in freeing the prisoners, he was in high demand.

However, he knew there was something he still needed to do.

NINETEEN

The Mission

Le's picture and story were in almost every major newspaper in the world, and on the cover of many magazines. His face appeared often on the internet and even on some billboards. All of America seemed to recognize the Vietnamese VIP.

Although he was still a little uncertain what the hubbub was about, Le kept his focus on one thing and one thing only—the pouch.

He set in motion the project he had to finish. He took the carefully guarded small bag from around his neck, studying its contents for a long time.

He had already received permission from military leadership and President Nathan Alexander to implement his plan. The authorities made the necessary arrangements for him to carry it out.

Le's first mission was to meet the family of Corporal Daniel Sparks, the soldier whose identity he assumed for four years. He was relieved to discover that Daniel's parents were still alive. With a heavy heart, he boarded a military jet to Butte, Montana.

At the airport in Butte, an official vehicle waited to drive him to the Sparks' home.

Le was uncertain how the family would respond to him. Would they see him as an enemy or friend?

The Army informed the Sparks family about Le's coming, but didn't tell them the reason for his visit.

As the car stopped in front of the simple, ranch style home, Le whispered a short prayer. *Please God, help me as I meet this family. I want to help them, not hurt them.* Climbing out of the car, he took a deep breath in the cool, brisk air.

Walking slowly to the door, he noticed the curtains shift to one side. He saw the face of an older woman peeking out. Seeing her sent a shiver down his back. *How will they react when they meet me? After all, my country was responsible for the death of their only son.*

He rang the doorbell and looked around at the freshly fallen snow. Three birds sat on a feeder nearby, chirping a cheerful melody.

The door squeaked open. An elderly couple stood in the doorway holding hands, drawing strength from each other. Le knew they were in their eighties. Although they moved slowly, they appeared to be well. *The Montana climate has been good to them*, he thought.

Smiling at them, Le broke the ice. "Hello. I am Le Huu Trang."

"Good Morning," they replied pleasantly in unison.

"Come in, please." Daniel's mother moved aside, gesturing for him to enter.

Stepping into the cozy room, Le noticed the lingering aroma of bacon from breakfast. The home gave the feeling of warmth and love.

"Would you like to sit?" the man said, pointing to an old, flowered sofa.

As Le sat down the woman offered him a cup of coffee.

"That would be nice."

"Sugar and cream?"

"No, thank you. Black will be fine."

She disappeared into the kitchen.

For a moment, it was awkward, sitting and waiting in the quaint surroundings. It appeared the couple lived a comfortable life, but certainly nothing elaborate.

Le noticed a lone picture in the center of the fireplace mantle. It was a photograph of a young man in military uniform. An MIA ribbon draped over the photo. He immediately knew the identity of the soldier. He walked over, staring at the picture. "May I?" he asked, pointing to the photo.

"Sure, go ahead."

Knowing how much it meant to them, Le picked it up respectfully.

The elderly man spoke in short sentences, never wasting any words. "That is our son, Daniel. Our only child. Doctors said if Mary had another baby, it would kill her. Danny was a good son. Great athlete in high school. Best high jumper in the state, two years in a row."

Le touched the ribbon, staring at the photo, and listening to the proud, but still grieving father.

"Joined the Army fresh out of high school...said it would pay for his college. He felt he had to do his part for America. My, he looked fine in that uniform. He was Army...like me. Went missing in Nam. They tell us he's dead. It's been forty years...they are probably right. We had a funeral...tombstone and everything...just no...no Daniel."

Tears welled in Le's eyes, listening to the father speak so admirably about his son. He studied the picture. It was almost as though he was looking at himself. *How will I explain the situation to these hurting parents?*

Daniel was a good looking young man, lean and tall in stature. In the photo, he was only nineteen years old—certainly too young to be fighting a war so far away.

Le carefully returned the picture to its original place, trying not to disturb anything else on the mantle.

He returned to the sofa, waiting for the right time to tell the young soldier's parents the reason for his visit.

The conversation changed to small talk when the host asked Le about his trip.

Finally, the woman returned with a steaming cup of coffee.

Le immediately stood as she handed it to him. He thanked her and brought it slowly to his lips.

As he sat down, his eyes were drawn to the photo again. He realized the hopes and dreams of these parents were shattered with the notice of their son's missing in action status.

Le closed his eyes and uttered another silent prayer. *God, give me strength. Please help me.*

"Is it too hot?" the woman asked.

"No. I like it hot. It is delicious. Thank you."

There was an uneasy silence as he sipped his coffee.

Finally, Le broke the stillness by explaining the reason for his visit.

Mr. and Mrs. Sparks already knew who he was and what he had done for the six prisoners. How could they not know? The entire world heard about Le and his friends. When the news first broke, they desperately longed for one of the rescued men to be their Danny. However, their hopes faded when the names were announced. On the other hand, they were excited for the families of the soldiers who were alive; it gave them a flicker of hope for their son.

Le found it painful to share his experience. With all his strength and with God's help he began. He told them what relationship he had to the men in the prison camp. He watched their reactions carefully as he told them each intricate detail. He explained how he and the guards before him assumed their son's name, Corporal Daniel Sparks. He confessed to being recruited by General Yo in order to listen to the conversations of the prisoners. He told how the prisoners knew him as "Saturday."

He related everything he knew about their son to the anxious parents. Le only knew the information the other guards passed down to him through the years. He believed some details should not be revealed. They did not need to know how badly the guards treated the young soldier after his capture, only how brave he was—that's all that mattered at this point.

The dreaded question came from Mr. Sparks. "How did my son die?"

"I am not certain, but I do know where his remains are. President Alexander assured me that his remains and those of twenty-six other missing soldiers would be returned to America."

Le took the pouch from around his neck. He opened the small bag carefully, and removed something, clutching it in his hand. Walking over to the proud father, he said, "Sir, with great honor and sorrow, I present this to you."

The bereaved father carefully took the item from Le's hand. He knew immediately what it was. He had received a similar set while serving in World War II. He held Daniel's dog tags, still attached to the chain. They were worn, but shiny and readable—the Army's means of identifying a soldier.

"When I received them they were rusty, but I tried hard to keep them in good condition in case this moment ever came."

The heartbroken father read the inscription aloud. *Sparks, Daniel M. RA 16917813 AB+ Protestant.* "My son's dog tags," the father lamented, tears filling his eyes. He handed the treasure to his wife.

She held them delicately. Of course, they weren't breakable, but they represented something precious to them. They were representative of their son's life, a tangible remembrance, possibly the last thing he touched before he died.

Mr. Sparks stood up slowly, facing Le; neither man knew what to say or do.

Le spoke from his heart, but was uncertain how the sorrowful parents would react. "Mr. and Mrs. Sparks, on behalf of myself and my people, I am truly sorry for your loss. Your son died trying to give freedom to my country, the Vietnamese people. Your great leader Abraham Lincoln, in the Gettysburg Address referred to a life not given in vain. Your son's life certainly was not given in vain."

The man and his wife stared at Le, concentrating on his words. Then the elderly couple embraced the former guard. "Thank You," they whispered.

Le was uncertain if their tears were out of gratitude for the dog tags, or because they finally had some information about Daniel's death—it didn't matter.

They released their grip on Le.

Sadly, he walked to the door. This hurting couple needed time alone to grieve their beloved son. Healing could come because now they knew with certainty what they always wondered.

As Le departed, he glanced back to see them still clinging to each other tearfully. How he wished he could have brought them good news!

Closing the door quietly, he headed to the car.

Le looked at the young military driver waiting for him. Sadness and compassion showed on Le's face, and the driver noticed how shaken he was.

Le's mind was reeling from the impact of what had just transpired. Reflecting, he stood at the limo. He laid his arms on the door, resting his head on his arms.

The house door sprang open startling the birds on the feeder.

Le heard the father shout, "Young man, please stop!"

He turned to Mr. Sparks, wondering what he would say. Le was afraid he would condemn him, leaving him shattered by his remarks. He knew how words could crush a man; he saw it repeatedly with General Yo.

In a shaky voice, the elderly man spoke, "Thank you, Mr. Le. God bless you."

Le smiled and replied, "He already has, sir. He already has."

The driver, deeply touched, looked through red eyes as he opened the car door for Le. Nodding his head, he smiled at the former guard, both of them feeling the deep emotion of the moment.

As he sat back in the seat, Le removed the small bag from around his neck, staring at the contents. Inside were twenty-six more sets of dog tags, each representing a man, a life who died at the hands of General Yo.

For the last couple of years in Vietnam, Le searched for, traded, and bought the tags, usually from other guards. Some he secured from Yo. Intending to send them to the men's families, the last thing he ever expected was to hand them to their relatives face-to-face.

The next three weeks would be busy and extremely stressful for him. He planned to visit each family of the twenty-six soldiers, apologize to them, and return the dog tags of their lost loved ones as a final remembrance.

After traveling thousands of miles and endless hours, Le visited the last family. He reached his goal, and met with representatives of each soldier's loved ones. Most were gracious, some were bitter, but all were grateful that they could close this chapter of their lives.

When he was finally finished, Le was exhausted. The ordeal had taken a huge toll on him; he felt drained physically, emotionally, and spiritually.

Leaving a small town in northern New Hampshire, he noticed a picturesque white church, which resembled a Christmas card scene, and asked the driver to stop.

The military vehicle pulled up to the church. Looking around, breathing in the fresh, crisp air, Le closed his eyes briefly and whispered, "I wish Sam was with me. He knew when I needed encouragement, and could always lift my spirits."

He strode toward the serene church. It surprised him to find the front door was unlocked.

Curious, Le opened the wide, wooden, red door and entered the foyer.

He looked around for a few moments. It was a homey church with a striking sanctuary. The old fashioned, wooden pews could probably seat a couple hundred people. He approached the altar. A large pipe organ was on one side, and a choir loft was in the center behind the carved wood pulpit. A piano and two guitars were nearby, ready for use on Sunday. On one wall was a large screen for videos and lyrics for congregational singing.

The wall on the other side displayed a large picture of Jesus standing in front of a closed door. Le had seen it before and it always fascinated him. As he studied the famous painting, he saw something odd, something he had not noticed before. There was no door handle on the outside of the door where Jesus stood knocking.

Le was startled when a well dressed man burst into the room. His warm smile instantly gave Le a feeling of tranquility.

"Hello. I'm Pastor Murdock. What can I do for you?" The friendly minister extended his hand to Le.

With a firm handshake, Le began to introduce himself.

The pastor interrupted. "I know who you are. Almost everyone in America knows who you are. I suspect you came to visit a family from our church."

Le nodded in agreement.

"Did they accept what you had to say with a good spirit?" Pastor Murdock inquired.

"Yes, they did. I told them what they already knew in their minds, but were unable to accept in their hearts."

"How many more families do you still have to visit?"

"I would like to visit all 58,000 plus of them, but only felt obligated to visit twenty-six. Well, actually twenty-seven. This was my last one. I have completed what I set out to do."

"You look exhausted."

"That I am. It has not been easy."

Le's attention drifted back to the painting. "May I ask you a question, Pastor Murdock?"

"Sure, go right ahead."

"That picture…I've seen it before, but never studied it up close."

"It's a beautiful painting. Holman Hunt was the artist."

"I have two questions. First, why all the vines? Second, why is there no handle on the door? That seems sort of strange."

"The painting is perhaps the most famous one ever painted of Christ, except for 'The Last Supper,' of course. Hunt painted the original in 1853 and named it 'The Light of the World.'"

Pastor Murdock pointed to the picture. "Look closely…it depicts Jesus knocking on a door, which is covered with weeds and vines. The overgrowth suggests the person on the inside has failed to look for truth. I understand it represents a human's conscience."

Le was mesmerized, hanging on to every word the pastor said.

"The door does not have a handle on the outside because the human heart must be opened from the inside. Only an individual can ask Jesus into his heart. He will not come in without an invitation, nor will He force Himself into any person's life. The lantern Jesus is holding is a symbol of the light He brings when He enters a life."

The words stirred Le deeply.

"The scripture that inspired the painting is Revelation 3, verses 19-21."
Behold, I stand at the door and knock; if anyone hears my voice and opens the door, I will come in to him and will dine with him, and he with me.

Silence reigned while both men reflected on the message behind the meaningful artwork.

The pastor continued. "Each person must decide whether to open the door of his heart and ask Christ in, or keep Him on the outside. Jesus still stands outside the door waiting. Will we invite Him into our lives? Sadly, many leave him on the outside, unwilling to surrender their lives to Him."

"Interesting. I can relate."

"What do you mean?" the pastor inquired.

Le continued to gaze at the picture; his eyes locked on the image. "When I was a guard at the prison, in the darkness of the cells, I would tap on the walls, trying to convince the prisoners to understand that I was trying to help them. They ignored what I told them. I knew freedom was close, and yet they would not trust me. One day they finally did. Because they trusted, now they are free."

Le added, "I'm not comparing myself to God. I'm just stating the similarities." He did not want to be misunderstood.

"I understand. In order to be free, we must trust and open the door of our hearts. Have you invited Jesus into your life?" the wise pastor asked.

"Yes. He changed my life, and now I am able to impact the lives of others."

"That's the way it works. Judging by what I have seen and heard, what happened in your life has helped change the world."

"What do you mean?"

"You have given America a fresh, new hope. Before you stepped forward to help the six prisoners, the world was getting darker. Many churches were dying. Religion was under attack. Public schools no longer allowed prayer. Even our national motto, *In God We Trust,* was being removed from some of our public places."

Looking directly into Le's brown eyes, he thought carefully before he continued his remarks to the young Vietnamese man. "I can only speak of what I have seen. Since you arrived in America with those six men, this congregation has doubled in size. People from all areas of life have come through that door. Giving has doubled and my workload has certainly increased." He laughed. "Trust me, I'm not complaining, I'm just stating a fact."

The pastor took a deep, calming breath. "America is beginning to experience renewal. It seems as though the nation is finally coming to its senses. You sir, have inspired America. I pray that the spiritual interest will continue."

Le nodded his head in agreement, listening intently as the pastor continued. "Many times in the past the same thing happened. The assassination of President Kennedy, Desert Storm, and 9/11 are all American tragedies, which resulted in people filling our churches and altars. However, a few months later, complacency took over. Many stopped attending services, and things went back to the way they were."

"And now?" Le asked.

"God is working—people are still coming. Who would have thought God would use a Vietnamese prison guard to lead the way to an American and worldwide spiritual awakening?"

"Who would have thought God would use a poor Jewish girl to bring His Son into the world?" Le added.

Pastor Murdock smiled broadly, nodding his head. "Good point."

Le reached his hand to the pastor. "Thank you for your encouragement. God knew I needed this time with you."

As they shook hands the pastor commented, "It was great to meet you in person. Thank you for all you have done. You made my day. It will make a great illustration in Sunday's sermon." He chuckled.

Le laughed heartily.

"May I pray with you before you leave?" Pastor Murdock requested.

"I would be honored. However, would you also pray for my friends, the POWs I came home with, as well as the millions who are imprisoned by something in their lives and do not know God. They desperately need our prayers."

"Nicely put…Nicely put. I may use that analogy in a sermon, too."

They bowed in prayer. The pastor prayed for Le, the six ex-POWs, and their families, and for those who are prisoners of something in their lives—drugs, alcohol, apathy, and other forms of bondage. They are prisoners of a different type, but enslaved nonetheless. Sadly, many do not realize it until they face a disaster in their lives or until they come face-to-face with God.

Le began to walk away deep in thought, when the pastor called, "Go with God's blessings, my friend."

Glancing back, Le said, "A few months ago I was a Communist guard trapped in a POW prison camp. Today I am a free American. I have my family and a host of new friends. I think His blessings have been abundant."

The pastor lifted his hand in blessing, "Then go in peace, my friend."

Le waved, as he walked to the waiting automobile.

The driver opened the door for him. "Do you feel better now, sir?"

Le paused. "Yes, much better. I feel as if a tremendous weight has been lifted off my shoulders."

Collapsing in the car, Le looked at his driver. "I feel…feel…free! Yes, that's it. I feel free!"

TWENTY

The Rest of Their Lives
Arlington, Virginia

As the day ended, there was a chill in the air. The sky was breathtaking. The clouds moved in creating a spectacular sunset with assorted shades of violet, pink, orange, and crimson.

Le sat on the cement bench in front of five grave markers. Buried in these graves in Arlington National Cemetery were brave men that Le was proud to call his friends.

Day after day, he typed thoughtfully on his laptop. He was almost finished with the account; it was a saga of freedom and of commitment to a goal.

A generation had passed. He vividly remembered the prison—the sights, smells, and sounds. Le recalled every detail of the harrowing escape, and the triumphant return of the prisoners to their homeland and families.

Le kept in touch with all the men through their fascinating lives. After all, he had an extraordinary history with them. They shared a unique bond.

Through the years, Le often reflected on the five words. Life...Hope...Faith...Love...Responsibility. He considered how they related to his six friends.

Life. The men lived free again. They appreciated every moment of life. They all realized they could never recapture their lost years. Forty years stolen from them! The time was gone forever, but the nightmares persisted. Even when asleep they could never forget the horror of their imprisonment.

Hope. During the years of confinement, the prisoners lost all hope. Freedom restored hope to them. Their country's welcome gave them a fresh appreciation and expectation for America—a new hope!

Faith. The men regained faith in their country, people, and God. They realized faith in God is what brought them home. Through the long, miserable years, when their own faith was shattered, others prayed diligently for their return. It may have been a family member, an unknown veteran, or someone who had lost a loved one in war. The result was answered prayer. God used Le and Sam to fulfill His purpose. Thank God, for the people who never lost faith and prayed steadfastly.

Love. Upon their return to America, love was awaiting each of the men. Perhaps it was a wife or child, sibling or friend, grandchild or elderly parent. Love sometimes came from a stranger, a community, or a nation. Love surrounded them, giving them the strength to live again.

Responsibility. The men had a responsibility to survive, which they did. However, their responsibility did not end with their freedom. They desired to share their account with others. Why? Shouldn't they put their horrible experience in the past and move on with their new life? The answer was simple—they needed to share their story to help prevent any captured American from being forgotten again!

Le's new life was an adventure—a dream come true for the former prison guard.

He followed his friends' lives to the ends. He attended each funeral with his head held high—confident that he had known a real hero.

Thomas Traber

Following the celebration in the nation's capitol, Sergeant First Class Thomas Traber returned to a gigantic homecoming in his small town in Kansas.

The popular senator, now in his eighties, attended his welcome home festivities. Together they recalled the days of drinking lemonade and lively conversation on the senator's back porch. The well known politician told Thomas about his political journey, which nearly took him to the White House. Thomas was enthralled with his stories, just as he was as a youngster.

His time in Kansas was a special time to reconnect with family and friends. However, he did not stay there long; nothing was the same as before his military days.

He had enough hot weather in the Vietnam jungle, so for a contrast, he moved to Alaska. He operated a commercial fishing boat in Juneau. He enjoyed the beauty and serenity of the area—outdoor activities occupied most of his time.

Thomas enjoyed a celebrity status. Often he would be the guide for Vietnam veterans touring Alaska. He considered that a special privilege.

He married a young, local Alaskan girl. At age sixty-two, his lifelong dream of becoming a father came true when he adopted his wife's twins. They were a close-knit family.

Every year on Memorial Day and Independence Day, Thomas spoke at schools and churches around the state. His message was always the same—patriotism and freedom.

Sergeant First Class Thomas Traber was the first of the returning soldiers to die. At the age of sixty-eight, a fishing accident took his life.

A tall, serene mountain overlooking Juneau was his burial place. His grave was nestled under a grove of giant pine trees.

The words on his tombstone were simple: Born April 12, 1950. Died August 10, 2018, at the age of twenty-eight.

The forty years in captivity were erased from his life, as if they never happened. As far as he was concerned, those years should be forgotten—as the tombstone etching stated.

Ronald Lomack

Sergeant First Class Ronald Lomack returned to Missouri to help his youngest brother, David, operate the family dairy farm.

He stayed isolated much of the time enjoying the solitude to which he had grown accustomed.

Every year on Veteran's Day, Ronald would meet the other five men, Le, and Sam in Branson, Missouri. They attended the ceremonies, and enjoyed meeting other veterans during Branson's patriotic festivities. Veterans are always welcome in Branson. One year each of the men received a key to that small Ozark city. They seldom had to pay for anything—somebody who recognized them usually picked up the tab. It was an appropriate courtesy for such heroes.

Ron continued to suffer from horrendous nightmares. He never married because of them.

He died in his sleep at the age of seventy-two. Le hoped it was a peaceful death and not a violent one, still fighting that war of long ago.

A small cemetery near his farm was his final resting place. His grave was located next to his parents and brother. The tombstone read, "Peace at last." That was fitting for him.

Anthony Williams

Sergeant First Class Anthony Williams was disenchanted with how much life in America changed while he was away. Nothing was the same!

His wife, who had been his childhood sweetheart, remarried after he had been missing several years.

He was too old to fulfill his dream of becoming a doctor.

His father died a year after he returned. Only then did he realize his calling was to become a minister. After additional schooling, he accepted the pastorate of a small Vietnamese church in Southern California. His knowledge of the Vietnamese language and customs he gleaned while a prisoner helped to equip him for specialized service for God. His forgiving spirit was a valuable asset and encouragement to others. The church grew in numbers, and God blessed his ministry.

In later years, Anthony became a missionary to Thailand. He assisted the people in the villages, sharing the gospel with them.

However, he never visited Vietnam again—the wounds were too deep, the pain too real.

He died of malaria at the age of seventy-four in a small village in Thailand. Le flew there to bring Anthony's body back to America. He believed his friend deserved that consideration.

Anthony was buried at Arlington National Cemetery.

Freeman, McCarter, Pfingston, Le, and former President Nathan Alexander attended his funeral. Hundreds of fellow veterans joined them. It was a full military funeral with a twenty-one gun salute—fitting for a man of outstanding valor.

Brent Pfingston

Sergeant First Class Brent Pfingston readily accepted the offer to be the representative for one of the Indy racecar teams. He married the widow of a famous racecar driver, fifteen years younger than he was. They lived a lively life, promoting racing across the nation.

Ironically, he died doing what he loved most—watching the Indy 500. During the fortieth lap, he lay back in his chair in his private booth, closed his eyes, and entered eternity.

Immediately following the race, his death was announced over the public address system. The entire crowd stood for a moment of silence. The drivers removed their helmets and joined in the emotional moment. Everyone stood at attention facing the gigantic American flag gracing the center of the racetrack as it lowered to half staff. It was a memorable scene.

Brent was seventy-seven years old.

His funeral was held at the Indy speedway; the stands were completely full.

The former president, Nathan Alexander, delivered the eulogy.

After Brent's funeral, some of his ashes were spread across the speedway using the same helicopter that had brought the six POWs to safety. The rest were buried at Arlington National Cemetery, next to Sergeant First Class Anthony Williams.

Robert Freeman

Sergeant First Class Robert Freeman lived a remarkable life. A couple weeks after he returned from prison camp, he had the opportunity to throw out the first pitch in the World Series. The President of the United States, scheduled to throw the ceremonial first pitch, proudly stepped aside to give the honors to Robert.

The New York Yankees organization hired him as a representative in public relations. He enjoyed traveling with the recruiters to check out prospective players. He knew it was not a real job, but he loved going to the clubhouse and talking to the team members. They also enjoyed bantering with him; his quick wit and uplifting spirit often encouraged them.

Le became a fan of the sport while listening to Thursday talk about baseball during his captivity.

One day James, Anthony, and Robert took Le to his first professional baseball game. Their seats were directly behind the Yankees' dugout.

Everyone stood up for the national anthem, except a nearby group of teenagers who remained in their seats, cutting up and joking with each other.

Freeman noticed that the teenagers were still seated and had not removed their caps. As the anthem began, Robert looked at them, and politely but firmly stated, "Show respect for the flag, young men. Stand up and take your hats off."

One kid sarcastically yelled back, "Are you going to make me?"

Robert eyed him and calmly replied, "Yes."

Another boy next to him yelled back the one thing he should not have said. "Hey, old man, you and what Army?" With that, the group of teens broke out laughing.

Very quickly, three old, proud veterans and a former Vietnamese guard were standing face-to-face with the four obnoxious, disrespectful teenagers.

People nearby watched, anxious to see how the scene would unfold.

Within seconds, three Marines who were sitting a few rows behind the rowdy teens rushed down to confront the boys. One of the Marines bellowed, "What Army, you ask? I'll tell you what Army—the United States Army and the United States Marine Corps. Do you really want to continue this?"

It was comical how fast their caps came off. The kids stood at attention, trembling as *The Star Spangled Banner* ended.

Unknown to the men, cameras filmed the entire incident and showed it on the giant screens around the stadium as spectators watched. Every eye focused on the screen as the three Marines turned toward America's heroes, saluting them. The men returned the salute, and then they all shook hands.

As the Marines headed back to their seats, the entire stadium erupted in a hearty applause. The players from both teams were standing in front of their dugouts clapping hands and cheering in a show of support for the well known soldiers.

One of the Marines turned to the teens. "See those four men. They are real heroes. I hope one day you will be half the men they are."

The young fellows were speechless and embarrassed by the whole scenario.

During the seventh inning stretch, the announcer introduced the heroes to the crowd.

Right after that, the teenagers came to them and apologized for their actions.

Robert smiled at the boys and pointed to the American flag flying high above the stadium. "That is more than merely a flag. To us, it represents life, hope, and freedom."

Le never felt more honored than at that moment. He was proud to be their friend and even prouder to be an American.

Television networks across America replayed the scene the following days. Spectators at the game would never forget the patriotism displayed.

Robert married a prominent actress. Together, they lived a full life.

He died at the age of eighty-one. His funeral was a massive event with well known ball players, Hollywood stars, and government officials attending.

James was there, but failing in health.

Robert Freeman was buried next to Pfingston and Williams in Arlington National Cemetery.

James McCarter

An airplane manufacturer offered a prestigious job to Colonel James McCarter. He declined the offer, so he could live near his family in Colorado Springs.

He worked with his son at the insurance company and resumed his former hobby—gliding.

He never turned down an opportunity to speak at a school or church. He shared what God taught him and his fellow prisoners about life and freedom.

James was honored to attend his great grandson's wedding, his namesake, who was born the day his family received word of the POW's rescue.

Le and James had memorable times together. Often Sam joined them. They fished in the mountains, went to ballgames, and observed holidays together. They reminisced, laughing about some of their unusual experiences.

However, they never talked among themselves about their time in the prison camp. It was a closed subject, never discussed.

Le was at James' side the morning he died at age eighty-seven. As his breathing became more labored, Le held his hand, thanking him for his enduring friendship.

In a weak voice, the old soldier replied, "Thanks again my friend, for all you have done."

Le was at a loss for words. He simply smiled back at James; tears stung his eyes.

"I'll see you on the other side," James whispered.

Le nodded his head, closing his eyes. He took a deep breath, ready to speak, but when he opened his eyes, James was gone.

Death ended an extraordinary life and an incredible chain of events.

Still holding his hand, the former guard stared at the lifeless body of his dear friend, and smiled. "Yes my friend, I will see you on the other side." Le looked heavenward uttering a silent prayer, and then lowered his head weeping.

The funeral was moving. There were politicians, dignitaries, and many old war heroes. Forty jet fighters from four different branches of the military streaked across the sky, each plane representing one year he was a POW.

After the sky quieted, four helicopters flew in a V-shape, known as the "Missing Man Formation." One lone chopper soared out of formation, away from the others, a tribute to the deceased. It was a remarkable sight.

Unrecognized, Le sat in the crowd at his dear friend's funeral. Le would miss him immensely.

James' body was laid to rest next to his fellow soldiers, Brent Pfingston, Robert Freeman, and Anthony Williams.

Samuel Jefferson

Samuel Jefferson married. He and his wife reared four children who all served in the U.S. Army Special Forces.

He was a proud father, but nothing made him more proud then the day he helped rescue the six POWs.

Sam died a few days after James.

Le often wondered what would have happened if he had not met Sam.

Many lives were changed because Sam introduced a Vietnamese guard to the One called Jesus. If it were not for Him, Sam would not have been at that orphanage. Le would not have met Sam, nor would he have done the "right thing." Those six men would have died POWs, never returning to America, their families, or freedom.

And Le...he would never have experienced freedom—physically or spiritually.

Now, he sits at Arlington, close to where his friends are buried, putting the final touches on the last chapter of his book. He has recounted the lives of six brave heroes. The details of the hardships they endured, and their jubilant return to America, will finally be available for the world to read.

Le meditated on the lives of the six men. When their government called them to service, they answered the call. They sacrificed their personal freedom for forty years of anguish, so people like Le and Linh could enjoy freedom. For that, all Americans should be grateful.

The grave markers Le sat in front of day after day were inscribed with the names: Sergeant Anthony Williams. Sergeant Brent Pfingston. Sergeant Robert Freeman. Colonel James McCarter.

The fifth tombstone read, "Samuel J. Jefferson. Captain, United States Army, Desert Storm."

His friends were home at last—their final destination. Home in the arms of Jesus. After all, home is where you lay your head.

Le looked skyward as he visualized the events of a night long ago. He clearly recalled every minuscule detail.

Following the incredible homecoming event at the National Mall the night of their return, the six men went to the Vietnam Veteran's Memorial. That snowy night Le followed the men and watched from a discreet distance. He was certain none of them knew he was observing their activity—they were caught up in the emotion of the moment.

It took a while, but each of them located his own name on the Wall. Their names had a cross in front of them with a circle recently etched around the cross. The cross represented a missing soldier. The circle—the symbol of life—meant the soldier returned home alive.

On that blustery evening, Le observed the men pay humble tribute to their fallen comrades.

Later, under the cover of darkness, he walked over to the Wall. His friends had left. He was alone; he looked around and made sure no one was watching.

Le stood in awe staring at the black granite wall, overwhelmed by the number of Americans who died fighting for his country's freedom.

He searched until he located the name of Corporal Daniel Sparks, the soldier whose identity he assumed for four years, also known in the prison as Saturday. He thought about Daniel's parents and the love they had for their son. He rubbed his finger gently over the etching, whispering a prayer for them.

Then Le bent down and brushed the freshly fallen snow away from the base of the Wall beneath Corporal Daniel Sparks' name. He stood, removing a small box from his coat pocket. His heart beat rapidly. Staring at the box, he reflected on the significance of its contents. Then he knelt and gently laid the box on the newly cleared area—inside it was his Medal of Freedom.

Le stood to his feet, looking heavenward.

The thousands of names inscribed on the giant monument captured his heart. What an incredible tribute to the brave men and women who paid the ultimate price for their service—people from all branches of the military who served for the great cause of freedom!

Why would he leave his cherished award at the Vietnam Veteran's Memorial?

He believed he owed a debt of gratitude to Corporal Daniel Sparks, and all the brave heroes whose names were engraved on the Wall. These men and women sacrificed their lives for the cause of liberty for all American and Vietnamese people.

The names on the Wall represent not just one person, but a family— brothers and sisters, sons and daughters, mothers and fathers. Each name symbolized a life, a calling, a future with dreams and goals—all cut short by a tragic death.

Le thought about his friends, the men he had originally known as *Sunday*, *Monday*, *Tuesday*, *Wednesday*, *Thursday*, and *Friday*. They had influenced his life enormously.

The lives of the men demonstrated honor... bravery... trust... courage... sacrifice. All for the cause of freedom—that most treasured of earthly gifts which is *never* free!

When Le placed his medal at the base of the wall, it seemed fitting. It was the right thing to do!

Dear Reader,

Many cannot forget the Vietnam War. Others refuse to remember it.

As a Vietnam Era Veteran, I experienced firsthand the anti-war sentiment. The protesters who held "Baby Killer" signs, their horrible insults, and the hatred on their faces are difficult images to erase.

Our military forces were not to blame then. They are not to blame now. Our courageous troops serve our country—for the great cause of freedom. Our troops deserve our respect, encouragement, support, and admiration for their tireless dedication to keeping us safe and secure.

It is our responsibility to support them. Next time you see a soldier, thank him or her for serving our country. If you notice military personnel in a restaurant, offer to pay his or her bill. Express your gratitude to a retired veteran.

Teachers, adopt a deployed troop from the community who is separated from his or her family. Perhaps the parent of one of your students is serving overseas. Gather supplies from the class for a care package. Mail it and save the family the added expense.

The families left behind also need our help. There are simple things we can do to assist spouses or parents of our deployed troops.

- *Provide childcare so the spouse can have needed time to himself or herself.*

- *Mow the yard.*

- *Help with repairs around the house or on the vehicle.*

- *Remove snow from the driveway or sidewalk.*

- *Take the family out to dinner or church.*

- *Take the kids to a ballgame or other entertainment.*

- *Use your talents to help wherever there is a need.*

- *Sometimes a family member just needs a friend—a listening ear.*

Less than one percent of Americans serve in our military. They deserve our support. One day that freedom may be gone.

Plan a trip to the Vietnam Veterans Memorial to pay tribute to America's heroes from the Vietnam War. Perhaps "The Moving Wall" will come to your area. Pay your respects—it will touch you deeply.

Remember those who have fought in other wars. World War Two, Korea and the Gulf. Visit their memorials and pay tribute to them also.

The internet has hundreds of sites dedicated to POWs/MIAs. There, you can find many ways to support our troops. Check it out. Become involved.

Above all, pray for our military personnel every day. Ask for God's protection on our brave troops and their families left behind.

Pray for all POWs, MIAs, and their families.

"You are not forgotten."

John L. Rothdiener

A NOTE OF THANKS

The author would like to thank Mr. Lawrence (Tazz) Tassone, who created the Prisoner Of War/Missing In Action program for the 1980 Air Force Sergeants Association International Division 13 Convention. Although intended as a one-time event to honor our missing and captured service members, this touching tribute has since been accepted as the formal ceremony for American POWs and MIAs.

With Mr. Tassone's kind permission, the POW/MIA ceremony appears in Chapter 16 of this book. I sincerely appreciate his generosity in allowing us to use it here, and the compassion and patriotism that he showed in beginning this find tradition.

— J. L. Rothdiener

ABOUT THE AUTHOR

J. L. Rothdiener was born in Syracuse, New York. Raised in Lakewood Colorado, he and his wife of thirty-eight years now reside in Bolivar, Missouri. They have two sons, and three wonderful grandchildren.

Rothdiener has had a lifelong passion for writing and began submitting articles to magazines and newspapers for publishing at an early age. He believes that God has given him the ability to write stories which can help change lives.

www.ingramcontent.com/pod-product-compliance
Lightning Source LLC
Chambersburg PA
CBHW020953180626
46814CB00003B/1075